I0691331

Wipe
My
Tears

Penelope S. Hession

Wipe My Tears
Copyright © 2005

Penelope S. Hession

This story is a work of fiction. All characters and events are a product of the author's imagination.

All rights reserved. No part of this publication may be reproduced, stored in a retrieval system, or transmitted in any form or by any means electronic, mechanic, photocopying, recording, or otherwise without the prior written permission of the copyright owner.

ISBN: 978-0-6152-0415-4

This book
is dedicated to Jesus Christ,
my healer,
who miraculously restored my eyesight
when I was going blind.

Other books:

Two Nights of Courage
Cast Your Nets
Jeep

The author can be reached at sdssolutions@msn.com

Calling

Rose laughed when her neighbor asked her to help. "Of course," Rose replied.

"I can get them picked, but getting them all rinsed and snapped, with the twins crawling around and grabbing at me, is more than I can do in a day. I'll blanch and freeze them tonight while they are in bed. And, of course, you can have as many quarts or pints as you need." Meredith smiled. "It is a circus trying to garden and then can or freeze everything. I just don't have enough hands."

"Or time," Rose commented. "You are right, the twins are too big and blustery for me to watch, so I'll snap and clean the beans. Bring them on over, the beans, that is."

So for the last hour or so Rose had been sitting on her shaded front porch, snapping green beans. The crop had been bountiful for Meredith's family. It was suddenly expanded, with the birth of the twins last fall and then with her sister's children, whom she and Tom had taken in after the accident. They were going to need all that they could produce in their garden to feed the family. Rose was happy for Meredith. The twins were born after ten years of marriage. An accident made orphans of her sister's five children. Now Meredith had the large family she had always wanted. It happened all in less than six months. Rose smiled at the blessings that God had granted Meredith and Tom. She thanked God for placing them as neighbors.

A car pulled up out front. A young man stepped out and waved. He took the steps two at a time and swooped down to hug Rose. "Jon Mark!" Rose cried out in joy. "What are you doing here?"

Jon sat down on the squeaky swing. "It needs oil again, Grandma. Is the oil can in the garage?" With a bound, he was up and off the porch before she could reply. He returned. "I couldn't find it out there."

"Well, if you hadn't been so quick, I would have told you it was down in the basement."

Jon grinned as he passed her and went inside to search for the oil can. He came back moments later and stretched his five feet eleven inches to reach the offending squeak with the oil. "There!" he said, as he sat back into the swing to test his work. Now the only sound was the creak of the floorboards under his grandmother's rocker.

"Meredith, my neighbor, has plenty of beans but not enough time. She asked me if I would snap them. I figured I'd just sit out here on the porch and do them." Grandma Rose looked at her third oldest grandchild. "You are graduating next weekend, aren't you?"

"Sure Gram. I've passed all my courses. You didn't think I wouldn't, did you?" Jon was smiling. "And you are coming to the graduation and

2

the dinner afterwards?"

Rose nodded. "Where is that pretty little girl you usually have with you?"

Jon looked down a moment then smiled. "She has one more final to take tomorrow. She needed to prepare for that."

"Yes, but I saw you look down. You don't fool me, Jon Mark. Are you going to give her a ring now or wait until she graduates?"

"Neither, Gram."

Rose stopped snapping beans and looked at her grandson. Something was wrong or different. "Want to tell me about it?"

"I am going into a seminary June 15th."

Rose ceased to rock her chair. She put the pot of green beans on the floor.

"You want to be a minister?"

"No, Grams, a priest."

Rose put her hands to her mouth, either in shock or maybe in sorrow. She had a similar conversation years ago with her son, Jon Nathan. It seemed like only yesterday. "You are going to be a celibate?"

"Yes, Grams. I have been praying about this for a couple of years. I made up my mind this spring. No matter what I would do with my degree, it would not be enough for God. I wanted to tell you first because of Uncle Jon. I didn't want someone to tell you, and you think I didn't know what I was doing." Jon Nathan had been a priest. When a war came, he signed up as a Chaplain. He died on a battlefield while giving a dying soldier the last rites. A sniper's bullet had done the job. Jon Mark knew the stories about Father Jon Nathan and remembered the funeral at the Cathedral after his body was returned.

"I'd sort of hoped you and the pretty girl would give me a great grandchild or two. You two seem so perfect for each other. Does she know?"

"Yes, I told her. She wants to remain friends, but I don't know for how long after her parents find out. They also thought we were so right for each other. She has been a good friend while I prayed and searched for what I should do with my degree and my life."

Rose's eyes were teary. She didn't bother to wipe the tears as they ran down her face. The memories of Jon Nathan's leaving came rushing back. He, too, had known what he was leaving for. "Celibate," she whispered.

"Yes, Grams, that is a part of what I had to decide upon. Don't cry, Grams, I'm not going away forever. I want to be a diocesan priest, working with the people. And my degree will be a big help to me. I'll be able to visit you and the rest of the family. I am not going stay in a monastery where all I do is work and pray. The Lord has a work for me to do."

Jon was now kneeling next to his Grandmother. He wiped the tears from her cheeks and then wrapped his arms around her.

"Do your parents know?"

"No, that is why I came to you first. You know what it is to give up a son to the priesthood, and Mom is going to have to learn to give me up."

"You want me to help you tell them?"

Jon rocked back on his heels. "Nope, just to be there praying for me, for all of us. It will be a shock, I am sure, to most of the family. But I think Dad has an inkling of what I have been seeking. Anyway, I hope he does."

"You're a big boy now, a man. It is right that you make your own decisions. I know it is hard for others to understand, but I guess I am the one most likely to understand."

Jon nodded. "Leslie understood, and that

4

was a pretty big hurdle for her, since she isn't Catholic."

"Did she try to talk you out of it?"

"She did at first. Then she saw how important it was to me. We prayed together a lot."

Rose sniffed and pulled out the handkerchief she always carried in her pocket to blot her face. "I guess that was what I saw in her that made me think she was ideal for you." Rose smiled. "I am proud of you, Jon Mark." She reached out and drew him to her bosom. "Remember me in your prayers."

Jon stood up and offered his Grandmother his hand. She stood up. "Let's go in and have a glass of iced tea."

Opening the screen door, they went inside.

Father George

Jon dropped his duffle bag on the floor of the small cubicle that would be his room for the summer. Four other young college graduates and he made up the 'class' for the summer at St. Michael's Seminary. He had been the last to get there that morning, after flying across country on a 'red eye' flight. The priest who met him at the door was aged and gruff. He said, "The others are already here!" as though Jon had deliberately been late to arrive. Jon tried not to take the comment personally, but it nagged at him.

As he unpacked his wardrobe and personal effects, there was a knock at the door. Before he could answer it, a thin piece of paper was slid under the door. Jon picked it up. It listed the schedule for the rest of the day. His name was at the end of the list of appointments with Father George. Jon wondered if Father George was the priest who let him

6

in.

A few moments later there was another tap on the door. A young man entered. He held his fingers to his lips until he had closed the door behind him. "Welcome, Jon. We were beginning to wonder if you had changed your mind about being here."

"We?" Jon asked.

"The other three and me. I know your late arrival made Father Grinch, er George, crotchety this morning."

"Storms cancelled my flight last night. I had to rebook on a 'red eye' for this morning," Jon said. "And you are?"

"Oh, sorry, I am Samuel." Samuel offered his hand.

"What is the schedule for us, Samuel?"

"Father G has us each scheduled for an interview with him. One every forty-five minutes after lunch. He picked me out to be his first. I think he is skeptical of a Jewish Catholic." Samuel's dark eyes snapped at the thought of the upcoming confrontation. "I've been a Catholic for over seven years, thanks to a wonderful friend, my foster-father. He took me in just at the beginning of the teen years. I hadn't been brought up in the Jewish tradition, so I didn't fight the idea. Best thing that ever happened to me. But I don't think Father G will see it that way."

"Is Father George that narrow-minded or that much of a grouch?"

"Just watch and see, Jon Mark!" Samuel laughed, "I'd better get back to my room."

Jon finished putting his things away. He thought about the intense interviews he had gone through and the psychological tests he had taken in order to be considered for this 'special class' that was entering in the summer rather than at the traditional time in the fall. They were an experiment this seminary was conducting, creating a 'fast-track,' year-round concentrated course of study for young men with college degrees. It meant giving up three summers, but with prayer and diligence, they would be ordained at the end of three and one-half calendar years. His track record at the university was impressive so when he was given permission to seek this intensive opportunity he had applied. Now it was beginning.

Somewhere in the distance a bell rang. There was a tap on his door, and Samuel peeked in. "That is the signal for prayers before dinner."

Jon nodded and tucked the tail of his shirt in before joining Samuel and three others as they walked toward the dining room. The others did not speak but nodded at Jon.

Like clockwork, every forty-five minutes one of the new candidates entered Father George's office as the previous one exited. It was a solemn process. No one smiled, going in or coming out. Jon waited, sitting on a straight chair and watching the slow passage of time. His mind was continually trying to guess what the interview process with Father George was like and considering how he would answer the priest's questions.

Samuel looked agitated when he exited but gave 'a thumbs up' signal to those waiting. Jon tried to read each man's face but was discomforted by what he saw.

Tom had gone in before him. A glance at his watch told him that it was nearly time for him to go in. He wondered where the others had gone after they left the office. The building was nearly silent, except for an occasional creak of old beams.

Promptly at four, Tom left the priest's office. Jon didn't have time to study his fellow seminarian's face. Father George stood waiting at the door.

"Come in, be quick about it, I don't want to be here all afternoon!" Father growled. "You are Jon Mark!" This was a statement, not a question.

"Yes, Father."

"Why do you want to be in this program?!"

"Why do I want to be a priest, is that the question?" Jon asked.

The older man's face was a pathway of wrinkles. His eyes peered out from under untamed bushy eyebrows. His cassock, appearing several sizes too big, hung from his wide shoulders. "No!" he said, "this program that starts at the wrong time of the year and eats up three summers!"

Obviously, Father George wasn't happy about the program. And everything he said was with an exclamation point after it. Jon reconsidered the question and said, "God is drawing me to the priesthood. This program was offered to me if I qualified, and I did. I decided I would take advantage of it."

Father did not say anything for several moments. Jon wondered if he had asked the other four the same thing. "Sit down!" the priest barked at him.

Jon sat on a very straight chair that offered no comfort other than providing a seat.

"Do you got a girlfriend?!"

Jon blinked. "I had a girlfriend."

"What happened? Did she turn you down?"

"No, we talked and prayed together and are in agreement about the direction my life is taking."

"Sex?"

Inhaling slowly, Jon looked deep into the face of the priest. "Are you to be my confessor?" he asked.

"For this summer term, yes!"

"We practiced abstinence."

Father George blinked. "You never had sex?!"

"No, we were friends, not lovers."

"Why?!"

"Isn't that what the Church teaches?"

"Doesn't seem to stop you kids much!"

Jon shrugged his shoulders slightly. "Well, it did mean something to me."

"Good!" Father George looked down at his notes and put his pen down. Then he looked over at the clock ticking on the sidewall. "I can't see why I have to spend forty-five minutes talking with each of you. Some need ten minutes, others three hours. And this is summer break!"

Jon wanted to laugh. He suddenly realized the old priest was mostly irritated by the summer 'special class'. "You would rather be somewhere else, Father?"

Father George mumbled something before he said, "I go for a month every summer to the beach. It is a time of rest and renewal. And I say Mass on Sundays at the little Chapel so everyone can attend while they are vacationing."

Jon leaned slightly forward and spoke softly. "You are going to miss that this summer because you have to stay here and teach us?"

The priest nodded.

Jon sat back in his seat. What a turn of events. "It isn't our fault."

Father George sighed and nodded again. "I know."

There was silence in the room, except for the ticking clock. Father turned several pages over and then began to fill out the questionnaire with Jon's answers. At four-forty, the priest dismissed Jon with a prayer and blessing.

Death Unexpected

There was not much time for more than studies and meditation on the topics of study. For Jon, the serious discussions with his mentoring priests stimulated him. The five seminarians were allotted a number of days when they could take leave of the seminary, besides the usual holidays. Jon was frugal in the use of his, leaving only for Christmas and Easter. By the end of the second summer, the group had dwindled to three, Jon Mark, Samuel and Thomas. The other two men elected to join the slower track of study.

As they were leaving the dining hall one noon, Father Randolph stopped Jon Mark. "You had a phone call this morning. You need to return it."

Falling into step beside the priest, Jon wondered about the call. Father Randolph was usually not so solemn. "Who called?"

Father Randolph used his key to open the administration office. "Your mother, I think."

"Something is wrong at home?"

"Sit down, Jon Mark."

The intense look on Father Randolph's face worried Jon. The priest pushed the phone toward Jon. "I'll wait outside the door while you call. Just push 'nine' before you dial."

"Hello?" The voice that answered at home was his Grandma's.

"This is Jon Mark, Gram. What has happened?"

"Your father had a heart attack while he was driving. Your mother is in the hospital with minor injuries."

"And Dad?"

"He is dead. He was dead before his car ran the red light."

Jon slumped in the chair. "Oh, Grams," Jon's voice broke. "What do I need to do?"

Rose's voice broke. She whispered. "Come home, your mother needs you."

Turning to open the office door, Jon beckoned Father Randolph in. "I'll call you back shortly, Grams. OK?"

After hearing the affirmation from his grandmother, Jon hung up the phone.

Father Randolph sat down in a chair near Jon. "I don't know what to say."

Jon Mark nodded. "My father is dead. Mother is in the hospital. That was my Grandmother who called you earlier."

"Yes, she did tell me what happened when she called. I am sorry. Can I pray with you?"

Jon Mark bowed his head.

After the prayer and blessing, Jon looked up. "Grams wants me to come home. For how long, I don't know."

Father Randolph looked through some pages on his desk. "You have not taken any extra days of the leave time you have. I can give you a release to spend some time with your family in view of these circumstances."

Jon shrugged his shoulders. "I don't have enough money for air fare."

The priest waved his hand. "It will be taken care of."

"And I don't know how long I will need to be there."

"I know that," Father said. "I'll call for a plane ticket and see that you have transportation to the airport and money for transportation at the other end. You call me in a day or two and let me know what is happening."

Jon Mark sighed. "What is this going to do to my studies here?"

"Nothing at present. Oh, you might be a little behind when you come back, but you are a diligent student, and I am not worried about that."

"Thank you, Father Randolph. I guess I'll go pack."

"Stop by the classroom and tell the others and Father Larry. That way they will have the information directly. My position will keep me from telling them."

"Yes, Father, I will go share with them." Jon stood up. "I do want to come back and finish my studies here."

"You will. God bless you my son." Father made the sign of the cross over Jon.

Jon stopped by the classroom and shared with his fellow seminarians. They prayed for him. Later that evening he was on the way to the airport. He had put in a quick call to Grams, who said a neighbor would be waiting at the airport for him.

His earthly father was dead. This phrase rolled through his mind over and over on the long flight home. What was this going to do to his studies and future as a priest? He remembered last Christmas, when his father had taken him aside and told him that there was some money in the bank in his name if he ever needed it. He had told his father that the Church was careful in caring for its priests, and he probably would never need it. Nonetheless, his father had taken him to the bank and had him sign a signature card so that he could access the money if necessary. As the plane circled for landing, Jon had formulated a plan for that money if it was needed by his mother.

Jenkins, a neighbor to his parents, was waiting for him in the luggage pick up area. "Sorry about your father," Jenkins said as he took Jon's luggage.

"I can carry that," Jon said.

"I know, but it is the least I can do for you," Jenkins smiled. "It will be strange not to see your father cleaning his golf clubs out on the back porch."

"You two did golf a lot these last few years, didn't you?" Jon asked.

"Yep, and he was the better player. I never understood why he put up with all my bogeys."

Jon grinned. "Still haven't conquered that slice, huh?"

"Car is over here." Jenkins led the way

"When was the accident?" Jon asked.

"Yesterday morning he was taking your mother to the store. She usually drove herself, but he had insisted. Then the heart attack and the accident occurred."

"She knew he had a heart attack."

"Yes, apparently he had just said something

about a strange pain in his chest."

Jon was studying the lights as they drove away from the airport. A pain in the chest was what his father had mentioned at Christmastime, while they were going to the bank.

"Had he ever complained before."

"Not that I know." Jenkins flipped his turn signal on to make the exit to the interstate.

"Had he seen a doctor?"

"Your Dad?" Jenkins turned his head toward Jon for a second. "Not that I know. You know he had no respect for medicine or doctors."

Jon nodded. He remembered the squawking his father did every time one of the kids had to have a physical or, worse yet, had exhausted all their mother's skills at nursing them and had to see a doctor. His father was reasonable about most anything else but the medical profession.

Grams had waited up for him. Jon clung to her for a long moment. "Well, Jon Mark, you look fit. A little pale and thin but otherwise healthy."

"Grams, did mother say anything about Dad's health before now?"

"She was a good daughter-in-law and kept her mouth shut about their lives together. You know that we never knew about an expected baby until it was obvious."

"Yeah, I've heard the stories over and over about how they fooled you with the upcoming births. But you would have thought she would have noticed something and not let him get to the place of a fatal heart attack."

"Oh, I don't know. He is probably in heaven, laughing at all the doctors who never got any of his money. I never understood his reticence in seeing a doctor every once in a while."

"Its too late now," Jon commented.

Rose nodded, tears in her eyes.

"Both of my sons are dead before me. It is almost too much to bear. Pray for me, Jon Mark. Comfort me."

Jon knelt as his grandmother sat down. He knew the prayers for the dying and knew the words of the funeral mass, but none of these were what would give his grandmother solace in this situation. For a while he just knelt in silence, waiting on the Lord. "Comfort Grams, Lord. She has borne the deaths of both her sons. Show her kindness and mercy."

Unto The Least

Father Jon stretched his hand. The most recently used pencil rolled to the edge of his desk and dropped off. From the sound, Father Jon decided it landed in the wastebasket. It did not matter. There were several other pencils sharpened and readily within his reach.

He had been at this parish almost since he was ordained. His two previous assignments were temporary fill-ins while assistant priests were on medical leaves.

He liked this small parish well enough, except for the monthly reports. The financial ones bothered him the most, so he put off the report each month until the last possible moment. Today was that time again. The weather was not cooperating. It was supposed to be sunny all week, but a cold front had come in, with dark clouds. The rectory had lots of dark woodwork and definitely was more conducive to serious work when the sun shone in the windows. This didn't help Father Jon. He felt the dark and gloomy room translate itself to the report.

This tiny parish barely paid the heat and other utilities. The Diocese provided a modest housing and living allowance. Father Jon was comfortable in the rectory.

He picked up a fresh pencil and tried once more to get the data written that this particular report wanted. The quickest way to be noticed by the Bishop's office was to send in a report that looked like he had not spent time and prayer considering each point. He had one phone call in the past about a previous report, and he did not want that to happen again.

Father Jon glanced at his watch. He had been working on this report for over two hours. Sometimes, he felt like his assignment to this parish was just a convenient way to keep him on the sidelines. Father Jon wasn't particularly ambitious for a more active parish, but he felt as though the Bishop had forgotten about him until he made a mistake on a report. He had asked the Bishop to consider him for a change of assignment. Either the Bishop was deaf or Jesus still wanted Father Jon in this parish.

The room grew darker. He turned on a lamp, glanced at his watch again, and shook his head. His watch said it was only eleven-fifteen. It was nearly midday, yet outside it was dark, like a storm coming in. Even the streetlights were on. Rain would really dampen his spirits today. He wanted to visit in the community. There were parishioners on the church rolls who never came to church. It was his intention to visit each one. So far this activity had netted one old member coming back into fellowship with the Church and several who were considering it. No one had reached out to those who quit coming in the past, so Jon's visitations were unique.

He could not keep his mind focused on the questions to be commented on in the report. He pushed back his chair to stretch his legs and thought about Mass that morning. The Harrison boys were his servers. Mrs. Toby Wilson had come to Mass as she usually did. Her best friend, Miss Lizzy, had died the previous day. Funny, he could not remember Mrs. Toby's first name. Everyone called her that, "Mrs. Toby," which was her long deceased husband's name. Father Jon made a mental note to look up her given first name in the old records before he had to preach her funeral Mass.

"Mrs. Toby, the Harrison boys and me," he said aloud. "What a group!" One of the Harrison boys was wearing a big bruise on his cheekbone. The boys had shown him many bruises over the time he had been their parish priest. Scotty Harrison was known as the 'town drunk.' He lived up to his reputation and got mean when he was drunk. Once Father Jon had seen Scotty nearly sober. He had been almost likeable.

"Poor Mrs. Harrison," he murmured. If the boys were telling the truth, and he was sure they were, Janey Harrison had many bruises and some broken bones too. Father Jon wondered whether maybe things would be better for the Harrison's if they just went to the other church across town where they did not believe in drinking alcohol. "Watch it, Jon," he said to himself, "That is dangerous thinking."

Father Jon knew the pastor from the tiny Pentecostal Church across town. The pastor and his wife had two very small children, and there was a third baby expected soon.   Their church barely supported them, while with humble hearts they served the community.   Jon managed to send excesses of food, donated to the priest of the rectory, to this couple. "With love from Jesus," the note that he included with the food always said.

Father Jon liked the words of Jesus in Matthew 25:40, where Jesus said, "Truly I say to you, inasmuch as you have done it to one of the least of my brethren, you have done it to me." He liked the entire passage so much that he had preached on it several times so far this year. He was sure the people of his small church were tired of hearing the same sermon.   However, until he saw them putting Matthew 25:35-39 into action in their lives, he supposed he would preach it again.

Sighing, Father Jon looked at the report in front of him. "What's this?" He had never before read the last question to be answered. "Describe a project for your parish that would affect the whole community." Again he was speaking out loud. *Now whatever could we do that would affect the whole community?* Jon picked up his pencil and drummed with the eraser tip on his desk. *I suppose they think we have money here to do whatever we would want.*

"A nice, sloping ramp, with handrail!" Father said aloud. "It really shouldn't cost much, and I'll get some men from the church to help me build it." A glance at the budget figures caused him to wince. "No excess anywhere!" he muttered. Nevertheless, Father Jon wrote in the idea for the last question on the report.

An amazing thing happened when he sent the report to the Bishop's office. A check large enough to pay for the proposed ramp arrived in the mail. The note from the Chancellor just said, "An anonymous donor." Within a few days, with the help of men

20

from the parish, Jon had a sloping ramp with handrail built.

It was just in time for Lorie Abrams' wedding. The family had expressed concern for the eighty-nine year old great grandmother who was wheelchair-bound. A joyous celebration was held. The grandmother took a spin in her wheelchair down the ramp with her new great grandson-in-law.

Two weeks later, a funeral was held for an important town official, with several persons coming to the service who used canes and walkers. Jon reflected on the goodness and timeliness of God. He tried to convince his congregation about how God was just waiting to bring a blessing to his people. Sometimes he feared they did not know the Lord in that manner. He prayed often that they would know Jesus the way he did and waited for a glimmer of response.

If I Should Cry . . .

       Nadine closed the door softly behind her before climbing the stairs to the third floor. She was glad to be home. Actually, this wasn't home, but it felt more like home than the place where she got her mail. The bed was neatly made. There was a flower in the vase and a comfortable chair. Yes, this was more like a home should be.

       Downstairs, Father Jon looked at the tasks before him on the desk. The bell tower needed repair. The kitchen sink was leaking. Mr. Colly was in the hospital again. Madeline J was clamoring for him to come to visit and have supper.

       Mass was uneventful this morning, with the usual three plus a couple of drop-ins for Communion. And there was the Bishop's report to be filled out again, which he dreaded. The conflict he felt within himself these days always showed up in everything he wrote on that form. Although he knew there wasn't any truth in his worries, nevertheless, he wrestled with his conscience as he wrote each line.

Nadine came unannounced, but that was all right. Her visits were always welcome. She was a breath of fresh air in the stuffy rectory. They had a relationship. Jon always made it a point not to think too deeply about that relationship and the Bishop's report at the same time. Nadine needed the peace and quiet of the rectory and the church to put the whirling nightmarish life she otherwise led into perspective. A few days exploring the dark recesses of the old church, the rectory, and him seemed to be what she needed.

She wasn't possessive of him and the relationship. She knew she was just a slight diversion and recreation for him from his mundane tasks of being a pastor of a church in a small out-of-the-way community. It was just an innocent relationship, causing no harm. And it was certainly beneficial to both of them. Jon knew others would call their relationship 'an affair'. He winced at that thought.

Startled by the shrill ring of the phone, he answered it, still somewhat shaken by his previous musings, "Father Jon, Christ Our Savior Church," he answered. It was Madeline J.

"Yes, I remember your invitation." Madeline J continued on non-stop. "No, I have a pressing need that I must take care of today. How about next Monday night?"

Jon was hopeful that Madeline J would respond and not question what 'tragedy' was taking place in 'her' community today. To her, a need for the pastor indicated a disaster, and she always wanted to know the particulars. He never told her details, but she seemed to ferret them out anyway.

"Oh, the bridge club meets Mondays. I had

forgotten. Tuesday, then?" More fluttering comments from Madeline J before she agreed that next Tuesday would be fine. Jon murmured a blessing over Madeline J and her house before hanging up the phone.

"Problem?" He had not heard Nadine come down the stairs. "Do you have to go out? I brought a book to read if you do, so don't be concerned about me."

Her voice was so nice to hear. Jon looked at her and smiled. "No, just Madeline J wanting me over for supper tonight." He laughed. "She seems to have a sixth sense about getting me out of the house just when I want to stay home."

"What kind of excuse did you give her this time?"

"A pressing need." He reached out to her. It was her turn to laugh. The embrace felt warm and satisfying.

"Do you suppose she believed you?" Nadine's voice came from somewhere near his chest.

"What do you think? Does she ever? She is a very nosey and gossipy old woman. I don't know that she ever believes what I tell her, and I only believe a small portion of what she says. Most of the town is that way. Everyone knows she gossips."

"Umm, are you saying that to reassure yourself and me that whatever she spreads about you isn't true?"

"Hey, friend," Jon pushed her away. "You are too close to the truth."

"You are unhappy I came!" Nadine tried to pout, but the smile in her eyes belied her words.

"No, of course not," Jon replied, returning to his desk. "I do have to get some bills paid, call the plumber, and make a hospital visit this afternoon."

He shoved the Bishop's report to the

bottom of the pile. "Make yourself at home but don't be too visible."

Nadine nodded and tiptoed from the room. Jon was right. He needed to do his normal activities. She picked up her book and let herself out the side door. The big bushes that surrounded the narrow brick church gave her adequate coverage from prying eyes. Slipping in between the brick wall and the bushes, she sat down in her favorite hiding place. She could watch the town from her vantage point and not be seen. Soon, absorbed in her book, she lost track of time.

Madeline J fussed and fumed. She talked to all her cronies, and no one knew what particular business the Father had that would involve him all day. Gracie had said a strange car was parked in the parking lot behind the church. Actually, Gracie said it was the same car that came periodically and stayed for a day or two. No one knew who owned it, but there was some speculation.

Mildred had asked Father Jon once about the car. He just laughed and said, "A friend comes to get away from big city stresses." At the bridge club, Mildred said that what Father does is his own business. The others in the club agreed with her. So Madeline J fussed and fumed alone, which probably annoyed her the most. No one believed her speculations.

The noontime ringing of the church bells brought Nadine back to the present. She wasn't too sure what she had been thinking or dreaming about. Her legs seemed to be asleep as well. She stretched and peered through the bushes at the side door just as Jon came out looking for her.

He grinned as she emerged from her hide-away. "I thought you might be out here. Did you get much reading done?"

"Probably less than the work you got done."

Together they reentered the house. One of their shared joys was cooking together. The kitchen was large enough for several people but too small for a dinette table. Jon solved that problem with a small pull-down table from an old ironing board closet. He opened the table and retrieved two chairs from the dining room.

"Any interesting phone calls?" Nadine knew full well that Jon would not tell her about anything but the most innocent, mundane calls. All other calls he kept private. That was one of the things that made him a good pastor. It also contributed to their relationship.

"Nope, but all work is done, except the hospital visit. I could put that off, I suppose."

"Oh no! That is so very important to the person in the hospital and the families." Nadine's voice took on a tone of urgency. "Who is in the hospital?"

"Mr. Colly. You know some of the treatment he gets has to be done in the hospital." Nadine nodded while biting into her sandwich. "Is the food alright? I didn't know you were coming. I am a little low on variety."

"Being able to eat with you makes up for the lack of variety. I really don't see any reason to complain about the food."

As the kitchen tasks were completed, Nadine stifled a yawn. "Time for your nap, isn't it?" She nodded. They climbed the back stairs to the second floor and then on up to the third floor. Nadine pulled down the covers and slid into bed. Jon tucked the covers around her before kissing her tenderly. "I'll wake you when I return," he whispered in her ear. She nodded and closed her eyes.

Down in his own quarters, Jon splashed on

some aftershave lotion.   At the foot of the stairs he listened to her even breathing. Satisfied that she was resting, he set out for the hospital.

Gracie pulled back from her curtains as she watched Father Jon leave alone.   Gracie had formulated a plan by the time Father Jon's car turned the corner. This one time she was going to have one up on Madeline J. Snooping was not her normal behavior, but now was the chance to check out that strange car.

Armed with pencil and paper and her garden gloves, she left her yard and headed purposefully toward the church parking lot. Once there, she put on her gloves before trying to open the car door. "No fingerprints," she reasoned to herself.

"Nuts!" she muttered. It was locked. Well, she could write down the license plate number. Charlie, up at the police station, could find out who it belonged to for her. She'd have to think up a good story, though, to convince him that this was indeed a good deed she had done.

Because the gloves made her hands too clumsy to hold a pencil, she removed them and placed them on the top of the car. After copying the plate number, she returned home. Sending up a quick prayer asking God to forgive her for snooping on the priest, she picked up the phone and called Charlie.

"Yep, I can find out who owns that car. You say it is parked behind the church? Maybe I need to come down and take a look at it. It might be stolen."

Gracie panicked. The last thing she wanted to happen was for the police to go snooping around. What would Father Jon think of her if he found out.

"No, no!" she almost shouted into the phone. "Just check out the license plate, would you please, Charlie. Just do it as a favor for your aunt."

"Well, all right. If you think it isn't stolen,

I'll do a check and call you back later."

Gracie fanned herself with the phone book. She hadn't realized how hard it would be or how guilty she would feel just checking out a parked car. After all, she had seen the car over there many times before, and she was just now checking it out. For a moment, she forgot her desire to top Madeline J just once.

If she had known it was going to be so difficult, she would not have crossed the street. It was then she remembered her garden gloves. Where had she left them? Surely not over in the church parking lot, she hoped. She was too ashamed and frightened to go look.

Later that afternoon, the first thing Father Jon saw when he drove into the church lot was a pair of garden gloves on top of Nadine's car. He thought Nadine had left them there. He took them into the rectory.

The rectory was quiet and still, just like it always was when he returned to it. However, there was a charge in the air, invisible but there. He knew it was because of Nadine's presence. His footsteps were lighter; his heart fluttered in his chest. It was during moments like this that he wondered about celibacy. Nadine certainly had changed his mind about living alone, but there was nothing he could do about it now. She would be here a day or two and then be gone again until the next time.

At the top of the stairs, he listened to see if she was awake. He could hear her even breathing. Silently, like a cat, he ascended to the third floor. She was still asleep, one arm dangling off the bed. Bending down beside her, he gently kissed her forehead.

Nadine stirred and looked up at him. "Back already?"

28

He nodded. She reached both hands up and locked her fingers behind his neck. He rocked back on his heels and slowly pulled her up to a sitting position.

"I picked up some food while I was at the county seat: steaks, salad, and ice cream. Does that sound good?"

Nadine nodded and rubbed the sleep from her eyes.

"How about a candlelight dinner for two about 7 PM? Think we can get it ready by then?"

Jon looked at the slender woman. She smiled at him and waved her hand toward the stairway. "I get the message," he said lightly. "Get out of here." She nodded.

In his second floor quarters, Jon changed to an open-necked shirt and trousers he wore only when he was not being official. Nadine joined him in the kitchen, where he was cutting a tomato for the salad.

"Let me," she reached for the knife. At one time, he would have argued that she was his guest, but now it was natural for them to prepare a meal side-by-side.

"How was Mr. Colly today?"

"Sort of discouraged. He had thought this was his last treatment at the hospital, but they told him he would have to come back again in two weeks. He said that it was getting harder and harder to make the trip. His spirits are lagging."

"I shouldn't wonder. That is an ordeal. Where is the lettuce and . . ."

Jon turned around from the stove, where he was heating the grill on which to sear the steaks. "Where do you think, silly, in the refrigerator."

Nadine was looking past him as though he was not in the room.

He turned around to see what she was looking at. There was nothing on the wall behind him that was any different. "Are you all right?" He stepped toward her. She seemed far away, but then she smiled.

"Of course."

"You weren't here a moment ago."

She murmured and gathered an armful of salad ingredients from the refrigerator. When she turned back around, her eyes glistened as she said too brightly, "Just where did you think I was?"

Jon wrapped his arm around her and steered her to a stool. "Sit while you work. It will make it easier."

Smoke from the overheated grill set the smoke alarm off. The previous somber mood in the kitchen changed as Jon removed the grill from the heat and the batteries from the alarm.

"You cause me more trouble," he scolded. "That thing never goes off, except when you are here!" A giggle came from the head bowed over the salad bowl. "I know you don't believe me, but that is the truth!"

"Sorry, you are so funny when that thing goes off. You're like a kid caught with the cookie crumbs and empty milk glass. You just fly around here setting things right." She giggled again and reached out to him.

Jon accepted her gesture and wrapped his arms around her slender body. "You're not mad at me, are you? For laughing at you?" her soft voice quivered.

"No, my little one. You have a way of distracting me while we are cooking, but I wouldn't want it any other way." He caressed her back and felt her shake as tears came down her face. Carefully he tipped her head and blotted the tears with a kitchen towel. If Madeline J saw him now, she would have the whole town in an uproar within minutes.

Nadine's tears slowly ceased. "I'm sorry," she whispered.

"You don't need to apologize. I understand. Was it the comments that Mr. Colly made?" She nodded. "No more talk along that line, OK? The grill is cold again. Let's see if I can get it heated without a disaster this time, OK?"

The candlelight meal went without a hitch. The phone didn't ring even once. Jon considered this a minor miracle, since his parishioners seemed to instinctively call about their most trivial concerns when he was eating.

Nadine talked about some songs she heard recently. They discussed the wave of harsher sounding Christian music around today and shook their heads. They agreed it was becoming unpleasant to listen to one particular radio station.

Nadine told Jon to go enjoy his time off while she did the dishes. Instead, he stood in the doorway talking to her. For Jon, talking with a friend was a wonderful treat. He put the dishes up as she dried them.

At dusk they retired to the summer porch to sit and talk. Jon pulled back the curtains to let in the cool evening breeze. They sat close together and talked in subdued voices. Nadine usually had many questions about life, but this evening she was probing his mind for answers about what happened after life. This disturbed him.

He held her hand as she told him of the last few weeks. She cried again. She tried so valiantly not to cry, but the tears came anyway. He blotted them and held her as she wept.

A movement out by the church attracted his gaze. Someone was walking around out there who didn't want to be seen. He touched her lips to silence her and pointed. From the darkened summer porch they could see a small figure darting from one shadowy area to another. "Do you think someone is trying to rob the church?" she whispered. He shrugged his shoulders.

The figure was now in the shadows of the bushes. "He is in the area where you often go." Jon said. "Look!" The figure was now running across the parking lot to where Nadine's car was parked.

"Is your car locked?" He could feel Nadine nod. "Who do you think it is?"

The figure ran all the way around the car, stopped to look under it, and then scurried back to the shadows of the bushes and church.

"The gloves," Jon said softly, "the gloves."

"What?"

"I found garden gloves on top of your car when I got home this afternoon. I brought them in, thinking they were yours. Obviously not."

"Garden gloves?"

Jon watched the small figure disappear into the shadows across the street. He shook his head.

"Go on up the back stairs but keep the lights off. I'll close up down here and be there in a minute. Meet me in the study."

Nadine tiptoed from the summer porch and felt her way along the wall to the back stairs. It was twenty-steps to the stairs and fourteen steps up to the second floor. She had counted them once when she was bored.

In the upper hall she moved along to the study door, the only one on her right. A quarter-moon gave some light to the room as she found the recliner and sat down.

Downstairs, Jon turned on lights and walked back and forth. He turned off lights in one room and moved to another. After checking all doors, he turned on the front hall lights and climbed slowly up the stairs. Anyone watching from the outside would have seen the pastor doing what he did every night before going up to his study. He mind churned with thoughts. Who was that figure? Who owned those gloves? And why were they left on Nadine's car? Did Madeline J have anything to do with it? The figure had been too small and spry to be Madeline J.

Gracie watched the priest's house from behind her curtains as the sun set. There was no sign of any activity. The sharp ringing of the telephone gave her heart palpitations. It was Madeline J. No, Gracie told her, she had not seen any activity over at the rectory. Of course, she would notify her if anything unusual happened. Wasn't she just a little suspicious, Madeline J wanted to know? Gracie said a little prayer and told her "no".

A short time later, Charlie called her from the police station. "Well, I've got interesting news." Gracie was all ears. "The car is registered to none other than our parish priest. Are you sure you got the right car?"

Gracie assured him that this was not the priest's car or, at least, not the one Father Jon drove.

Charlie said, "Well, it's parked at the right address. I guess he owns it," and hung up.

Gracie was frantic now. She was sure she left her gloves over on the car in question. How she was going to get them back worried her. Finally it was dark, with only a trace of moonlight. Putting on a dark sweater, a scarf, and her sturdy garden shoes, she let herself out the back door. There were no lights on in the rectory. Either Father was asleep or?

She really didn't want to think too much on the other possibility.

Madeline J's suspicions had already caused her too much grief. Darting from shadow to shadow, she scurried across the street. The car wasn't in any shadows, but she had to find her gloves.

She hurriedly circled the parked car. There were no gloves in sight. She thought she had put them on the roof, so she stooped to see if they had fallen on the ground. She found nothing.

She retraced her steps from shadow to shadow until she was back in her house. Shaking like a leaf, she collapsed on the sofa, tears of guilt, fear, and shame mingled with the upholstering of the sofa. She pleaded in her anguish. "God, I'll never do anything like this again."

How would she ever again be able to receive Communion? Father would know because she always took Communion. He would know! Maybe a visiting priest would come, and she could go to confession. She certainly couldn't go to Father Jon. Gracie cried all night.

Nadine and Jon talked in the darkened study for several more hours before kneeling together and praying. Jon escorted her up the stairs. He noticed some hesitancy as she walked that had not been present during her last visit.

"I'll see you after Mass in the morning," she whispered. He embraced her briefly before going back down the stairs.

Nadine dropped wearily into bed, while on the second floor Father Jon knelt in fervent prayer for his houseguest.

The early morning bells woke Nadine. She knew Jon was ringing them for her. The sound of the church bells comforted her. She felt so peaceful when they rang.

34

When she got to the kitchen, she laid out bacon in the skillet and a carton of eggs on the side board. She began heating the skillet. The aroma of cooking bacon soon filled the kitchen. She heard voices of the few parishioners who attended the early Mass as they left the church.

Suddenly, Jon bolted through the back door, locking it behind him. "Get upstairs!"

Nadine moved quickly to the back stairs and went up. She could hear knocking on the back door and then, a few moments later, the ringing of the front door bell.

Jon stirred the bacon once, turned down the burner, and removed his cassock. He took his time walking from the kitchen to the front door. "Oh, Madeline J, I completely forgot you said that you had brought some breakfast rolls for me. I'm so sorry."

Madeline J stood at the front door and glared at him. She moved forward like she was going to enter the rectory, but Jon stood his ground and blocked her entrance.

"Thank you for bringing them to me. I am sure they will be up to your superb standards." Then he shut the door in her face.

Madeline J's mouth fell open, and she muttered, "Why, I never!" She went slowly down the steps, her mind awhirl. He was hiding something, that was for sure, and she was going to get to the bottom of it. It had to be a woman. Father had a woman in the house! Father was having an affair!

She wandered toward her car and only slightly remembered that Gracie had not been at Mass that morning. Pulling away from the curb, she clipped the maple tree at the corner and ran through the stop sign at Main Street.

Gracie knew she could not go to Mass that morning, although she had made her peace with God during the night. No makeup could ever cover the large dark circles that encircled her eyes.

Gracie watched Madeline J's clumsy departure from the rectory door. When Madeline's car grazed a tree, Gracie wondered what Madeline was thinking. She didn't have to look out toward Main Street when she heard the screech and crash to know that one of the cars was Madeline J's.

Up in the upstairs study, Jon and Nadine heard the crash too. Nadine mouthed, "Madeline J?" Jon shrugged his shoulders and hoped to God it wasn't.

Looking out the window, he could see two cars sitting in the middle of Main Street. People were running toward the cars. One of the cars was Madeline's. "You'd better go," Nadine said softly.

Jon nodded. His heart pounded, and his legs felt almost too weak to move at the thought of being confronted on Main Street by an injured Madeline J. "I'll pray," Nadine said.

The frantic ringing of the doorbell increased Jon's anxiety as he hurried down the stairs. An excited neighbor stood at the door. "Father, come quick, one of your parishioner's has been hurt in an accident!"

The EMT said that Madeline J would probably be all right. She had a bump on her head and wasn't making much sense in what she was saying.

Father knelt beside her and anointed her as he prayed for her. She clung to his hand briefly before allowing the medics to put her into the ambulance. She didn't say anything to him.

Shaken, and his mind confused by Madeline J's silence, Jon returned to the rectory.

"Will she be all right?" Nadine's face was etched with concern. Jon breathed slowly before

36

nodding.

"Did she say anything to you? You told me how angry she was when you shut the door on her."

"It is in the Lord's hands."

"I turned off the bacon before it became a burnt offering. The smoke alarm wouldn't have gone off because you didn't put the batteries back in last night . . ."

Before she could finish her sentence, Jon turned abruptly and went into his office, closing the door behind him. His mind churned. What was his responsibility for Madeline J's accident, Nadine, the garden gloves and the figure in the dark? For a long time he knelt before the Lord, confessing his sins, hoping that a measure of peace would return to him.

He called the hospital and relayed his concern for Madeline J. He was sitting in the darkened room, still groping with his thoughts when the phone rang. It was the doctor attending Madeline J. The news was neither good nor comforting. He continued to wait before the Lord.

A faint knock on the door reminded him that he had left Nadine alone to cope with her pain and thoughts about how she may have contributed to the accident. "Come in," he spoke in a near whisper.

Nadine entered, her face stained with tears of her distress.

"Oh, my dear Nadine."

She sat on the edge of a chair, not looking at him. Her eyes had that far away look he had seen the day before. "I am going to leave before there are more problems," she announced.

"Leave?"

She nodded. "I'm sorry," she sniffed, as the tears poured out from behind the dam of her shut eyelids. She sobbed. "I have no right to be here. It has caused you nothing but pain, and now this accident."

Carefully, Jon blotted her face with a tissue. "No, I am the one to say I am sorry. I left you alone out there with your tears and fears. I promised you when we started this that I would 'blot' your tears and be with you until . . ." His hands gently caressed her face. "I made a promise to you, and that promise will not be broken because others do not understand. Do you understand that, Nadine?"

"But, . . ."

"No 'buts', I am committed to our agreement. Nadine, how could I leave you alone now that you are so much closer to the end than the beginning? No, my little one, we are a twosome. Is that clear?" Jon's voice was gentle but stern.

"What about Madeline J? Wasn't it the anger, caused by her suspicions, that led to the accident?"

"Probably not. She has suffered from high blood pressure for years and has refused to take the medication the doctor prescribed. That phone call was from the hospital. She had a stroke, which may be why she couldn't stop her car at the corner. This is not her first stroke.

"Oh." Nadine's voice sounded soft and muted.

"Now, don't you think it is about time we had a meal around here?" Jon's voice had a lightness that belied his true feelings.

Later that afternoon, Gracie observed Father Jon and a young woman getting into Father Jon's other car. The priest was driving. "Must be his car, like Charlie said," she announced to the living room. Satisfied, she went upstairs to take a much needed nap.

After the commotion of the accident at Main and Maple had settled, Charlie drove around town.

He tried to make it look like he was just out patrolling when he passed the church. Father Jon's car was parked in its usual spot. There was no other car. Charlie checked out the lot behind the church and rectory. No other car there either.

Then, just on a sixth sense or whatever, he wrote down the license plate numbers of the priest's car. A short while later, he looked at the faxed report from the Bureau of Motor Vehicles. Both cars were registered to Father Jon. He put the information in his desk drawer and sat frowning at the discolored and out of date calendar on his wall. He phoned Gracie. There was no answer. "Dear Aunt Gracie, you are on to something and don't even know it."

Seventy or eighty miles away, a young, distinguished-looking couple shared a dinner in a small restaurant. They talked and talked. Nadine was past her tears now and appreciated Jon's attention. She said she would leave early in the morning before Mass. She told him her schedule for the week or so to come.

He nodded and watched her. Her eyes flitted from his face to a blank spot on the wall and back all too often. He knew the time was not long now. She did not talk about the pain or the fears. If she was not at peace with life and the situation, she was doing a courageous job of hiding her feelings.

"I want you to know how much I cherish you," she dared not look at him. "I was so mixed up, so confused, and so alone. And I know what a price you are paying, and will pay, for your friendship with me. I am sorry to have caused you so much trouble but also grateful that you wanted to be part of what I am going through."

Jon reached out and took her hand. She looked at him and quickly glanced away. Tears were brimming in her eyes again. His voice betrayed his attempt to be nonchalant. He sounded as if something was choking him. "Nadine, you have meant more to me than you can ever imagine. I am the one who is so very appreciative of having the privilege of knowing and caring for you. You have taught me so much about myself, others, and life. Thank you." He reached out his napkin and blotted her tears before dabbing at those in his own eyes.

Appearing as discreet lovers, they lingered at a small park and watched the sun go down. It was dark, as they had planned, when they returned to the rectory. The telephone answering machine was blinking. "Seven messages! The whole town must have been trying to get a hold of me."

"Aren't you going to listen to them? We can talk more upstairs in the study."

Jon reluctantly punched the play button. The first and third were from the hospital. Reports on Madeline J, who was in stable condition, and Mr. Colly, who wasn't very stable. The old man's voice cracked and wheezed as he told the priest he was going to go home and never come back to the hospital. He had made up his mind. "Enough was enough!" he gasped.

Nadine had left the room. Jon hoped Nadine hadn't heard that one.

Two calls were from the Bridge Club, informing the priest of Madeline's accident. The other two callers just hung up. It was the last call that concerned him. Charlie, the local police officer, said there was something important that he needed to talk with him about. He said it was about Father's 'other car' and then hung up. Jon decided that there was no reason to call at that late hour. The 'other car' would be gone by daybreak anyway.

Upstairs, pad and pencil in hand, Jon listened to Nadine. They planned the funeral and burial. He

40

showed her the picture he had taken of the spot in the cemetery.

She smiled and said it was to her liking. She asked how he had explained his need for a single plot to the caretaker.

"Easy. I told him that a distant relative who is getting along in years wanted to be assured of a spot."

"He bought that?" She giggled. "Getting along in years? I sure hope he never looks in the casket."

"No, I bought it, the plot." Jon's grinned. "You said it was to be a closed casket."

"Uh huh. That's OK, isn't it? After all, it will be only me in there."

I am going to preach the funeral Mass. Anything you want to pass on?"

Nadine hugged her knees and rocked back and forth on the floor. Her breathing ragged. Jon prayed for relief from the pain.

"I try not to yell and scream, but sometimes it is so hard." Her words came in short broken bursts.

"It's a lot closer, isn't it? Jon was kneeling beside her. She nodded. "I counted your pills this visit. You've eaten them like candy."

Nadine, her head bowed, answered in a tiny voice. "Yes, I was trying to not let you know. But you guessed." Her voice was just a whisper now.

Jon cradled her in his arms. "Do I need to take you to the hospital now?" he whispered.

"No, just wipe my tears."

Charlie was at home when the priest called. Father Jon said very little, just come now. Jon knew Charlie was needed for police business, but would he drive his own car?

Charlie asked, "It's all over?" Jon's voice

affirmed.   Charlie called Dr. Richart, the county coroner, and asked him to meet him at the priest's house.

Dr. Richart came immediately. After a brief examination, he accepted a package of documents from Father Jon. He had known about the situation for some time. "She prepared well. She was a brave woman," he commented.

Charlie didn't say much, except, "You know, my Aunt Gracie was getting really close to knowing?" Jon smiled as he thought of the gloves.

It wasn't an ordinary day for the town. Everyone knew that a young woman had died at the rectory. Charlie and Dr. Richart were seen leaving the rectory before the Mathias' Funeral Home hearse drove up.   Without Madeline J to distort the news, most of the people in town accepted it with reserved interest. Father Jon prepared for the funeral Mass.

The church was packed, which was amazing since none of them there had even known Nadine. "Who was this woman?" Jon began. "She was any woman, or man, or child. She was a child of God, but on this earth she was alone." The somber crowd listened attentively. At the end of his message, Jon's voice became soft but distinct.   To the silent congregation, he whispered, "What would Jesus have you do?"

The Bridge

Jon laid his pencil in the little groove at the back edge of the desk. Stretching his tired and tense muscles, he straightened the small notebook in front of him. During the past thirty days he had faithfully written in the journal. Tomorrow he was to meet with the Bishop. He was afraid to think about that appointment, yet that was all that had cluttered his mind since he was relieved of his parish work after the funeral.

Nadine had died in his arms after a long struggle with cancer. He had befriended the lonely young woman at a retreat over eighteen months ago. She had questions about mortality and her approaching death. He had searched scripture and Church writings to answer her questions. In the end, she was peaceful. He had ministered to her mind and her soul. It was "the rest of the story," as the saying goes that caused the Bishop to send a replacement the day Nadine was buried.

43

Some in his parish had begun to raise questions about the strange car that was often parked overnight at the rectory. Someone, possibly Madeline J, had called the Chancery to report the "incidents". No one had ever asked him or seemed to even care, he mused over and over.

Then, so it seemed, the whole town turned out for the funeral Mass of a young woman no one else knew. Dr. Richart, the coroner, had known, and also Charlie, the police chief. They were sworn to secrecy as Nadine had requested.

She had transferred ownership of her car to Jon almost a year ago. She didn't care much for the few family members she could trace, who lived several states away. They didn't respond when she called them less than six months or so ago.

Jon wondered what they thought when they got the official letter from the coroner's office confirming her death. As she requested, he mailed her final letters to them the morning she was buried.

All this was in the past now, or was it. Father Jon was to go to the Chancery in the morning. Would he leave the Chancery as a priest? Only the Bishop could determine that.

He could hear the afternoon prayer bells sounding. Hurriedly, he put on his cassock before leaving the small, sparse room. With slow, measured steps the priests and brothers in residence at the monastery moved toward the chapel. As the prayers began, Father Jon took his assigned place at the end of the pew where the least of the brothers knelt. He felt sorrowful as the Psalms were read. This was the last of the afternoon prayers he would attend, maybe the last time he would read them as a priest.

The next morning, a bright, sunny day greeted Jon as he entered his car. The short drive to the Chancery passed in what seemed like split seconds. A wrought iron fence surrounded the church offices and Bishop's residence.

The door opened before he reached the top step. A severe-faced priest ushered him into a small sitting room. "The Bishop has been delayed a few moments," he said.

Jon was alone. Fear climbed up onto his shoulder and sneered in his inner ear. "You dummy, you thought you could follow the ways of that book you read and have an agape love relationship with that girl just because she was dying. No one believes you, and she is dead now. What are you . . ." It took Jon that long to know who was talking. It wasn't self, and it wasn't God.

"In the name of Jesus, stop!" he spoke in a low voice. An outsider would have thought he was talking to himself.

Almost instantly, the door opened, and the same stern-faced priest beckoned him to follow. Jon knew the routine, having visited with the Bishop on less stressful days.

"Your Excellency."

"Jon." The Bishop nodded and indicated a chair across the desk from where he sat. The door closed behind him with a small click.

Silence permeated the room. The Bishop tilted back in his chair and shuffled the papers in a large folder on his desk. Jon scarcely breathed.

Suddenly, the Bishop sat up straight and snapped the folder shut. "Father Jon, all I see in these papers are accusations of irregularities, but no deliberate sin. Answer me one question. Is your conscience clear?'

"Yes, your Excellency."

The Bishop responded, "Bishop James Paul." He swiveled his chair halfway around and stared out the window. "You made your confession while you were at the monastery?"

"As a sinful man, a confession of my daily sins. Specifically involving Nadine, no. There was no sin."

Only the deep breathing of the two men filled the room now. He was sure the Bishop could hear the pounding of his heart as he waited expectantly to be challenged about his last statement. None came.

After what seemed to be a long period of time, Bishop James Paul turned to face Jon again. Jon noticed that his stern continence seemed to have softened. "I find no statements against you to be true. I accept your word without reservation, Father. I only wish that I were younger, and not of this office, so that I could more often do what my conscience tells me Jesus would do."

Jon released a deep sigh and let his eyes meet the Bishop's eyes. Bishop James Paul had accepted his statement. A spark of hope jumped within him. Jon said, "Nadine needed to be loved, taught, and cared for in her last months."

Bishop James Paul held up his hand. "Enough said. I find no fault in your actions. Now the problem is where to place you. I have two needs in the diocese, and they are both not without grave danger for a priest such as you who listens so closely to Jesus' heart. Over near the sand hills is a small community in need of a pastor. There are about 24 families who are served on rotation by the four other priests within the general area. They need a permanent priest."

Jon relaxed slightly as he considered what the Bishop said.

"However," James Paul continued, "in the urban area, there is a nearly bankrupt parish in the heart of the most undesirable part of the city. There

46

are fewer than 20 members left, all elderly, all staunch believers, even though they are not exactly orthodox in their faith. A few years back, in an attempt to preserve the church and parish, an elected official was prevailed upon to have the site declared a national historical building. Now it is nothing more than a skeleton of its former self, surrounded by a chain link fence to keep the 'undesirables' out. That is their word, not mine," the Bishop continued. "I have yet to find a priest capable of restoring that church and parish and of cutting through all the governmental red tape that was created by the preservation of this ancient building."

To himself, Jon considered the parish at the edge of the sand hills as what he was used to, a small, rural, tightly knit community with families. That meant children and life for the parish. It certainly would keep him active in all facets of life, and he considered that ideal. He was aware of silence in the room and looked at his Bishop. Had he missed something while he was thinking about the sand hills, he wondered? No, the Bishop was looking out the window again. How long had the silence been? He waited.

"Father Jon," the Bishop turned back to look at him. "I am going to assign you to St. Ignatius Parish in the city. I suspect you are what those people need."

If the Bishop had expected a response from Jon, he wasn't disappointed. "The inner city?" His voice sounded pinched and high.

Before he could utter another sound, the Bishop raised his hand to silence him. "Yes, you and Jesus are needed there." Then, changing the subject slightly, Bishop James Paul hurried on. "Father Malcom packed your personal belongings and will have them here this afternoon. If you find anything

47

missing, just make a note of what he has overlooked and send it to him. If anything needs to be returned to that parish, please bring it by here at your convenience, and I shall have it returned. It is best that you do not return to your old parish."

The look in the eyes of the Bishop clearly commanded obedience. Jon nodded his assent.

Less than an hour before, he had left the monastery, not knowing his fate. Now, with his car keys in his hand, Jon stood outside the Chancery. The last 30 minutes had passed so quickly that he could hardly believe all that had taken place. He was still Father Jon, he had a new assignment, and the Bishop had given him his blessing. "Inner city, St. Ignatius, red tape, unorthodox parishioners, chain link fencing, a historical building, politicians, obstinate custodians," . . . too many conflicting thoughts and emotions crowded his mind. Jon wanted to dance in the driveway like he had seen someone do in a movie one time.

When he crossed the bridge that led into the bowels of the city, Jon sensed a profound change. The joy he had when he left the Chancery vanished as dark, grimy buildings crowded the narrow streets. He could feel the helplessness of those who lived in the ramshackle structures. He wondered what St. Ignatius would be like.

St. Ignatius

Just before dusk, Jon turned onto the narrow one-way street called 3rd Avenue. The brownstone and dirty red brick tenement buildings crowded the trash-strewn sidewalks. In spite of 'no parking' signs on one side of the street, cars were parked on either side, reducing the flow of traffic to a single lane. Occasionally cars were even double-parked, nearly blocking any vehicular traffic on the street.

Jon parked in the narrow alley-like drive that ended at the back door of the St. Ignatius rectory. Broken glass, crushed pop cans, and paper trash littered the walkway to the front door. Jon attempted to use the key he was given to open the cumbersome lock of that door. Nothing happened. A voice spoke from a group of youth loitering in front of the church. "Try the back door, Father."

Jon turned to look at the 13 eyes watching him. One youth had a black patch covering one eye.

"You're Patch?" Jon asked.

"What's it to you!" snarled the one-eyed youth.

"I was told you would be here and . . ."

"I don't know nuthin," responded the boy.

Jon shrugged his shoulders and started for the back of the rectory.

"Hey you, don't leave until he says so!" shouted a dark haired youth, whose long hair failed to cover the scar that crossed his forehead.

Jon stopped, "And you are?"

"Scar."

Jon nodded.

"Let him go. He ain't nothing but a sissy priest. He won't last any longer than the others." The boys laughed.

Jon shoved hard with his shoulder on the back door. It opened with a groan. Stale air greeted him. He groped for the light switch and found none. "You'll have trouble with the lights," the Chancellor had said as he handed him the key and a dark gym bag. "Extra bulbs and a flashlight." The Chancellor was never one to say a whole lot. Putting the gym bag on what appeared to be a table, Jon fished in it for a flashlight. Soon the beam of the light confirmed to Jon that he was in the kitchen. He shut the back door and slid the deadbolt in firmly. He did not want any unwelcome guests.

Cautiously, he explored the rooms on either side of the hall that ran from the kitchen to the front door. He found a dining room, a small parlor, and an even smaller office. He banged his shins on a small stool and then again on a chair. The light switches were the old kind, round with a twist knob. None responded to his efforts to turn on the lights. In the parlor he found a lamp with a bulb and tried to turn it on. No luck. He found the cord, and with his flashlight beam followed it to the wall. It was unplugged. "Figures," Jon said to the musty air. The bulb flashed when he plugged in the cord. "Extra light bulbs!" Feeling a little like the cartoon character with a light bulb exclamation point hovering above his head, Jon made his way back to the kitchen and the gym bag. *Oh oh.* Jon felt a tinge of concern. There were three full packs of bulbs in the bag. Armed with one pack, he returned to the parlor. Once the burned out bulb was replaced, a warm glow lit the room. Satisfied, Jon knelt and prayed.

Outside, the group of young men watched with distained interest as they caught sight of a light beam that moved from room to room. They saw the flash behind the closed blinds of the front parlor and snickered. They expected the priest to return to his car in a hurry.

Across the street, from the fourth floor window of the building, a stubble-bearded man watched the group in front of St. Ignatius and the car parked beside the rectory. He wiped his runny eyes on his shirtsleeve. "Bishop has sent another priest."

Down at the corner, the proprietors of a little grocery also noticed the car at the rectory at St. Ignatius. Miss Claire and her sister, Agnes, operated a little store in the basement of the building. They lived in the windowless storeroom behind the grocery. A heavy chain link grill protected the front window from intruders, and at night a barred door was secured from the inside in front of the regular door. A ventilation shaft from the roof of the building allowed some air to seep into their basement apartment.

The backroom had been a coal bin in

previous years. A rusted iron door covered the old coal chute opening that they called their "secret escape hatch." They had reasoned they would climb up the steep chute and crawl out into the alleyway if they couldn't get out the front door. Of course, that was the plan when they were in their 30's and 40's. Now, at the age of 78 and 72, neither could climb well, and Agnes weighed over 200 pounds.

They rarely made the effort to go up the few steps out front, cross the street, and go into the side door of old St. Ignatius. Claire complained about her arthritis hindering her so. Neither knelt for prayers anymore, Agnes because of her size, and Claire because she was the older one . . . and her arthritis. In reality, Claire weighed only 98 pounds and was incredibly healthy. So they missed church, except for 'high holy days,' whatever that meant to them.

After replacing a few more bulbs, Jon went upstairs. One large bedroom with linens on the bed seemed to be the priest's room. After more light bulb replacements, he found the bathroom. The water was dark and stale in the commode from lack of use. Musty towels were in the linen closet. It would do for now until daylight revealed the true condition of the rectory.

Before dawn, the incessant alarm on the clock he had propped on a chair woke him. Picking up his flashlight, he made his way to the bathroom and began his early morning routine. At least the water ran in the sink, and there was a mirror. The stubble on his chin seemed to defy the razor. After a couple of minor nicks, Jon smoothed the irritated skin with an antiseptic stick and considered growing a beard. That idea didn't last long, considering what the Bishop had said in his last communication with the priests.

52

A change of clothing made him feel better. He was now ready to make his first entrance into the church next door. Lifting a key off the hook in the kitchen, where someone had used a marker to write 'church side door,' he saw the second hook was marked 'house door' but held no key. He dug into the bag the Chancellor had given him and pulled out a mass of keys strung together with twine. He hoped one would work on the side door. After a few false tries, a satisfying 'click' released the door lock from its prison. Once outside, he took four steps and stood at the church door. The key went in smoothly. Before he could turn it, the door was jerked open.

Facing him was a small, thin man more in need of a shave than Jon had been. "You were coming over here?" Squinting eyes, barely visible behind wire-rimmed glasses that sat lopsided on a bony nose, stared at him. The thin lips barely moved as the man spoke.

"Yes, I am."

The man in the doorway did not move.

"I am Father Jon, and I am coming to the church to celebrate Mass."

Still the man did not move.

"I would like to come into the church, please."

"I am Angus Cosstilla, custodian and keeper of St. Ignatius." Angus made a movement that indicated he was going to close the door before Father Jon entered.

Jon put his foot in the way of the shutting door and gently pushed it back open. "Please close it after I am in, Angus. That will keep it secure inside."

"Oh." Angus's eyes actually blinked.

Amazing, I almost thought his eyes were frozen in that squint. Fascinating!

Jon turned toward the sacristy. The old

53

man's hand snatched at his arm. "This way, floor is weak."

Negotiating several steps, the two men were in the Sanctuary. The morning light was just beginning to show through the few remaining stained glass windows. "Beautiful!" Jon spoke in almost a whisper.

"Yes, it was."

Genuflecting before the ornate altar, Jon noticed the Sanctuary lamp burning. "Who will come to Mass this morning?"

Angus looked downward and mumbled something.

Jon continued into the sacristy. It was sparse and clean. Vestments were laid out. The Chalice and cruets sat ready on the side table by the door.

"Who will serve . . ." Jon's voice trailed off as he saw Angus pulling on a worn garment. He could hear the sound of voices in the church. They were all there, fifteen elderly parishioners who shuffled in through a side door. Slowly they took seats in the worn pews. Each one was dressed in Sunday best of years gone by.

With methodical care, Jon vested in the garments while his heart sought Jesus. Angus thought the priest was slow for a young man and cleared his throat, trying to hurry him.

Jon rang the bell as he stepped into the Sanctuary and listened to the rising of fifteen elderly bodies. There were scrapes and coughs and thuds. When he looked out over the small congregation, they were all standing expectantly, even as they clutched the pews in front of them for support. "Good morning."

After he returned to the rectory, Jon dug through the bags of food he had brought with him.

He found his choice of breakfast food was a box of dry cereal. The doorbell rang. It seemed the bell was being twisted incessantly. "I'm coming!" He called out to no one. A quick look through the peephole revealed two women who had been at Mass earlier. They were holding a box of food. "Well, this looks innocent enough," said Jon, opening the door.

The heavy-set lady greeted the priest with gushing words of how wonderful it was to have a priest at the rectory again. The very thin lady thrust the box of food at Jon and said something about a store on the corner, in the basement, or something like that. Then the two turned and hobbled away, one clutching the rail for support and the other one clutching her. Jon called out his thanks and realized he did not know their names. They hurried away as fast as their conditions allowed them.

Thinking back to the Mass, it seemed to have gone well, even if he had to carry the Host to each one where they sat. He was fearful that they could not stand or walk without a pew to hang on to. Those two ladies sat in the third pew on the left.

Jon found a quart of milk in the box of stuff from the ladies and happily used most of it on his cereal. After a quick check of the refrigerator, Jon decided to drink the rest of the milk.

Gang Encounter

A loud bang and the sound of breaking glass came from the front of the house. Jon went to investigate. A brick and broken glass bottle littered the front porch. On the street, the gang of 'thirteen eyes' stood defiantly holding bricks, rocks, and sticks in their hands. Across the street, an equally defiant group stood. Only the narrow, cluttered street separated the two gangs. A flash of sunlight on a knife blade in the hand of one of the gang across the street caught Jon's attention. Jon hesitated only long enough to whisper 'Jesus, help me' as he unlocked the front door and stepped out on the porch. His appearance caused a mild stir among those on the other side of the street. One of the 'thirteen eyes' said, without looking around, "Get back inside, Father, this is our fight."

Sirens could be heard in the distance. Maybe they were coming here, Jon thought, or going some place else. In any event, the sound mobilized both gangs, and they disappeared. That was when Jon saw a boy lying face down in the street. He quickly moved to the inert form, making the sign of the cross as he went. The boy was bleeding badly. "Still bleeding, still alive," Jon muttered as he looked for the wound. It was deep in the young man's stomach. Jon pulled off his own shirt and pressed it against the gap. He looked up as he heard feet running toward him. It was another youngster. Her face was white with fear.

"The police are coming," she cried out. "Quick! Move him inside where they can't find him."

It took a few seconds for the request to sink in. It didn't make sense as the boy would probably die without some medical attention. The girl was now tugging at the inert figure, trying to get him up. Jon stooped, picked him up, and followed the girl inside one of the tenement buildings. "Down here, in here!" she instructed. After passing through two cluttered rooms, Jon was in a small room behind a bathroom. "Put him here."

"Why are you hiding him? He may die from his wound?"

"You don't understand! He is my brother! He will be kept by the police if they take him to the hospital! I would never see him again!"

"And if he dies here?"

"He won't," the girl said with confidence. "There is a doctor who will come here and take care of him. And besides, you are a priest, you will pray for him."

"Yeah, a priest who just carried a badly injured young man from the center of the street into this." He waved his hand to include everything in sight. The room was far from clean. "Who is this doctor? How will he know to come here?" Jon realized he had no idea who the boy was, who the girl was, who the doctor was, or even how this part of the inner city worked. An involuntary shiver ran up his bare back.

"Don't worry, the doctor will come. That gang in front of the rectory will notify him. You'll see." She looked down at the unconscious form on the filthy bed and patted his arm.

Jon stepped back and considered leaving, except he had no shirt. He could see the headlines in the paper. **'Priest Rescues Injured Youth,'** and a picture of him without shirt or Roman collar. He wished the Bishop had sent him to the sand hills.

Sirens stopped outside. The knot in his stomach made him want to vomit. "Keep quiet and stay here," the girl commanded, closing the door to the bathroom as she left them. The boy moaned. Jon, holding the makeshift bandage against the gap in the stomach, knelt beside him and prayed.

Sometime later, after the police had left without finding the injured boy, a small, dark-skinned man came into the room with the girl. He looked at the priest and nodded. Feeling dismissed, Jon moved away from the boy. "Here, Father, wear this shirt to get home." One of the 'thirteen eyes' gang appeared behind the doctor and girl. "Think it will fit to get you across the street."

Once back in the rectory and in clerical garb again, Jon unpacked the rest of the food he brought with him as well as what had been brought to his door. He retreated to what appeared to be the office in the rectory, fell on his knees, and later on his face, before God. He had never been in such turmoil in his whole life. The conflicts in his spirit while caring for Nadine were nothing compared to the things that had happened in the short time since he took up residence in St. Ignatius Rectory. The phone rang. Only a dial tone greeted his 'hello'.

In the silence of the kitchen, a rat gnawed on the food left there. Jon fell asleep on the office floor.

The constant ring of the doorbell woke Jon from his sleep. He had slept a long time as it was dark out. Stumbling to his feet, he considered removing the bell from the door as his first act of restoring the parish. The peephole revealed the gang member called Patch. Pulling the door open to the extension of the safety chain, he greeted the young man.

"Father, here is your shirt. We tried to get the blood out."

A quick glance at his watch was all that Jon needed to confirm it was nighttime. "Is he alright?"

"The doc says you did the right thing."

Jon repeated himself, "Is he alright?"

"Well, sort of."

"What do you mean by that?"

"He needs a blood transfusion."

"Are you alone, Patch?" Patch nodded. "Just a minute," Jon closed the door and released the chain. Opening it again, he beckoned Patch to enter the rectory.

"I can't, Father, we took an oath to never enter a church."

"This is not the church, this is my home."

Patch looked around him, as if to see if anyone would see him enter the rectory, before stepping inside the door. Jon promptly fastened the door shut.

They stepped into the tiny office and closed the door behind them before Jon turned on a light.

"This room and the kitchen have no

windows." Jon explained. Patch was staring at the various religious symbols in the room. A large, wooden crucifix hung on the wall behind the desk. To the left, the wall was covered with books. On the desk was a dusty bottle of something. Indicating a chair for Patch, Jon sat on the edge of the desk.

"What is that?" Patch pointed at the dusty bottle.

"It is for Holy Oil. I imagine it is empty right now." Jon picked it up and shook it, nodding in agreement with his previous statement.

"Now, tell me about the blood transfusion."

"He lost so much blood. The doctor wants to give him a transfusion. But he can't."

"Let me guess, the doctor is not a real doctor."

"Oh, yes he is! In his home country, he was a fine doctor, but here they do not recognize his degrees."

"So he is the doctor on call for the gangs?"

"No, he is not!"

"Couldn't he just turn the boy over to a recognized doctor who could get the blood transfusion done."

Patch looked straight at Jon, "Geez, Father, then the police would get him!"

"Who, the doctor or the boy? So why did you come here, besides to return my shirt?"

"Well, we sort of hoped you could do something."

"Like a miracle?" Jon said lightly.

Patch nodded then stood, "I gotta be going before anyone knows I am here."

"Who is going to tell them? No windows, remember? Besides, we haven't solved the problem of the blood transfusion." Jon's mind was racing, trying to figure out how to help the young gang

60

member and not compromise either him or himself. "Does the doctor know what blood type?" He asked this question without expecting an answer.

"Yeah, he does."

"Dare I ask what type?"

"He said he needs 'O positive,' whatever that means."

Jon groaned and dropped to his knees. Patch, startled by the sudden move, stared wide-eyed at the priest. "Oh, Father in heaven, why this type, and why now? What would you have me do?"

"Are you sick, Father?"

"No," Jon fished for his wallet from his hip pocket. Flipping it open, he pulled out a blood donor card. "What does it say on there?"

Patch squinted his one eye and studied the writing.

"Can you read?"

"Some," mumbled Patch.

"What letter is on the line?"

"Zero"

"That is also known as an 'O.' What comes right after that 'zero?'"

"A plus sign."

"Put the two together."

"O plus."

"Also known as 'O positive'."

Normal Days

After Mass in the morning, a very tired priest entered his house with one thing in mind. He was going to go to bed, at least for the rest of the morning if not the whole day. He turned the ringer off on the phone and closed the bedroom door. His last thought, before falling into a deep sleep, was, "Please, Lord, don't let anyone ring that doorbell."

Hours later, Jon awoke to the sound of tapping some place in the house. At least it wasn't the doorbell ringing or the phone. A short time later, Jon listened to the two calls on the answering machine. This rectory, in spite of its primitive light fixtures and doorbell, did have a few modern devices.

The first call was from the Bishop's office inquiring about his needs at St. Ignatius. He noted the time and decided that he would call back in the morning. The second call was from the local police

Precinct asking if he was aware of the gang fight in front of his rectory yesterday. And would he please return the call to Detective Janski as soon as possible. He wanted to erase that call and say he never got it when the Detective called again, but his conscience wouldn't let him. The tapping sound started again. It seemed to come from the kitchen. Jon, relieved to have to investigate the sound and not call the Precinct immediately, followed the sound to the back door.

Making a mental note to get a peephole for the back door, he called through the door. "Who's there?" There was no answer.

A short time later Jon crossed the street to the store on the corner, kept by Miss Claire and Miss Agnes. They were thrilled to have the priest come. He picked out some canned goods, a chunk of cheese that looked like it had been in the store since it opened, and another quart of milk. The two sisters argued about taking the money he offered. He was a cash-paying customer. They had so few of those that the temptation was to take the money. But then again, he was the new priest over at St. Ignatius, and should they give him the food as a tithe, so to speak. All of this was discussed in front of Jon as though he was not even there. At last Miss Agnes won out and refused his money. Jon picked up the items, and as he left the counter he tucked some money under a jar of pickles where Miss Claire could see it.

After such a tumultuous beginning to his assignment at St. Ignatius, life took on a humdrum tone. Detective Janski came to see him about the gang fight in front of the rectory. Father Jon said very little, and the detective didn't pry. The Detective also was aware of the difficulties of St. Ignatius Church since it had been declared a historical site. He wished the priest well and advised him to keep his doors locked. Jon agreed.

Angus was reliable, to a point, as a server for the Mass. He lived across the street from the church. When he was not in the church itself, he was watching it from his fourth floor flat. Angus appeared to have the only key to the side entrance fence to St. Ignatius. When Jon asked him if he had the key to the front-padlocked gate, Angus acted like he didn't know what gate or what padlock Father was talking about.

During the first few days, nearly all the living congregant members attended the Mass each morning. Then one morning only three people were in the church, Father Jon, Angus, and a frail ninety year old.

The refrigerator did not work, so the first order of business with the Chancery was to request a replacement and for permission to hire a housekeeper or a cleaning service. The refrigerator came within a few hours. The other request seemed to have been overlooked.

During the afternoons, Father Jon walked around the neighborhood, meeting the people and getting a sense of how this part of the city functioned. He learned that police rarely come to the street fights like the one that occurred on his second day. Only when there was a death or injury too severe for the injured person to leave did the police come. Most of the neighborhood knew Father had carried the last victim inside a building. This made Father Jon a part of them since he had not told the police where the young man was. The shopkeepers, all struggling against the poverty of the neighborhood, offered Jon something when he went into the shops. Jon accepted the gifts. He often found someone on the street to give the gifts to.

Thirteen eyes were eleven since the street fight. They watched Father as he moved among the community, giving a word of encouragement or a helping hand. Along about dusk Father returned to the rectory. Eleven eyes followed him. "Hey, Padre"

Jon stopped. The six crowded in around him. Scar spoke for the group. "Thanks, bro, for taking Mighty inside and what else you done."

"Bro?"

"Yeah, you know, brother. You are almost a blood-brother now."

Patch spoke up. "He is a blood-brother, his blood is in Mighty."

"How is he, Mighty?"

"Aw, he'll get better. Doc says you saved Mighty's life twice."

"Then what?"

"Then we get even with the Street Rats for knifing him."

"The Street Rats?"

"Yeah, that's their name. They live like rats, eat like rats, and try to come in our territory like rats."

"Oh." Jon could not think of anything else to say.

Across the street, from his fourth floor window, Angus watched the group of hoodlums that surrounded Father Jon. His rubbed his eyes, hoping his foggy vision would clear. If only the Father would just go into his house and stay put. Angus had no use for any of the young thugs of the neighborhood. It was because of them that he had gotten the city to put the eight-foot high chain-link fence around St. Ignatius, and he kept the only key to the side entrance. No one was going to damage God's house while he was custodian.

The discussion in front of the rectory broke up, and Father Jon went inside. Angus muttered at the boys who remained standing around outside.

65

"No good, up to no good."

Jon asked Angus again about the missing key to the front gate. Angus refused to talk about it. Father asked for the key to the side entrance. Angus reluctantly identified the key in the bundle of keys held together with twine. It was then that Angus made up his mind. If Father was going to open the doors to anyone, like the gang, he was going to be prepared. It took him a few days of rummaging through old boxes sitting in the corners of his apartment before he found it. It was still shiny and felt good in his hand. It seemed like just yesterday that he had bought it at the pawnshop. He tucked the gun into his belt. He was prepared now.

Changes Coming

The Chancery left a message on the answering machine. Jon poked the play key. The Bishop had earmarked some money for the beginning of the restoration of St. Ignatius. The first step had already been taken by the Chancery. The Bishop's office hired **Restoration Now, Inc.** to inspect and determine what structural repairs had to be done now and those that could wait until donors were found for specific needs. **Restoration Now, Inc.**, experts in historic restoration, would be contacting Father early next week. Also, in regard to the need for a housekeeper or cleaning service, the diocese had contacted **Mary Jane Cleaners,** who promised to be in contact with Father Jon this week. This was good news. Jon had tried his hand at doing the laundry and decided that was not a gift God had bestowed on him.

Mary Jane Cleaners phoned early the next morning. A woman named Linda, who seemed to be the owner, asked Father Jon many questions about the kind of housekeeping he needed done. She said her workers either were general cleaners or special-skill cleaners, such as kitchen clean up after banquets. Jon made it clear he needed a cleaner to cover the house from top to bottom, at least initially, and also do laundry. Linda said her cleaners did not do personal laundry, but she could recommend someone who would clean, including laundry. Since the Bishop's office had made the contact with *Mary Jane Cleaners,* Jon was hesitant to hire someone outside of that cleaning service. Linda assured him she could pay this particular woman through *Mary Jane Cleaners*. "But I have one important question I must still ask you. Can you guarantee the safety of our worker? I understand from the newspapers that St. Ignatius is in a very undesirable area of town."

Jon took a deep breath and prayed for wisdom before he answered the lady. He wanted to tell Linda that he didn't need her help, but then that would have been a lie. "Your worker will be as safe as I am."

The answer seemed to suit Linda, so she said she would be contacting the person and give her his phone number. "Thank you for using *Mary Jane Cleaners*." And the line went dead.

Jon stood for a while, holding the phone. "I wonder who Mary Jane is."

The *Restoration Now, Inc.* people spent two days looking into all the nooks and crannies of St. Ignatius. A nervous Angus followed behind Jon and the 'experts'. Angus tried to halt the inspectors with misleading answers or questions that had no reference to St. Ignatius. Jon took mental notes about the eccentric behavior of his custodian and server.

Several trips were made into the bowels of

the basement. It seems there was no basement until about 60 years ago, when the church decided to put in a heating system. That was the cause of the weak floor outside the sacristy. Wishing to make it easier for the priest to get to the coal furnace, a tunnel was cut, allowing entrance from the basement of the rectory to the basement of the church. This meant a trip into the basement of the rectory. Jon was glad he had others with him as he descended into the dank and musty basement. Evidence of rodents was everywhere. The old tunnel from rectory to church building was filled with debris.

Angus was astounded that the two buildings were connected. When the new heating system was installed with an automated fueling system, the original furnace, coal chute, and tunnel where abandoned behind the newer furnace. No one had ever taken it out. Jon watched the experts and could almost see dollar signs as they calculated how much it would cost to remove the old furnace, close up the tunnel, and shore up the weakened floor outside the sacristy. The experts left that afternoon with a promise to be talking with the Bishop's Office and assurances that St. Ignatius could be saved.

Of course it could be saved! That was the whole purpose of making St. Ignatius an historical site. Jon wondered if the politician who was responsible for designating St. Ignatius a national historical site was still around. He doubted it. He understood something about politics, especially if someone wanted to be re-elected.

On one of his late afternoon walks through his part of the inner city, Jon was joined by a small, dark-skinned man. He recognized him as being the doctor who had come to care for Mighty when he was knifed. They talked about the weather, the narrow streets, the crowded sidewalks, and other things. Finally the man said, "Mighty wants to see you."

Jon nodded. "Where is he? Is he still in the building across from the rectory?"

"No, will you go to see him?"

"Sure, but how, when, and where?"

"Patch will take you there tonight."

By this time they were standing in front of an abandoned building. "The newspapers call this building an eyesore," Jon commented.

"It is just an old building, not an eyesore. It can still have a purpose. People in this area need this building. Back home the people would be glad to have such a sturdy building."

"Tell me about 'back home'. How did you get here, and why?" For a moment Jon was afraid the man would just turn and walk away.

"Back home, I was a doctor, a real doctor. The regime, the dictator, hated all educated people. He killed them if they did not escape to the mountains and across the border. My wife and I fled one night. We walked for many nights. We always hid in the jungles during the day. We had nothing but our clothing and this." He held up a small silver cross. "I was a dead man if they caught us so carrying this wasn't something that would hurt me."

"You are a Christian?"

"Yes."

"What about your wife."

"She was, too. The missionaries gave us this cross when we were married. She is not anymore."

Jon just waited. The small man hesitated, then went on. "When we reached safety, we were put in a 'camp' with lots of other persons from our country.

A church here in America offered to sponsor

70

us to come to this great country. We were very fortunate to be selected to come. But I cannot be a doctor here. I have to work at other things. It is a great difficulty."

For a while the two men just leaned side by side against the old building. Two derelicts came down the street, arguing over who had the last swallow from the now empty bottle. When they saw Jon and the doctor, they tried to get them to give them some money for another bottle. Failing to obtain money, they continued on down the street, still arguing over who had the last swallow.

"Sad, they do not know how rich and fortunate they are."

Jon looked at his friend and nodded. "What happened after you were sponsored to come to this country? Why are you living in this neighborhood?"

With a slight grimace, the doctor continued his story. "It is, how you say, 'someone dropped the ball'. The sponsors stopped sponsoring."

Jon winced. "I am sorry. How did you get to this area of the town?"

"There are other people from home country who live around here. We help each other out. I have papers to live here in this country but no way to work. It is difficult."

"And your wife?"

"She is bitter. She does not want to be a Christian anymore. This hurts my heart." He touched his chest. "It would almost be better to not have come." Then with a sudden brightening on his continence, he said, "But here we are free from fear. It is definitely better life."

"Free from fear," Jon thought aloud. "In a part of town where people are afraid to visit and work, and where the police rarely intrude. It is interesting to see this fear or lack of fear from another's perspective. Thank you for sharing with me."

"You are a Christian, too, no? What does that mean for people like me?" The doctor suddenly stopped. "I must be leaving. Go see Mighty tonight, yes?"

"Yes, when Patch comes to get me, I'll go see Mighty."

An outstretched hand grasped Jon's. "Thank you." The man was gone, lost from sight in the milling of people in front of a storefront across the street. Jon stood and looked one more time at the 'eyesore' he had been leaning against before heading back to St. Ignatius.

The Bishop called about mid-morning to inform Father Jon that he would be at St. Ignatius shortly after eleven and that this was a visit 'without ceremony'. Jon had been down on his knees, trying to level the new refrigerator. He looked down at his soiled jeans and decided the best he could do was a quick shower and change. *Without ceremony,* mused Jon. "This is different."

Jon had just put his tools away when a dark car pulled into the rectory drive. He met the Bishop at the front door. Dressed in simple clothing, no one would have known this man was the Bishop. "I decided to come see for myself what is the true condition of St. Ignatius, that would require two hundred thousand dollars just to stabilize the church building."

"Two hundred thousand?" Jon echoed.

"That is what ***Restoration Now, Inc.*** has estimated. Does that surprise you, Father?"

"I could hear their minds adding up the dollar signs, but that is a bit more than I had guessed."

"Show me what they found. I came dressed

72

to dig around if necessary. Lead on, my man."

"I must warn you that Angus may be over in the church building and will wonder who you are."

"The obstinate custodian," the Bishop chuckled. "Just tell him I am an overseer following through on the **Restoration Now, Inc.** inspection. He'll believe that, won't he?" There was a twinkle in the Bishop's eyes.

"He probably will, if I don't slip and call you Bishop."

"Then see that you don't. Lead on, Father."

They started with the basement of the rectory and the old debris-filled tunnel. "Does it go all the way through?"

"It did when it was new."

"Rat trap, isn't it?"

"I wish I had a few rat traps. They ate all my cereal and bread the first few days I was here."

"They aren't eating any more?"

"They haven't figured out how to open the new refrigerator, although they had eaten their way into the old one. At night I can hear them gnawing on something. I try not to listen too hard."

The two men were back in the kitchen. The Bishop noticed the crudely labeled key hooks. "Did you label that?"

"No, but it helped that first morning when I went over to St. Ignatius." Jon pulled keys from his pocket and opened the side door. A second key opened St. Ignatius. "This way, Bi . . ." Jon caught himself. "The floor is weak here. I will show you why after we go into the sacristy."

Both men genuflected as they enter the main church Sanctuary. They acknowledged the presence of Christ in the Tabernacle before passing on into the sacristy. "Look here at this corner of the room," Jon indicated. There is a drop and displacement of the floor and wall. I imagine that was in the report."

Kneeling to examine the displacement, the Bishop could put his hand deep into the crevasse. "What keeps this place standing?"

"I'll show you more when we get downstairs. It has to be a miracle of God that this building hasn't fallen in on itself sometime in the last ten to twenty years."

Angus appeared suddenly in the sacristy doorway. "Oh, it is only you. Who's that?"

Before Jon could answer, the Bishop said, "An overseer."

"He is following through after *Restoration Now, Inc.*"

Angus nodded his head. "Oh."

"Would you show me the way to the basement and furnaces?" The Bishop was speaking directly to Angus. Almost in a daze, Angus led the way. Father Jon followed after the 'overseer' as they descended the crumbling steps to the original furnace. The evidence of the tunnel to the rectory was clear.

Father pointed to the cut beams overhead that allowed the monstrous old furnace to sit in the cramped chamber. "Why the original installers didn't dig a deeper basement so they would not have to cut into the beams puzzles me? You would have thought they could have dug two more feet deeper."

"Yes, but it was all by hand. I wonder if they hit rock. There are some massive rock formations under this city, as most builders of the 'high-rises' will tell you." Angus stood nearby rocking on his heels and watching the overseer look into everything. Finally the overseer pushed a narrow stick up the crack that was the end of the crevasse in the sacristy. "Goes all the way through, I suspect."

Jon pointed to the narrow wall that separated

the old furnace from the present one before they climbed back upstairs. Angus was eager to lead the way to the second set of stairs that led down to the current furnace area. Poking around behind the more modern furnace, the overseer found an opening that allowed air to pass from one furnace room to the other. "They just built a wall to hide the old one when they put in this one. This one is certainly more efficient and smaller."

"And self-fueling," Jon spoke. "No need to shovel coal into this one."

"It is an oil furnace, so where are the oil tanks?" Angus pointed to a narrow passage that went toward the back of the church. An oil line ran down one side of it. The overseer squeezed himself into the narrow passage and followed it as it ascended to ground level and a locked steel door. "Where is the key for this padlock?"

Angus shrugged his shoulders. The three men climbed back to the church level. Jon indicated that he might have the key in the collection he had at the rectory. Angus stood mutely by, peering at the other two though his glasses. "Show me the oil tanks, Angus." Angus did not move.

Father Jon cleared his throat and moved toward the side door. Angus bolted ahead of him. Jon was startled by the sudden activity of the custodian. "Can't go out there!"

"Why not, Angus?" asked the overseer.

"No tank, gone. Riff rats."

"The tank has been stolen?"

Angus by now had his small body jammed against the door. His eyes blinked continually.

Jon backed away. Angus reminded him of a trapped animal that was ready to make his final defense. Something was not right, and Jon did not want to find out what at that moment. The Bishop acknowledged Jon's move, and the two men retreated to the sacristy to see if they could feel the stick that had been pushed up in the crack from below. Both were praying and watching for the reappearance of Angus at the sacristy door.

They heard the outside door open and close and the outside padlock snapped into place. The two men continued to pray for the disturbed custodian for a long time. The Bishop moved around the Sanctuary of the church, praying. He noted the beauty of the architecture. Jon remained on his knees in front of the altar, listening to his heart commune with the Lord. He had felt fear for the first time since he had been assigned to St. Ignatius. That fear came off of a trapped animal, Angus. He hadn't been afraid when the gangs fought in front of the church, or even walking around the inner city area. But here in the church, he had confronted fear. This disturbed him.

The Bishop's thoughts were on the need to repair the foundation of this magnificent old church and where he could possibly get the money. He had also observed the fear that Angus exhibited and prayed that Jon could overcome this obvious hindrance to the restoration of St. Ignatius.

After a light repast, the Bishop and Father Jon discussed the possibilities for the reconstruction of the foundation and the obvious interference that Angus might pose to the overall restoration.

Across the street on the fourth floor, a frantic Angus was digging through the boxes of saved stuff, looking for the shells for the gun. He knew he would never go back into St. Ignatius without the gun in his belt. And he intended to use it first on the 'riff rats' that stole the oil tank from behind the church.

Confrontations

Father Jon kept a wary eye on Angus during Mass the following morning. Angus said very little, except when spoken to. He left immediately after the four other parishioners had vacated the church. Jon felt relief as he heard the padlock snap shut behind Angus. At least he would not have to contend with him any more this morning. Jon passed over into the rectory and shoved the long unused deadbolt shut on the rectory door. Jon had an appointment with several of the gang later in the day.

The weather left much to be desired by the afternoon. First the wind blew, and then torrents of rain flooded the street in front of St. Ignatius. Jon wasn't particularly surprised at all the trash that was blown into the gutters at the edge of the street. The streets were empty as Father Jon set out toward the meeting with the gang, his umbrella twisting this way and that. He wondered if they would be there, with the sudden change in weather, but decided that he was not going to be the one missing this meeting. At the edge of a wet and trash strewn alleyway, Jon hesitated before entering. It had all the markings of a good spot for a mugging. A few feet in, Patch appeared, seemingly out of nowhere. "Hi, Padre!"

If Father Jon had been the tense type, he would have jumped at Patch's sudden appearance. Jon closed his umbrella and followed. Patch led to a cellar door of an abandoned building. A quick tap, a rustling and scraping noise from inside, and the door opened. The two stepped into inky darkness as the door was shut behind them. An interior door opened, revealing the rest of the group.

They greeted him as their brother. "You saw Mighty last night?"

"You are not like any other priest we have ever known."

"We didn't think you would come."

"Most people are afraid of us."

"You are different."

"We really think you're cool."

The boys clamored on for several minutes. Patch lifted his hand for silence.

One boy popped the cap of a beer and passed it to Jon. Jon looked at it and then at the under-aged teen who had handed it to him. Silence reigned in the room for 30 seconds or so. "You don't have to drink it if you don't want, Padre."

Father Jon looked up. It was at moments like this that his heart was beseeching the will of God for what he should do next. He placed the beer on a table.

"Sit here, Father." Patch directed the priest to a chair next to him. The others sat on chairs and boxes.

Jon wondered who would speak first. He had asked to meet with the gang, and they indicated they were willing to meet with him. Patch broke the silence. "You are Mighty's blood-brother. You are our brother now 'cause of Mighty. You have done what no other person would do for us, brother." Patch hesitated. He twisted on the box where he was seated and looked at the floor a long moment before continuing. "We owe you. Whatever you have come for, you can have."

This was not exactly how Jon had thought this meeting would go, but then that was just Patch speaking. How would the others react? Jon was still ignorant of the authority the gang leader had over the members. With deliberateness, Jon looked at each of the members present. He watched them each meet his gaze before dropping their eyes downward. He searched each face for hostility, for uncooperativeness, for anger. All he saw was acceptance and possibly some discomfort in the presence of the priest.

"I asked to meet with you so that I can know each one of you better. I know Patch, and we have talked. I know Mighty, and we have talked. I did for Mighty what I would have done for any of you or anybody else that had the need he did as he bled in the street. I am a priest. My vows include the care of all, whoever has need. I know the God who created everything and everyone. It is my obligation as a child of God to introduce, teach, lead, and care for those he, God, puts in my charge. The Church, of which St. Ignatius is a part, specifically directs me to care for all of the children of God." Jon paused, letting his words sink in. There was little sound but the breathing of seven people in the room. "You all are children of God."

"Geez, Father, you sure don't know us! We

79

can't be God's children. We took a vow to never enter a church! We hate the Church. It has never done nothin for us. It is our enemy . . ."

"Shut up and listen," Patch snapped.

Jon focused on the boy who had interrupted. "What is your name? How old are you? Who is your mom, dad?"

The thin boy with dirty blond hair looked at the floor. "You. . ."

"Answer the questions," a now soft-spoken Patch directed.

Jon realized he was holding his breath. This was the confrontation he had expected. Slowly he exhaled and waited to see if the boy would answer. Patch was staring at his gang member.

Later Jon wondered how long the silence was before the members began to talk, to share, and to trust him. Hours later the rain had stopped. Jon walked home in the damp dark of the evening, marveling at the outcome of the meeting.

When he reached St. Ignatius, he noticed a light on inside the church. He had not remembered leaving any light on. The side gate was closed but unlocked. Angus must be inside. For a moment John wanted to go check on the church building, but something in his spirit said to just go back to the rectory. He knew he would know soon enough whatever Angus was up to. He was willing to wait until whenever that time was.

Early morning Mass was celebrated without Angus. Jon found the gate unlocked and the side door open when he got into the church. After a quick look around, he found Angus had laid out everything in preparation for the Mass. A scrawled note that he could not decipher was on his vestments. The words 'riff rats, tank, water, trash' were all he could make

80

out. Angus had signed it, but what it meant Jon had no idea. Several members of the church arrived. Jon hurried into his vestments, praying all the while that Angus was all right and not lying in some dark corner of the church.

After the five had left, Jon toured the building. The basement smelled. Jon found that the trash strewn sewers had pushed water back up into the furnace rooms. He saw where Angus had cleaned it away from the furnace and had made a makeshift dam to hold any more that might bubble up the sewer pipe from reaching the furnace. That explained the light he had noticed on the evening before and the note upstairs, except for the mention of riff rats and tank.

On the way back up the steps, Jon met a disheveled Angus. Angus stopped with a jerk, then mumbled something about being up all night cleaning the mess in the basement. Father complimented the old man and helped him turn and go back up the stairs. At best Angus always looked like he had just gotten up and probably hadn't washed in days. This morning he also smelled like the sewage he had cleaned up during the night. Jon steered Angus to the side door that led to the rectory. Angus balked at first, but Jon's youth and strength won as he took him into the kitchen of the rectory and sat him at the kitchen table.

While Jon pulled bread, butter, jelly, cereal, and juice out, Angus dropped his head on the table and began to snore. He woke when Jon set a steaming coffee cup in front of him. Grabbing the offered sugar, Angus poured half of it into his coffee. By then the toast was ready. Jon sat across from Angus and pushed a pile of buttered toast and the jelly toward him. Angus stuffed his mouth with the first piece of buttered toast and then reached for the knife and jelly for the second piece. For at least twenty minutes Angus ate, belched, and ate some more. Jon wondered when the man last had a meal.

Like a child, Angus suddenly said 'bathroom' and pointed to his lower body. Jon half lifted the man up and propelled him down the hall to the small bathroom on the first floor. Angus didn't wait until the door was shut to begin his business there. Jon stepped back and turned to inhale less perfumed air in the hall.

The scripture, Matthew 25, came to mind: *'Assuredly, I say to you, inasmuch as you did it to one of the least of these, My brethren, you did it to Me.'* Jon moaned softly. This was becoming his habit when he heard the Lord give him distinct instruction that was contrary to what he would rather do. "OK, God, I hear you."

He turned back to the bathroom to rescue Angus from a wad of toilet paper that had wound itself around the old man's hand. While he helped the man clean himself, Jon was not breathing too deeply. After that task and a wash down at the kitchen sink were completed, Angus headed for the table again. Jon fixed a bowl of cereal for himself. Angus started on the last of the toast.

The phone rang before Angus had finished the toast. Jon hurried to the office and grabbed up the portable phone. He did not want to leave Angus unsupervised for very long. "Father Jon, St. Ignatius."

It was *Mary Jane Cleaners*. "I have found you a housekeeper who is willing to come to your area of the city." The voice continued. "She will need taxi fare to and from. This seems to be the safest way. Can you pay for her taxi fare the first week until we get arrangements with the Bishop's Office?"

82

"When can I expect her?"

"She can be there today at 11 am. She normally would be there between 8 am and 4 pm, with an hour off for lunch. Is that suitable? You wanted someone to do housework and laundry, didn't you? This will give her ample time to keep the house up after the initial cleaning. We are charging an extra fee for the first week's deep cleaning. The Bishop's Office has already approved that."

"Yeah, right. Then I can expect her at 11 today? What is her name so that I know I am paying taxi fare for the right woman?"

"Hilda Anne Cynder, spelled C-Y-N-D-E-R, pronounced like 'cinder' in Cinderella. She is very capable. I assured the Bishop's Office of her integrity. I am sure 'you' will be satisfied." The way the caller emphasized the word 'you' annoyed Jon. He was watching Angus lick the jelly from the knife and his fingers and plate.

"Thank you, I will be expecting her at eleven." Jon pushed the off button on the phone before slapping it down on the kitchen sink. The lady at *Mary Jane Cleaners* annoyed him every time he had to talk to her. He hoped Hilda Anne Cynder, like cinder in Cinderella, was more human than that woman on the phone.

"I gotta go home." Angus was standing, looking at the door that connected to the church.

"Let's go out the front door here, Angus," Jon looped an arm around the old man and steered him down the hall.

"I gotta go lock the gate! Gotta keep out the riff raff." Angus' voice became pinched.

"I'll do it after I get you safely home and back to bed. You didn't get much sleep last night. With a full stomach, you ought to sleep well now."

Angus did not resist the strong arm

supporting him as they crossed the street and went up the four flights of stairs to Angus' flat. The odor that assailed them as they opened the door nearly knocked Jon over. He wished he had remembered to breathe more deeply when he had been out on the street.

"Gotta take out the trash."

"I'll do it, Angus." Jon deposited Angus on the broken down couch that served as a bed. At least there was a sheet and pillow on it. Jon wondered when they had last been washed. Angus slumped over and was asleep almost before Jon could lift his feet off the floor. It didn't take him long to find the several offending trash bags stuck in between boxes in one corner. He closed the door and hurried down the stairs, carrying the bags as far from him as possible. Just outside the back door of the building was an overflowing trash bin. Jon stuffed the bags in among all the other smelly trash. At the opening of the alley, Jon stopped and breathed deeply. He could not get the smell of that apartment out of his lungs.

Turning the corner, he went down to the building where Miss Claire and Miss Agnes had their store. The bell on the door gave a feeble 'tink' as he entered. There it was by the cash register, peppermint chewing gum. He grabbed a package, opened it, and thrust several pieces into his mouth all at once just as Miss Claire came from the back room. He was now fishing for change from his pocket to pay for the gum.

"Are you that hungry, Father?" The cash register clanged as she put his change into it. "I can get you some cheese and bread and ..."

"Yes, I need bread and jelly today, Claire. And, no, I am not that hungry. I just had a very strong taste in my mouth and wanted to get rid of it."

He smiled at his description of the foulness he had experienced.

84

"Oh, just bread and jelly? Do you need milk? And would you like one of these oranges? They will do wonders for a bad taste. Here, Father, take one."

Reaching for his wallet, Jon realized it was still across the street. "Guess I'll have to come back to get this. My wallet is over there." He pointed at the rectory.

"No problem, your credit is good with us." Agnes had joined them. "Isn't that right, Claire?"

Claire scowled at her sister but nodded her head.

Jon put away the bread, milk, and new jelly and ate the orange before he returned to pay Miss Claire and Miss Agnes. He left a deliberate gap of time to give them time to quarrel about taking money from the priest, which they did every time he bought something from them. Since the time they had quarreled in front of him, he made sure they had privacy for their quarrels.

At eleven sharp, a gaudy yellow, orange, and purple taxi pulled up in front of the rectory. Jon nodded at the choice of transportation as this particular taxi company was owned and run from this part of the city. A woman climbed out of the backseat carrying an umbrella and a small gym bag. Her energy, smile, and appearance reminded him of Mary Poppins. The driver opened the trunk and set out two large boxes of cleaning supplies. After he had paid the driver, Jon carried the boxes into the rectory. Hilda was chattering at his heels. "I took the liberty of picking up what I thought a long neglected rectory might need in the way of supplies. *Mary Jane Cleaners* assures me that the Bishop will pay for them.

"The Bishop's Office," Jon corrected as he

carried in the second box. "Let me show you around, and then we can decide together what areas would be best to start on first."

Hilda plopped the gym bag on the kitchen table and hooked the umbrella on the back door knob. "Your laundry?" she asked with a mischievous glint in her eyes.

"Yes, that is a primary need, but so is the bathroom down here and the one upstairs. I can change my own bed if the linens in the upstairs closet are freshened and if that will be of help to you. My mother taught me well. It is just that I seem to have my hands full here," and he waved his arm to include the church and local area, "so that even simple cleaning tasks seem to remain undone."

"It is no small wonder, and this building has been unoccupied for any length of time for years."

Jon pointed out the washer and drier before touring the first floor. He held his nose in mock concern as he opened the necessity room door. The odor left behind by Angus was mostly gone. "I will want you to sweep and dust my office, but only when I am around. I don't want you to throw out anything you find anywhere until I can see it. There are so many loose ends here that no one knows where the pieces are. I'll take the trash out each day."

Hilda nodded vigorously. "Burned out light bulbs are a problem, but there are plenty on one of the shelves in the kitchen. Please change any that need to be replaced. If I am not in the rectory, any incoming phone calls will be recorded, so you can ignore a ringing phone."

They were back downstairs. Hilda picked up his basket of dirty laundry while they were upstairs and piled several sets of musty, dusty sheets and towel sets on top. She headed to the washer as Jon went to his office.

It wasn't until later in the day that he remembered the unlocked gate and door at the church. And that Angus was not wearing his glasses when he had come down the basement steps this morning. Jon could easily remedy the gate and door problem but wondered about the glasses. It puzzled him. A light tap on the door announced Hilda, with vacuum cleaner in hand.

Most of the house had a clean smell, and dust balls were not in the corners of the rooms. All in all, it appeared Hilda knew how to clean. His clean laundry was neatly folded on his bed, and she had remade the bed with clean sheets. Jon had given her enough money to pay the taxi home and back again in the morning. She promised to be there by 8 am. He wondered what else she would have to do, and she assured him that she had just begun. Hilda Anne Cynder, as in Cinderella, seemed to be everything he could want for getting the rectory in shape.

Jon checked on Angus about dark and found the man still sleeping. He took an orange, some dry cereal, and a couple bottles of fruit juice to the flat. He left them on the makeshift table in the corner near the couch. He hoped Angus would find them when he awoke. The flat didn't smell as badly as in the morning, but it still took Jon a few minutes of deep breathing when he left to clear his lungs and nostrils of the putrid odors.

Angus was not at Mass. Jon found him disoriented and still on the couch in his flat. He asked Angus about family or friends, and his glasses. Angus only muttered nonsensical gibberish. Puzzled, Jon asked Miss Claire and Miss Agnes what they knew about Angus. They only said that he owed them money and that he stopped coming to charge anything new. Did they know when he had last eaten? Both shook their heads 'no.' A call to the Social Services that served the area was met with a thirty-day or more delay and a request for papers to be filled out on Angus. Jon resorted to prayer before the altar in St. Ignatius. It was there that Angus, with his glasses on, found him. Jon was elated to see Angus up and walking. The old man seemed not to remember anything from the day before. Jon took him down to Chico's Place and fed him lunch. He carried clean sheets and a new pillow up to the flat and helped Angus pick up some. Angus was reluctant to talk and got agitated whenever Jon got too close to the boxes piled in the corners.

Jon threw away the sheet and pillow he brought back, with Hilda's blessing. Again the rectory smelled fresher, and he could see Hilda's touch in the arrangement of the what-knots on a shelf in the living room.

Restoration Now, Inc. phoned and left a message on the answering machine. They inquired about a mutually acceptable time to go back over the areas they felt needed to be worked on first in the church. Jon wondered if he should include Angus in their return visit or try to keep him away and distracted. When he returned their call, an appointment was set for the following week.

Angus was ready in the sacristy when Jon arrived in the morning. He still seemed a little disorientated but, with a little coaching, served Mass. Ten were there that morning. Two were new to Jon. After the Mass, he hurried to catch up with them, but they had already left. When he asked Angus about them, Angus just stared at him.

Later in the day, Patch stopped by. He said the gang wanted to come to the rectory that evening. Jon agreed. Patch said it would be after dark. "So no one can see you?" Jon asked.

"Something like that," and Patch smiled.

Across the street from the fourth floor apartment, Angus rubbed his blurry eyes and dirty glasses. He thought he had seen one of the riff rats at the rectory door. "Not good, not good," he muttered to himself.

When the doorbell rang that evening, Jon hesitated, noticing that the street light that normally lit up the front of the rectory was out. "It's me, Patch," called the voice through the door. Relieved, Jon opened it with the chain on to confirm and then hurriedly let Patch in.

"I don't suppose you know what happened to the street light outside?" Jon asked.

Patch grinned. "The electric company will fix it in the morning."

"Is that a confession that you had something to do with it?"

Patch nodded his head and pointed to the tapping at the backdoor. "They didn't want to be seen coming in here."

"So you put the light out?"

Patch looked at Father Jon and shrugged his shoulders. "You'd better open the back door before they change their minds."

The five other members of the gang, plus one being carried, entered the kitchen and yelled "Surprise! We brought Mighty with us."

Jon pulled a lounge chair from a closet for Mighty. The others sat around the table or on the kitchen counter. Jon pulled snack food from a cupboard and opened the refrigerator to reveal two shelves of soda pop. "Help yourselves. I thought it was best to buy these goodies out of the area so that no one would get suspicious of the unusual groceries for the rectory." He grinned at them. "And the kitchen has no windows, so you can feel more secure."

They opened bags of chips, pretzels, and popcorn and popped the tops of the sodas like any group of hungry teenage boys. For a short while all that could be heard was the rustling of plastic bags and deep gulps of soda. Mighty drank a soda slowly and nibbled on a handful of chips. He was a long way from total healing, and the effort to be there showed on his thin face.

Jon waited and watched the gang satisfy their hunger and thirst. At last the boys looked at Patch and Mighty and then at Father Jon. Still nothing was said. Jon was not surprised. These kids still were unsure of civil type conversation.

Patch dug the toe of his shoe into the floor. Jon wondered if there was going to be a hole there when the gang left. Finally Patch looked up and cleared his voice. "We want to be your friends. All of us, we talked about it, and what you said to us the other night makes sense."

Jon waited.

"Yeah, you said we were making our own prison, even if the cops don't nab us for anything."

"You said we could be free. I am free. But you said that I didn't have any peace. Someone was always after me."

Jon nodded.

"So who is this very best friend you told us about?"

"Is he a judge or a cop or . . . ? "

"How can he be our best friend?"

"I don't know nothin about religion or this place!"

"What are you, some kinda shrink?"

At that remark, Jon laughed. "No, but this very best friend might be!"

90

"I'm outta here!" declared one, who headed for the back door.

"No you ain't, you took an oath to come here and listen!" shouted the rest in unison. A couple of them moved to block the one going toward the door.

"He can go if he wants," Jon said.

"No he can't! We took an oath to do everything together, Padre, and we decided to come here to talk and listen and to be your friends." Patch stood in front of the back door, blocking the one trying to leave.

Jon was wondering how they would keep him from leaving when he saw the flash of a knife in the hand of one of the others. "Help, Lord Jesus!" He could see the headlines in the papers in the morning, '**Gang Fight In St. Ignatius Rectory!**' and could hear the phone ringing from the Bishop's office. His outburst of prayer brought instant results. No one moved. No one said anything. Jon looked at the boys one by one. The one with the knife put it away. The dissident stopped his forward motion and sat down. Patch moved back to where he had been seated. "Sorry Padre."

Jon didn't trust his voice to acknowledge but only nodded. For a while they all sat in relative silence. Mighty groaned when he tried to move a little. His condition brought the gang back to the unity they had with the priest. The priest was their blood brother. Whatever he said or needed, they were ready to respond.

Someone crumpled an empty potato chip bag and tossed it toward the trashcan. It missed.

"Padre, we don't know nothin' about this Jesus man, or this place, but you are our brother. What do you want us to do?"

Jon considered the question carefully, his heart and mind in constant search of the right things to say and to do with these boys. "I want you to come back and visit again." Then an idea came to his mind, so he continued. "I need the oil storage tank that was behind St. Ignatius returned."

"You mean that big ol' tank that was out back of the church?"

"Yep, the one that is missing."

Patch said in a steady voice, "It will be back in the morning."

"The one that used to be here or another? Do not take one from someplace else. That would be stealing."

"We know that, Father," one of the other boys said.

"Yeah," another said.

"OK, no questions asked. Just do not steal a tank to replace the old one."

Patch spoke up. "We know where to find it. Trust us, Padre."

Jon nodded. The boys cleaned their trash up. Mighty grimaced when a couple of the guys started to pick him up. "Put him back down. I'll care for him here. He is my blood-brother." Jon wondered at his sanity, but the words were out.

Patch hesitated but for a moment and indicated that they were to leave Mighty there. Like shadows, the gang left by the back door and disappeared into the night. Jon turned the deadbolt on the door.

Once he had carried Mighty bleeding from the street; now he carried Mighty up the stairs to the second floor. He placed him in the room next to his own. Jon had wondered what he would ever do with the guest room, but now he knew. Hilda had made the bed up and placed clean towels in the bathroom just that morning. Mighty clung to Jon after he laid him down.

92

Jon sat down on the edge of the bed and checked the wounds. They did not seem to be disturbed by the trip to the rectory. Mighty moaned softly. "Don't leave me." Jon nodded and held the boy. He wondered if this was going to be another Nadine, with Mighty dying in his arms. He began to pray, first softly, and then aloud and boldly, interceding for the young boy. The boy drifted into a quiet sleep, still holding Jon's hand. Mighty didn't seem to be feverish. Jon pulled an extra pillow down to the floor and stretched out, still holding Mighty's hand. He thought of the prophet in the Old Testament who had lain on the widow's dead son. God had restored her son. He hoped he didn't have to do that for Mighty, but it was on his mind as he fell asleep.

Once back on the streets, the gang separated, each one with a task to do and a meeting place to be at in an hour. They all arrived under the viaduct within minutes of each other. Patch checked with each one, and, satisfied that all plans were ready, he led the gang stealthily through the backside of an industrial area. When they arrived at the tall fence around Buddy's Salvage, they clasped hands in a secret ritual, confirming their solidarity. "Remember Mighty," Patch said softly, "and Padre." They nodded.

"What about the dogs in there?"

Patch pulled out a small bottle and a blow dart gun. "Watch," he said.

"Will it work?"

"TNT thinks so." Patch put some of the liquid onto the point of a dart. "Sort of like playing darts at Smalleys," and he blew hard into the tube. The nearest dog yelped when the dart hit it on the flank. It jumped up, only to fall over almost instantly.

"Wow! What's in that stuff?"

"Shhh!" hissed Patch as the remaining three dogs stood up, barking. He aimed at another, and that dog fell. Now two dogs were racing up and over the assorted junk iron pieces to reach the fence where the gang stood.

Phaft, phaft. Those dogs dropped in their tracks. Patch put the bottle away and tossed the blowgun into a dumpster.

"Are they dead?" Patch just helped Scar up over the fence.

"You got the truck?"

"Yeah, parked over there." The dirty blond-headed member pointed to a dark object beyond the farthest dumpsters.

"You pulled the wires on the lights?"

"Sure, you think I am dumb or something?"

Scar was busy inside the fence locating the missing oil storage tank. When he found it, he made a sound like a cat calling. Patch and the others moved to the closest point outside the fence. Don't Call Me Charlie pulled out a fence cutter and went to work.

"Didn't the priest say not to steal the tank?"

Patch nodded. He began peeling the wire back to open a hole large enough to get the tank through. "We ain't stealing it. We are taking it back to its rightful owner. Besides," hissed Patch as he tugged at a particularly stubborn wire, "Buddy has never paid us for it. We are just taking it back."

The hole was big enough for the tank. Two others joined Scar in moving the tank to the fence. They worked hard at keeping the noise to a minimum. When car lights suddenly approached on the street out front, they all hid in the shadows of the salvage yard. "Hurry up, we ain't got all night!"

94

Shortly before the sky began to lighten, the gang wrestled the tank into place behind St. Ignatius. Having almost total darkness there, with the street light out from earlier in the evening, made the job easier.

Before the first deliveries were made on the street out front, the gang had clasped hands again in their ritual and departed.

Jon could not figure out what was tapping on his back as he awoke. He was cold and stiff. "I need to go to the bathroom." It was Mighty. Carefully he helped Mighty up and to the bathroom. After Mighty was back in bed, Jon slipped into his own room to continue to pray for the boy and the others out there somewhere.

Mighty was sleeping soundly when Jon let Hilda in early before going to say Mass at the church. He told her a little about Mighty and that Mighty was upstairs asleep. She nodded as Father Jon hurried over to the church. It was unusual for him to be late. Three parishioners sat in their usual spots. Angus was pacing the floor in the sacristy. He glared and followed Father Jon as he vested and hurried out to the altar. Jon began with his usual 'good morning' and briefly apologized for his tardiness. The people in the pews seemed to nod their acceptance, although Jon wasn't sure they were not just nodding off to sleep. He kept his homily very short and served each one at the pews. Angus, breathing heavily, followed along with the paten. If he had actually dropped a Host, Jon doubted that it would have landed on the paten.

After the Mass, Angus lingered. Jon looked at the man and realized that, if the people hadn't been asleep, surely his server had been. Angus' eyes were matted more than usual, and his glasses were incredibly dirty. "Let's go down to S&S and get a cup of coffee and something to eat."

Angus just stared at him. Jon revised his impression of Angus from the beginning of the service. What he had taken for a glare was probably no more than a stare. Guiding Angus by the arm, Jon steered him out the side door and gate. Angus did not even offer to snap on the padlock hanging there. Seating Angus on the step in front of the rectory, Jon rang the doorbell. Hilda did not bat an eye when she found Father at his own doorstep.

"I need my wallet. I am going to take Angus to S&S. It is in my office, second drawer, on the left side. I don't think I had better leave him sitting here by himself."

Hilda nodded. "I can stay with him."

"No, just get my wallet," Jon grinned. "I'll have to find a new hiding place for it, I suppose."

Hilda scurried away and returned. With an impish look, she said, "I took out my allowance before bringing it to you."

Jon laughed. "Thanks, I needed something to lighten me up. Any noise from upstairs?"

Hilda shook her head 'no' and closed the rectory door.

Pulling Angus to his feet, Jon steered the man across the street and to S&S. Bill looked up as Father Jon came in. He would have turned Angus away if the Father had not been with him. Jon put Angus down in a booth and beckoned to Bill. "Breakfast food and black coffee for us both."

"Cereal, eggs and toast, or both?"

Jon nodded, "All of it. Leave the cereal in the little box for him."

"Light was out." Angus spoke.

"What light?"

"One in front of . . ." and Angus waved his hand.

"I suppose the power and light people will be out to fix it."

Angus scowled. "Work of riff rats!"

"Why do you say that?"

Bill slammed the cereal bowls and little cereal boxes on the table. The pitcher of milk slopped over.

"It's always one of the gangs puts it out, that's why!" Bill answered the question.

Jon was taken aback by Bill's anger. He knew Bill didn't like Angus, and probably for a good reason. But the harshness of his remark was very evident. Helping Angus open a box of cereal occupied his time and conveniently covered having to respond to Bill's remark. One thing he had noticed since coming to the parish was the latent anger in many of the people. He supposed it was due to the lack of adequate income, or maybe insecurity, and it was then Jon realized he had never addressed that source of anger in his quiet time with God. He made a mental note to do so as soon as time would allow.

Leaving more money than the actual cost of the breakfasts, Jon steered Angus toward his flat. After helping Angus with necessary toiletries, he covered him with the now dirtying sheet and a blanket. Angus was asleep immediately. Jon stood on the street, breathing deeply the polluted air of the neighborhood and enjoying the less potent air of the apartment upstairs. He stopped by Agnes and Claire's store for another package of the peppermint gum before crossing toward the rectory.

Before he went for the back door, a quick glance toward the back of the church revealed an object sitting there. Standing on three legs, leaning on the back of the church, was the oil tank. He felt along the bottom side of the tank and found the imprint of the Diocese there. Patch and the others had come through. He felt good about them.

Upstairs, Hilda went about cleaning the priest's room and the bathroom. She hummed and sang to herself. The door to the one bedroom was shut. She knew that a young boy was in bed in there. Ever since the first light of dawn, when Father Jon phoned her and asked her to come early, she had been thinking about how much Father did, and how worn down he seemed.

Inside the room, Mighty heard the humming and singing of a woman. At first he thought he was dreaming, but it really sounded like a woman. He didn't know a woman lived in the house with the priest. Patch had never told him that. A tap on the door, and a voice called out, "Are you covered up?"

Mighty managed to pull the covers over him and responded feebly. Hilda entered with a smile. "Hello, Mighty. Would you like breakfast?"

"How'd you know my name?"

"Father Jon told me about you and how sick you are. How about some cereal, buttered toast, and a glass of milk?"

Mighty made a face. "Don't like milk."

Hilda thought for a minute, "Coffee?"

"Yeah."

"OK, I'll be back in a few minutes. Do you need me to help you to the bathroom?"

"Naw," Mighty answered. After she left, he dragged himself out of the bed and, using the wall to keep his balance, made his way to the bathroom. He was still in the hall coming back when Hilda returned with a tray of food. She put it down and let Mighty lean on her the rest of the way back to the bedroom. "Longer trip than you thought, huh?" she said, helping him lift his legs back up on the bed. Mighty moaned. She stayed and helped Mighty with the food. He seemed to have no strength at all after the

98

hike to the bathroom. When he had drifted off to sleep, she took the food tray back to the kitchen. Father Jon came through the back door.

"Mighty ate?" he inquired.

"After a fashion," Hilda replied. She scraped the dishes and poured out most of the coffee. Jon nodded. "Would you like a cup of coffee?"

Pulling out a kitchen chair, Jon sat down. "That sounds really great." Picking up a wad of paper toweling left from the meeting the night before, Jon got rid of his gum.

Hilda grinned. "Apartment still stinks?" She handed him a full mug of hot, aromatic coffee. "This should help a little, I suppose. Sugar?"

Jon scooped a couple of spoonfuls into the cup, taking the liquid to the brim. With his head down nearly to the tabletop, he slurped the hot coffee. When he looked up, Hilda was hiding her laughter behind her hand.

"Not so graceful or pretty, but it does the trick," Jon acknowledged. "Sit down and have a cup yourself. All work and no rest will make you old before your time!"

"You know," Hilda said as she sat, "I was thinking the same thing about you. You sometimes go on twenty-four hour days with no rest."

Jon nodded soberly. "I don't know if the Bishop had all this activity in mind when he sent me here. Sometimes I feel like two or three different priests as I am confronted daily, sometimes hourly, with the needs of St. Ignatius parish."

Hilda just nodded. She had seen that in the time she had worked at the rectory. "You really have a full time job upstairs with that young boy."

It was Jon's turn to nod. "Not to mention the rest of the gang, Angus, Claire and Agnes, the daily routine of Mass and reporting to the Bishop, a certain doctor in the area, social workers who are too busy to stop and see Angus, a missing oil tank, and **Restoration Now, Inc."** Jon suddenly felt very tired.

"I've been thinking," Hilda ventured. "When you called this morning, I remembered the old housekeeper who used to live here when Father Vincehetti was here. That was years ago. This house does have a housekeeper apartment. It used to have a door to the outside. That was sealed when the gangs got so plentiful. They made part of the apartment into the utility room, but the room behind and the small bath are still intact."

Jon was now looking at Hilda. "Are you suggesting I need a live in housekeeper?"

"At least someone to care for that poor boy upstairs until he is fully recovered," she said.

"And how would I justify that in my weekly expense report to the Bishop?"

"You mean, tell the Bishop about the boy?" Hilda asked sweetly.

"Umm." Jon didn't want to trust himself to answer that question. It did seem the Bishop knew most of what was going on at St. Ignatius, but so far there had been no mention of the gang or the injured boy. Then there was the policeman who had come to talk with him after Mighty was injured. That seemed so long ago, and yet he had been at St. Ignatius only six weeks. He rubbed his hands through his hair, leaving it standing straight up. He had had no time to shower that morning so, other than a cleanly shaved face, Jon felt intensely grubby.

"More coffee?" Hilda busied herself at the stove. "Can I make a suggestion?"

"Any more pointed than the one you have already made?"

"No change in the salary. I'll just stay around the clock until the boy is able again. You'll get some rest, and the boy some nursing and mother-love. Both of you need that."

"What about where you live now? And that gaudy cab that comes two times a day to this house?"

Hilda laughed. "I am not going to give up my apartment. And as far as that cab, it is owned by a distant cousin. I guess I could get him to drop by twice a day as though I am coming and going. Would that help?"

Hilda continued, "My grandparents on both sides lived in this neighborhood when I was young. I know something about how the area works. People here won't pay any attention, for the most part. When that boy upstairs is able to walk by himself and climb stairs, then I'll go back to being just day help."

It must have been the coffee, for Jon's head was swimming, or maybe it was the lack of sleep. Jon heard himself say, "OK, it's a deal."

Fear Walks In

The phone was ringing in the office. Jon had no idea how long he had slept in the recliner. Hilda had taken over the care of Mighty for the past two days. He had enjoyed some needed rest in the afternoons after caring for Angus each day. The answering machine droned, and he heard Patch's voice. "Padre, I . . ." The machine cut the boy off before Jon could get to the phone. No telling from where Patch was calling. He played the message, spoken in almost a whisper. "Padre, I, we did not do it." Then the caller hung up. Jon knelt and bowed in deep prayer for all the members of the gang, including the one upstairs.

There was disturbing talk in the neighborhood that someone had slit the throats of the dogs at Buddy's Salvage the night the oil tank had been brought back. He hoped against hope that the gang hadn't done it. The office at the salvage yard also had been broken into that night, and a large sum of money had been removed. Buddy was claiming it was 'that gang,' the one with a one-eyed leader. The boys had not contacted Jon until now, and he had not been available. He was very annoyed with himself. Jon wept for the lost boys and continued in prayer until the phone rang again.

Grabbing it up, he responded with "St Ignatius Rectory." It was the Bishop's office, wanting to know if the repairs to the oil tank had been completed successfully. Jon assured the caller that all parts were reconnected and the furnace had been tested. He was reminded that *Restoration Now, Inc.* would be coming on Thursday to begin their preliminary work.

Jon sighed as he hung up the phone. He wondered how he would work *Restoration Now, Inc.* into his already crowded schedule. Then he laughed to himself. This was what the Bishop had sent him to St. Ignatius to do. Restore the church. But what was the church? Was it the actual building, the aged parishioners, the obstinate, self-proclaimed custodian, the lost living in the parish area, the gangs? Jon retired to the recliner to pray and think. The phone rang again. He bolted to the phone. "St. Ignatius Rectory."

The voice on the other end was familiar. For a moment Jon searched his mind as the caller identified himself. Detective Janski asked if the priest had time to answer some questions.

"On the phone?"

"No, I will stop by shortly. I just wanted to make sure I would find you in."

"Hmmm," Jon replied. "Is this to give me time to get rid of the evidence?"

A hearty chuckle came back over the

receiver. "I wouldn't think that your vows would allow you to do that. I'll be there in thirty minutes, OK?

Jon agreed, before hanging up the phone. His mind whirled, trying to figure out exactly why the detective was coming and why he gave him a thirty-minute window. Police seemed to like to use the 'surprise, we are here to talk with you' tactic rather than to call for an appointment.

Mighty! He was hidden away upstairs in the rectory. Was this the reason? Jon took the steps two at a time. Hilda was watching a video with Mighty. Jon called Hilda out of the room and told her of the expected visitor. She nodded and said, "He is about to fall asleep. I will turn the TV volume off and stay with him. If he is still awake when the detective comes, I will do my best to keep him quiet. I shouldn't think he would want the detective to know he is here." Jon nodded his agreement and retraced his steps down the stairs.

Not usually one to pace the floor, Jon forced himself to sit at his desk and pray. When the doorbell rang exactly thirty minutes later, Jon slowly walked up the hall to the door. The detective showed him his badge, a procedure recently instigated by the police, even though Jon knew the detective. Janski accepted the invitation to enter, and they went into Jon's office.

"I am still having difficulty remembering I have to show my badge to everyone I interview. They all mostly know me, and I them. It is sort of awkward. I sometimes think it hinders the relationship." The officer was apologetic. "I am here on official business."

Jon said nothing. He noted the general ease that Detective Janski seemed to have with the priest's office.

"The gang that usually hangs around out front, have you seen them?"

Jon considered the question, Mighty was here, but not the gang. "No."

"When did you last see them?"

"Monday."

"Did they say anything to you about their plans?"

Jon knew the answer before the detective uttered the question. "You know I can't answer that."

The detective laughed. "It was worth a try. I had to ask."

"There are some questions a priest can never answer."

"I know, Father, and I am glad when it is my sins."

"You're Catholic." Jon made it a statement, not a question.

"Yes, with my last name, are you surprised?"

"No. Do you have any questions that I might be able to answer?"

"Do you know where they are or might be?"

Jon just shook his head.

"I didn't think you would tell, but again, I had to ask."

Jon breathed a prayer, "I wish I did know where they are." Looking the detective straight in the eyes, Jon said, "Let us talk about the rumors that are abundant in the neighborhood. We might be able to learn something from one another."

"Fair enough. Buddy's Salvage was broken into on Monday night. The throats were slit on the big dogs he kept to protect the place. A sum of money was stolen from the office."

"Was anything else taken? Besides the money? How many dogs had their throats slit?"

Detective Janski grinned. "You sound like an interrogator. Four or five."

"Hmm. And no one heard any commotion?"

"Buddy lives in the building on the next street. He said he knew nothing until he found the dogs dead the next morning and the office broken into."

"How did the intruder or intruders get in?"

"You tell me, Father, you seem to know something."

"The talk in the neighborhood says a side window was broken."

"That is what we found when we were called."

"And no one heard it break or saw anything?"

"Father, it was in the middle of the night. Not many people travel on that street after dark."

"Why is this gang being sought? What about the other gangs around here? I have met a few and seen several, the Street Rats, for instance."

"Now it is my turn to ask a question," Janski said. "Why is it that the gang led by the boy with a patch over his eye is in hiding? Can you answer that, Father?"

"No, unless they did commit the crime. Or they did not commit the crime and are afraid they will not get a fair hearing. Either reason would keep them in hiding."

"I am open to that, Father Jon."

"But Buddy of Buddy's Salvage is a powerful figure in the area."

"Good assessment, Father."

"Wouldn't you say he is a sort of 'godfather' of this area?"

Detective Janski winced and nodded. "You have learned a lot, for living here only five weeks."

106

"Six plus."

The detective pulled out his handkerchief and blew his nose. "Sometimes the stench in this area is almost overpowering. You know what I mean?"

Jon nodded, thinking of Angus' fourth floor flat across the street. "Maybe that is why you and I are having this conversation, to enlist one another to help deodorize the stench and give this area back its self respect. I understand that St. Ignatius parish was once the apple of the high society of this city."

"The current problem, Father, is a break-in, a gang being accused, and said gang being in hiding. Until I can talk with the gang . . ."

Jon interrupted, "Interrogate."

"All right, interrogate the accused. I have to assume they did this deed."

"Whatever happened to the American principle of being innocent until proven guilty?"

"Oh, for Pete sakes, Father, you know they did it, just like everyone else knows. Why are you trying to hide them?"

"St. Peter has nothing to do with this. Scared young men and a powerful overlord are at odds. I am not trying to hide them. I have no idea where they are."

"They haven't contacted you?"

"Yes, one phone call, which told me nothing about where they are."

"I suppose I could have your phone tapped."

"Why don't we just trust each other and work together. My goal is for their eternal souls. That does not mean hiding or permitting sin to go undiscovered. It does not mean hiding a sinner from justice. It does mean listening to, talking with, and counseling, praying, hearing confessions, and using wisdom in all of the previously named activities." Jon's expression was intense.

Detective Janski raised his hands in surrender. "Alright, alright, let's work together on the same page. You find out as much as you can and do that which you are bound to do as a priest to save these young men from hell, and I will do likewise. Maybe the grace of God will be seen in all of this." As a professional police officer, Janski was less sure of himself than he had been when he was a rookie. Something about this priest triggered anxiety and old memories from childhood of the terror of being sent by Sister to confess his misdeeds to Father.

Jon saw the anguish in the detective. "Let's pray for a good and fruitful end to this conversation." Detective Janski bowed his head as Jon prayed. He ended the prayer with 'the Lord's prayer,' which Janski joined in reciting, and the Sign of the Cross in a blessing over the detective. The two men clasped hands before parting.

The front door had barely closed when down Mighty staggered down the stairs. Hilda was close behind. The boy fell into Jon's arms. "I tried to stop him, Father."

Jon propelled the lad into his office. Mighty was shaking with rage, fear, and pain. "I've got to go to them. We are all one. When one is in trouble, we all stick together. The whole gang is in trouble. I've got to get to them."

"How are you going to get to them?" Jon asked. "You can barely walk now?"

"Let me go. I can find them. No one is going to keep me here!"

"Well, first you will need some clothes on. Hilda, go get his clothing."

"But, Father, he can't possibly go out in his state."

"Go get his clothing," Jon commanded.

Hilda hurried up the stairway.

Mighty swayed as he stood, "You will let me go?"

"If you insist, but the police will have you before you are a block away."

"Did you tell them I was here?"

"No. But when you stagger down the street, someone will call the police, and they will pick you up, if you are still alive."

Hilda arrived with Mighty's clothing and left the room. Jon allowed Mighty to struggle to dress, knowing that everything he did by himself would soon tire the boy. Mighty was breathing fitfully. Jon noticed a fresh flow of blood seeping through the abdominal bandage. As Mighty stuck his hand over it, trying to hide the evidence, he moaned loudly and collapsed unconscious onto the floor.

"Hilda!" Jon stooped to pick up the boy. Hilda appeared at the door. She looked at the unconscious boy and the white-as-a-sheet priest.

"Is he dead?"

"No, not yet." Jon groaned as he carried Mighty up the steps. "Get something to hold his abdominal wound shut. Pressure, like a bath towel. Keep him still." That hardly needed to be said. Mighty was very limp now.

Jon knelt on the floor beside Mighty, holding the wound until Hilda could replace his pressure on the wound with the bath towel. Kneeling always sent Jon into prayer. Hilda dropped down by him, crying softly for Jesus to help Mighty and them.

"I am going for the doctor. The doors will be locked; don't answer them, or the phone."

Jon took off his bloodied shirt as he ran to his room. He pulled a clean, non-cleric shirt over his head while running down the stairs. "Father, God, help me find that doctor."

Across the street, on a front stoop, a man watched Father leave the rectory. He followed the priest for four blocks. Another man joined the priest as he walked. He followed the two as they walked on. Jon told the man, the doctor, about Mighty. Suddenly they stopped, and the man following was left out in the open. The doctor said, "See the man behind me?"

Jon nodded.

"He is an informer. He probably followed you from outside the rectory."

Jon agreed. He had seen the man there several times.

"He will be calling in soon and telling someone that we have met up. It will not be good that we go back to the rectory together. We must pretend that we are having an argument. I will leave, and you will go back angry. I will follow, but that man will not know it is me. I will go to the church side entrance. Meet me."

Jon looked at the doctor in amazement.

"He will get his throat slit someday," indicating the man, "and no doctor will be able to help him." Then the doctor pushed Jon away and yelled, "Get away from me, I don't know what you are talking about." Jon reacted with a grab at the doctor's shoulder. The doctor and he struggled and broke apart. The doctor turned and ran down the street, pausing to look back before running on. Jon shrugged his shoulders and made a big deal of wiping the dirt off his pant legs before striding toward home.

Back at the rectory, Jon could hear crying upstairs. Reaching the top, he found Mighty crying and moaning while clinging to Hilda. She was as pale as Mighty. "Hold me!" Mighty cried out. Hilda relinquished her position to the priest. Jon wrapped strong, warm arms around the frightened and deeply hurting boy. Mighty sobbed. "I'm scared! I don't want to die!"

For what seemed an eternity Jon interceded for the boy. Slowly he became aware that Mighty was talking to God. He spoke of his past deeds and asked to be forgiven. Jon looked down at the boy nestled in his arms and prayed. Within moments Mighty was at peace, resting in Jon's embrace. "Hilda!"

Hilda appeared almost instantly. "Get me a glass of water and a couple bath towels." Hilda scurried away, returning with the glass of water.

Still holding Mighty, Jon turned Mighty's face upward and said, "Mighty, I baptize you in the name of the Father, and of the Son, and of the Holy Spirit." He poured the water over Mighty's head, catching the runoff with the towels. "Welcome to God's family, Mighty."

To Hilda, he said, "Hold him, keep him warm and still. I have to let the doctor in."

Bounding down the steps, Jon raced to the church. Outside the side door, kept locked by Angus, there was a commotion. Jon raced to the front doors, yanked the crossbar off, and threw them wide open. At the apparently locked side gate, an old woman stood, crying and screeching for the priest to hear her confession. Jon tugged at the lock, and it popped open. He had not closed it tightly when he took Angus home that morning.

The old woman staggered through the gate, and Jon helped her to the front doors of the church. Once inside, with the crossbar back in place, Jon turned to find the doctor and a medical bag unveiled from his disguise. "Kindly take me to the boy."

Jon had this phenomenal urge to laugh hysterically. The doctor grinned. "Pretty good, yes?"

"Yes," Jon said as he led the doctor to the rectory. Upstairs, the doctor examined Mighty. The wound in his abdomen had torn open.

"I am going to have to close that again. I have nothing to put him to sleep with. It would be too dangerous anyway." The doctor looked down at the wide-eyed Mighty. "It's going to hurt – a lot."

"How can I help?" a very pale Hilda ventured to ask. "I have done volunteer work in the hospitals, sometimes in the emergency rooms."

The doctor looked toward Father Jon. Jon nodded his head slightly before he said, "Can we wait a few minutes before you start? I would like to give Mighty Communion and anoint him."

"Yes, Hilda and I need to get some things ready."

Jon hurried down to the sacristy to get small bottles of holy water and oil, his stole, and the elements of Communion. Back upstairs, the doctor cautioned Jon about giving very much by mouth to Mighty before he worked on him. Jon just said, "God knows exactly how much he needs to endure this time."

By now Mighty was fearful again. Jon came beside him, wearing his stole. Father Jon explained that he was going to give him very small amounts of the Host and anoint him with Holy oil.

"The last rites?" Mighty asked.

Hilda gasped.

"No, the Anointing of the Sick for healing and life." Jon was now down on his knees beside the bed. Only Jon's quiet voice could be heard as he ministered to Mighty. The doctor and Hilda watched as the priest spoke the words of healing to Mighty. They watched as Mighty relaxed following Communion and the anointing and seemingly went to sleep.

The doctor checked the boy's breathing and heartbeat. It was more normal and no longer strained and stressed. "I shall begin now."

Jon placed himself partially over Mighty's chest, thinking again about the old prophet of long ago. The doctor was efficient, with Hilda's help. Mighty whimpered occasionally but never offered to open his eyes. After all, God was holding him, and that was what mattered.

"I think we have done it. He didn't lose a lot of blood. We will have to watch for infection."

Jon rose from his half-kneeling position and settled heavily into a chair. "God was here." He was spent. The phone rang. Jon didn't move.

"Father?" Hilda questioned.

Jon just remained seated.

The doctor started to check Jon's pulse, but Jon pushed him away. "I am alright. Let the answering machine take the message. Life in this room is more important."

Detective Larry Janski sat moodily looking out the small window in the door to his cubicle. Ever since he had returned to the Precinct Police Department Headquarters, he had been thinking about the challenge of the priest at St. Ignatius. Periodically he would pick up a pencil and worry a paper clip around his desktop. Momentarily he would forget the interview with the priest as he concentrated on pushing the paper clip under and over obstacles on his desk. The coiled cord of the telephone occupied considerable time.

Finally he jabbed the pencil point deep into his empty notepad, breaking the lead. With an excuse to sharpen the pencil, Larry meandered out into the hubbub of the outer office.

"You look like you lost your best friend,"

one of the clerks said.

"Nope."   With a sharpened pencil, Larry retreated to his privacy in the cubicle. Why was he so perplexed? He had known the answers that the priest would give, even before he went. The priest, that priest, was obviously hiding something or somebody. His informants indicated that. Was it the gang, or was it that woman who had become his housekeeper and seemed to be there full time now. "Jesus, forgive me for thinking it is a woman," he whispered to the empty room.

Then there was Buddy. The priest had accurately identified Buddy's role in the neighborhood. All the police officers knew Buddy and tried to avoid having to confront him on anything. There were rumors of people disappearing, money being extorted, houses of prostitution, and anything else that was illegal connected to Buddy's Salvage. The problem with the current situation was that Buddy had called the police about a teenage gang who apparently had robbed him and killed his dogs. This did not fit. Normally Buddy would have taken care of the situation without the police.

Who was Buddy trying to get to? The gang, led by the one-eyed leader, but who else? The priest? Possibly, but why? Buddy had nothing to do with St. Ignatius Parish. He attended the same parish Larry did. It was the upbeat parish of The Little Flower, located at the edge of town. Larry and his wife had a modest house on one of those dinky lots in so-called suburbia. It got Larry far away from his Precinct and gave Sally a place to grow flowers.

Larry slammed his hand into his forehead. Buddy didn't actually live in that parish. He lived in the building behind the salvage yard. Buddy had a house out beyond suburbia, with land, iron fences, and a locked gate. Mostly, though, Buddy lived in a palatial, remodeled building in St. Ignatius Parish. Maybe that was it.

Now Larry was thoroughly confused. His thinking had led to an impossible point. His phone rang. "Detective Janski." He listened to the caller before he slammed the phone back down.

Down the street, in a hastily created hideout, the gang considered their options. Go out on the street and be arrested and jailed. Go out on the street and run and be killed, or stay put and appear to be hiding. Well, they were in hiding, but not because they had done what all the neighborhood talk said they had. They were scared because of who was accusing them. Patch arrived, looking very gloomy. "All I get is the answering machine."

"Did ya say anything this time?"

Patch sat down and shook his head 'no.'

"Mighty is there. Do you suppose something has happened to him?"

Patch shook his head again. "Padre will take care of him."

"Are you sure?"

"He and Mighty are blood-brothers, remember."

"Maybe it doesn't mean the same thing to a priest."

"Shut up!"

Father Jon accepted the suggestion that he go to bed. The doctor and Hilda were going to sit up with Mighty. Assured that they would call him if there was a change, Jon stretched out full length and was instantly asleep. The occasional ringing of the phone did not awaken him. The doctor had put a pillow over the upstairs phone. Whoever was calling did not leave a message on the machine in the office.

Near dawn, Father awoke. He was still dressed, but in his bed. Mighty! He moved for the door and was met in the hall by a tired but happy doctor. "He is doing just fine. I think we shall have a full recovery without another blood transfusion. Hilda fed him about 2 am. I took a short nap."

"Father?" a weak cry came from the other bedroom. Jon entered. "Thanks." Mighty's eyes glistened. "You are the best brother."

It was Jon's turn for eyes to glisten. "Yeah, Mighty, Jesus came through for both of us. I have much to celebrate this morning at Mass."

Angus, still unsteady on his feet but doing better from the ministrations of Father Jon over the previous days, muttered to himself when he found the outside gate unlocked. The padlock was still on the side door, so he guessed all was OK inside. Once in the church building, he thought he saw something or someone at the back of the row of pews. It didn't move. He hurried into the sacristy so he did not have to see it. Maybe it was a body, maybe it was the death angel coming for him, or maybe it was riff rats. Whatever it was, he was going to stay in the sacristy until Father came.

He heard the side door open and close. Someone coming to Mass, he thought. He began to ready items for the Mass. He heard a footstep at the sacristy door and looked up. "Riff rats!" In almost slow motion, he pulled the gun from under his shirt and pointed it at the first of several young boys now standing in the sacristy.

As Jon entered the church from the rectory, he saw the discarded disguise on a back pew. He was starting toward the back when he heard a voice in the sacristy. "Riff rats, you can't come here!"

"Put the gun down, old man, we aren't going

to hurt you"

That was Patch's voice. Jon ran toward the sacristy, leaping over the weakened floor to enter from the rectory side. Angus was pointing a gun point blank at Patch.

"No, Angus, don't!"

Angus pulled the trigger as Jon lunged across the small room, hoping to deflect the shot. Silence followed after the gun went 'click.' No shot. No explosion. No bleeding, dying Patch. Jon took the gun away from Angus, who just sat down on the floor, mute.

"Thanks, Padre,"

Jon looked at the six standing there. "How did you get here?"

"We aren't dumb. We came last night and hid under the oil tank. Then, when he came in, we did too."

The murmur of a few voices in the Sanctuary alerted Jon to the reason he was in the church. Looking down at Angus, all he saw was a very tired old man in too much shock to be of any help or hindrance. Signally to the boys to keep quiet, Jon vested for the Mass. He tucked the gun in his belt and went out to greet the three parishioners waiting on him. He began with his usual 'good morning' and announced that Angus was not feeling up to serving this morning. Three heads nodded and then seemed stirred by something behind Jon. Jon was almost afraid to look. Turning slowly around, he found Scar, dressed in the cassock and surplice and waiting expectantly for Jon to begin the Mass. He stepped forward to the boy. Scar whispered, "Relax, Father, I have done this before."

Jon spoke in a quiet voice, asking God to bless the Mass, and began. Scar did not miss a point.

After giving all three Communion and

117

ending the Mass, Jon remained in the Sanctuary until each had left. He then bolted the door from the inside. He was kneeling before the altar, asking for wisdom and guidance, when he became aware all six boys were watching. "Where is Angus?"

"Still sitting on the floor. He seems very afraid and doesn't make any sense."

"I don't imagine he expected to see you still standing, Patch, after he pulled the trigger."

Back in the sacristy, Jon removed his vestments and knelt down on the floor beside the old man. "Let's get you something to eat before you go home, OK?" Angus sat motionless.

"Padre, the gun?" Patch pointed at the gun, still tucked in Jon's belt. Jon stood and removed it, fumbling as he tried to open it to remove the shells. "Let me," Patch offered. After a short hesitation on the priest's part, he handed it to Patch. Patch comfortably opened the old gun and dumped out five bullets. They looked at each other.

"Is there one stuck in the barrel? No, don't look or pull the trigger. We can deal with it later." Jon cautiously took the old gun back.

Patch was just staring at the gun. If there had been six shells in it, where was the one that was supposed to fire at him?

"A miracle, huh?" Jon said softly.

Thirty minutes later, Angus had eaten a hardy breakfast in the rectory kitchen. The doctor volunteered to take him over to his flat and see that he was comfortable.

The gang had gone upstairs to see Mighty, who told them all about the night before, about being baptized, having Communion, and being anointed for healing. They stood spellbound around his bed. He showed them the new stitching on his abdomen.

They were impressed.

Hilda, the doctor, and Jon conferred about the arrival of the 'wanted fugitives' and what should be done next. Jon expressed the need to seek the Lord's heart in the matter. The doctor took Angus back to his apartment.

The gang was cautioned to stay quietly on the second floor and under no circumstances come down until Father called for them. They were agreeable, since Hilda provided food and drinks for them in Mighty's room.

The rectory was strangely quiet when Jon returned from a time before the altar in St. Ignatius. Tiptoeing upstairs, he found sleeping youth in Mighty's room and the other bedroom. Hilda whispered, "They were awfully tired. They told me they hadn't slept since the night of the incident."

Jon nodded and retired to his room to refresh and plan the strategy needed for the next several days. There was a soft tap at his door. "Father, I need to talk." A barefoot Scar was standing outside the door.

"You're not mad at me for what I did at Mass, are ya?"

"No, where did you learn to serve Mass."

"When I lived with my grandma, she went to a Catholic Church and made me go too. I went to Catechism and served Mass sometimes on weekdays. It was a small church, and there weren't too many boys there to do it."

"Have you been baptized?"

Scar looked down embarrassed, "I said I had."

"So you haven't?"

"No."

"Mighty has."

"Uh huh, he told us."

Jon wondered which way to take the conversation next. Scar solved that for him. "I told them about the church being a sanctuary. That you could go to it and be safe. I mean, others couldn't take you away."

"Where did you learn something like that?"

"I can read, and I used to spend a lot of time reading books my grandma had. I read the stories in the Bible about running to the altar to save their lives."

"Grabbing hold of the horns of the altar. That is in the Old Testament."

"I know! I ain't ever seen horns on an altar. What do they look like? Are they covered up?"

"Since you can read, I have plenty of books that will explain that more clearly. But did you six actually come believing you would be safe in the church? I thought you had taken an oath to never go into the church?"

"Yeah."

Jon nodded, wondering how this was all going to work out. When Detective Janski found out the whole gang was hiding in the rectory, would he be arrested along with them? And the Bishop, what will he think? Jon wished that all this was done and over with, but he knew that was wishful thinking. "How did you get them all to go into the church?"

"Patch did that. He said you were Mighty's blood-brother and you would figure something out."

"I appreciate the confidence." Jon said dryly.

"We thought Patch was a goner when that old man pointed the gun at him."

"Yeah, I did too."

"You jumped in front of the old man."

"I think I did something like that."

"He would have kilt you instead."

120

"Remember, I am a blood-brother."

Scar paused, as though looking at Jon in a new light. "Yeah," he said, with great emotion in his voice. "Thanks."

"Now you can do something for me." Jon paused and waited on a positive response from Scar. He let silence just fill the room.

Scar shifted from one bare foot to the other. "What?" he said in a soft voice.

Jon said nothing, while he prayed for Scar to answer the knocking of the Lord in his heart.

"Oh that." Again Scar's voice was soft. "What I said I had."

Jon nodded, still maintaining silence.

"And Mighty did."

"Uh huh," Jon said so very softly. He was now down on his knees, beseeching the Lord for Scar.

"Geez, Father, I have never confessed face-to-face to a priest." Scar was now on his knees beside Father Jon.

Sometime later, Jon left Scar to wrestle with God and what God wanted him to do next. The front door bell was ringing. Jon stepped into the parlor where he could see who was at the door. It was a woman he did not know. "Hilda," he called out quietly.

He opened the door. The woman gushed, "Oh, I am so glad you are in, Father. My son is here, isn't he?"

"I don't believe I know you. You are?"

"Lorraine, Lorraine Smith."

Hilda arrived in the hallway as Jon invited the woman into the parlor. "Smith, Miss Smith?"

"No, Father, of course not, that is just my professional name. I was married when my son was born."

"What is your son's name?"

"Wayne McIntyre, he is 13, or is it 14 now. He is always talking about you, Father."

Hilda's eyebrows arched. From her position in the hallway she slowly moved her hands to her lips, signaling Father Jon to be careful of what he said.

"I don't believe I have met your son. You said his name is Wayne? Does that ring a bell, Hilda?"

"No, Father."

Miss Smith seemed uncomfortable and surprised that Hilda was listening to the conversation. "Well, I seem to be mistaken. I am sorry to have bothered you, Father." Lorraine moved toward the hallway and door. She paused and looked up the stairway.

Jon thought of nothing to say other than "God bless you" as the woman scurried down the front steps and almost ran up the street.

"What do you suppose that is all about?"

Hilda had a strange look on her face. "I know that woman."

"You do?"

"She wasn't here looking for a missing son, I can guarantee you that."

"Another informer?"

Hilda's head came up quickly, "You know about them?"

"The doctor showed me one, and then I thought back to other times and people who always seem to be hanging around, no matter where I am in the area."

"Somebody is awfully interested in what the priest at St. Ignatius is doing," Hilda commented.

"Police?"

Hilda shook her head 'no'.

"Then who?" Jon asked. As soon as the words were out of his mouth, he knew who. "Oh. Am I in danger?"

"I hope not, but you never can tell. I pray for you all the time."

"Thank you, Hilda. It is nice knowing someone is constantly praying for me."

"The boys upstairs, are they in danger?"

Hilda nodded. "I think so. Buddy usually takes care of his own dirty business in his way. To start such a rumor through the neighborhood, accusing someone to the police, is not his way."

"Well, let us work hard and see if we can keep those boys invisible for a few more hours or days."

Hilda nodded again. "As long as they are as scared as they are, it will be pretty easy to get them to cooperate."

"I'll go out grocery shopping in a little while, some place away from here. Do you have enough food to cover until nightfall?"

"Yes."

Sanctuary At Last

Jon sat in his office, thinking about the early afternoon caller. Who was she, and who sent her. He could readily believe she was sent to spy. Her long look up the stairs told him that. What was he supposed to do with seven wanted teens hiding on the second floor? He almost wished that Detective Janski would call or come by again. That wouldn't work. The six that came that morning had come because they sincerely believed Scar's story that the sanctuary of the church was a safe haven. Jon wished he knew more about law, and if that was still true. But then he would have to keep them over in the church building to meet that requirement, and tomorrow *Restoration Now, Inc.* was due to begin the preliminaries of restoring the sagging floor. He already had figured this was going to put a crimp in morning Mass, but with his few elderly parishioners he thought he could manage with them clustered to the extreme left of the altar. Then there was Angus. Jon buried his head in his hands. "Help, Lord!"

The Bishop looked at the note the Chancellor handed him. It was handwritten on a piece of dirty meat wrapping paper. What it said caused him to pause and ask the Chancellor, "Who delivered this?"

"It came by private courier. I have his name and number. I did not recognize the company name on his uniform."

The Bishop did not take threats lightly, and this one wasn't threatening him but the priest at St. Ignatius. Dismissing the Chancellor, the Bishop prayed before picking up the phone. He wondered whom to call first, Father Jon or the police. He elected to call Father.

Jon jumped when the phone rang. "St. Ignatius Parish."

"Bishop James Paul."

Jon's heart did flip flops, partially out of fear and partially in awe of the answered prayer. "Yes, Bishop, I am glad you called."

"You are doing something right, and, although I don't want the details, I guess you'd better tell me what is going on."

Jon inhaled slowly and told the Bishop about all that had been going on since he had arrived that was not in the official reports.

The Bishop only interrupted him to clarify a point or two. When the whole story was out, Jon said, "Forgive me, Bishop, for not telling you sooner. I . . ."

The Bishop stopped him. "Jon, this is grave, graver than you can imagine. I am not speaking of the extra things you have done, but I am holding in my hand a note that threatens the priest at St.

125

Ignatius."

For Jon, the threat for the priest at Ignatius didn't sink in at first. "Oh," he said at last.

"You mentioned a Detective. Do you believe he is trustworthy? Remember, several lives are dependent on this trust."

"I think he can be trusted, but I could be wrong."

"You asked about the legality of sanctuary in the church. Yes, it is legal and has been used in this city once or twice, a long time ago. But the laws haven't changed. Didn't you show me a tunnel connecting the old furnace room with the rectory? Was it ever sealed off, or could it be opened easily? Opened, it would make the rectory technically a part of the church."

Jon sat back in amazement. The Bishop was answering his questions and giving him direction. The Bishop gave him a few more instructions, asked for the full name of the Detective, and gave Jon his blessing before he hung up.

A light tap on the office door announced Hilda. "Scar says he wants to talk with you some more." Seeing the distressed look on Father Jon's face, Hilda asked, "Are you alright?"

"I am now, I think. The phone call was from the Bishop. He knows about everything."

"How?"

"I told him." Jon considered the threat on him and decided just to tell Hilda not to answer the door or telephone and to keep the boys quiet upstairs for now. "Tell Scar I will be up shortly. First I need to do some exploring in the cellar."

"Watch out for the rats."

"Don't worry, I intend to make lots of noise and turn on all the lights. Are the extra bulbs still in the cupboard?"

126

Down in the dank basement, Jon found and replaced burned out light bulbs and the old tunnel. He made noise with everything he found, fully expecting the rats to jump out and overwhelm him. Once inside the narrow passage, he yanked and pushed debris aside, moving deeper in toward the church. He had to stoop a little to pass under what he thought was the foundation of the rectory. Once close to where he supposed the church was, he began to push a broom handle he had found into every possible crevasse. "Eureka," he shouted when the broomstick went deep into an opening. He shoved it as far as he could.

Returning to the rectory basement, Jon took the steps two at a time into the church building. Circumventing the weakened floor, he descended the stairs to the basement that housed the old furnace. There, sticking through the wall behind the furnace, was the broomstick. He almost jumped up and down with joy as he pushed it back through and heard it hit the floor of the tunnel. Back in the rectory basement tunnel, he confirmed the broom was back on that side before he went up to see Scar and the others.

The Bishop depressed the button on the phone only long enough to break the connection. He called the Chancellor for the phone number of the Precinct of Detective Janski. Within minutes he was asking for the Detective.

"Janski, here," the voice replied. The Bishop let no time pass in niceties. After identifying himself, he asked the Detective to make a house call at the Bishop's residence. Larry Janski would have thought it was a prank call if the voice on the other end of the line had not been so commanding.

"Can you be here within thirty minutes?" The Bishop went on to describe how to locate the residence and which door to use. After receiving an affirmative, the Bishop said, "I will be expecting you to be prompt."

The Detective looked down at his worn pants and mismatched shirt. His shoes were scuffed, and his socks drooped. He chastised himself for not dressing more carefully in the morning. He was going to see the Bishop, the Bishop of the Catholic Church, his Bishop! He wanted to run out into the outer office and announce his destination, but he knew that was not proper. He wanted to call Sally and tell her, but she would probably ask him what he was wearing. He stopped by the police garage and picked up an official car with plenty of gasoline in it.

A solemn-faced Chancellor met Larry at the door and ushered him into a small, pristine waiting room. Larry fidgeted wishing he had taken more time to dress that morning. "The Bishop will see you now." The Chancellor escorted Larry to the door and promptly closed it behind him. It occurred to Larry that he did not know what to say, what the proper etiquette for meeting the Bishop was. Did he kiss his ring, did he genuflect, how was he supposed to address the Bishop?

"Detective Janski, I am Bishop James Paul, please have a seat."

Relieved, Larry sat on the indicated chair.

"My office received this today by special courier. I believe the priest being referred to on this paper is the one at St. Ignatius, Father Jon."

Detective Janski stared at the crude message. This was serious. He noticed the Bishop was handling the paper very carefully by the outer edges. He now became the police professional. "Who has handled this besides you, your Excellency?"

"Only the Chancellor. Are you going to check it for fingerprints?"

128

"Yes, and we need to take yours and the Chancellor's so as to eliminate those on this." Detective Janski placed the paper on the desk. "Do you have the envelope this came in?"

The Bishop nodded and buzzed for the Chancellor, who arrived immediately. "How will you take our fingerprints? Can it be done here in this office?"

"May I use your phone, your Excellency?" Quickly, Detective Janski arranged for a fingerprint technician to come to the Bishop's residence. "Does the priest at St. Ignatius know about this?"

The Bishop dismissed the Chancellor until the technician arrived. "Yes, we have talked."

"Does he want protection, or do you want protection for him from the police department?"

"At the present time no. I think he will be extremely cautious and careful. I am not sure what we are dealing with. Do you have any ideas, Detective Janski?"

"Yes and no. How much do you know about what has been going on at St. Ignatius since Father Jon came?"

The Bishop paused. "I have weekly official reports, and I have talked with Father by phone and in person. I visited there one day anonymously and walked through the possible reconstruction problems with him."

If the Detective had thought the Bishop might give him any information about what was going on inside the rectory, he had been wrong.

"By the way," the Bishop asked, "do you know anything about a company called *Restoration Now, Inc.*? They are scheduled to begin work tomorrow on the church building, but I am going tocancel them until later. They have been pressing us to go ahead with the needed repairs, while I have continually stated that we do not have the money. Their persistence has concerned me, even though I keep telling them to wait. In light of that," he pointed to the threating note, "I don't want them in there at this time."

"Wise move, your Excellency, very prudent. I am not familiar with them, but I can run a police check on the company if you would like."

"I would."

"Are you going to tell him, the priest, that you have contacted the police?"

"He knows I was going to contact you. He gave me your name. Oh yes, you said 'yes and no' to the question about having any ideas about this matter. Would you care to elaborate on them?"

"May I use your telephone again? I do not want to forget to run a check on *Restoration Now, Inc.*"

The Bishop nodded and sat amused as Larry made his request and asked that the results be phoned immediately to him at his cell phone number. Larry must have realized what he had said, for he reddened in the face. "So why are you using my phone for your calls?" the Bishop asked.

"I guess I wasn't thinking. I am sorry, your Excellency. I was flustered by your request to come here, being as how you are my Bishop. I just wasn't thinking."

"You're excused. Now, why the avoidance of 'yes and no'?"

The piercing eyes of the Bishop never left Larry's face as he gulped a few times before speaking. "I work in a world that does not tell the truth, where to put up a smoke screen is normal, and I am supposed to find out what is real and what is not. After a while, most of us police officers get cagey when we are interviewing. You would be amazed at

130

how proficient lawbreakers are at getting information out of us. They are far better than we are sometimes."

The Bishop nodded.

Larry continued. "So if I think I have accidentally implied too much information, I work other areas, hoping the other person has missed the implications."

"I didn't miss any," the Bishop remarked. "So since we are now assured I am neither a criminal nor a dishonest person, let us talk confidentially about all that may pertain to St. Ignatius and Father Jon."

"But you will not tell me what I probably need to know about Father Jon and what is going on in that rectory. How fair is that?"

"Does the priest tell others your sins?"

Larry blushed. "No."

"Then neither will I. 'Yes and no,' Detective Janski. I suspect you have knowledge that may protect my priest. I want it."

"Off the record, we never discussed this?" Larry was sweating. First the priest at the rectory, and now the Bishop, had brought up all the old memories. Maybe he had stayed too long in police work. It was getting harder and harder to look people in the eye.

"Off the record, we never discussed this," the Bishop said. At that moment the detective's cell phone rang. They both looked startled.

"Janski here," and he listened. He grew pale, and beads of sweat popped out on his forehead.

"Please tell his Excellency, the Bishop, what you just told me." He handed his phone to the Bishop.

"Bishop James Paul. Yes Ma'm, I asked that to be checked on. Who is the parent company? I see.

Thank you." He handed the phone back to Larry.

"How soon will the tech be here? The fingerprint tech, that's who! Well, get one here now!" Larry ordered, before shutting his phone off.

"Who is Vincent Sardoni?"

"He is known as Buddy in the neighborhood." Larry took a deep breath, "A sort of 'godfather' of the neighborhood around St. Ignatius."

"Not a very nice man, from what I can recall in the papers. And never spent anytime in prison for anything, has he?"

"No."

"And you are afraid of him?"

Larry hesitated before nodding. "You don't cross him."

The intercom buzzed, and the Chancellor announced that the tech was here from the police department. Picking up the phone, the Bishop spoke to the Chancellor, instructing him to show the man in.

The next ten minutes were spent taking fingerprints of the Chancellor and the Bishop so that theirs could be eliminated from any others found on the threatening note. The tech took the note in a protective wrapper and the new prints with him and left. The Detective had regained some of his composure and tried to avoid looking the Bishop in the eyes. It didn't work.

Quietly, the Bishop interrogated the police officer concerning all he knew about this 'Buddy' and the possibility that this man was behind the note. The Bishop gave Larry Janski absolution after a very contrite confession. At last the two men shook hands as fellow workers, teamed together to see to the bottom of the trouble.

Before the Bishop went to the Cathedral to

pray, he instructed the Chancellor to cancel the appointment at St. Ignatius with **Restoration Now, Inc.** and to inform Father Jon not to let them in if they did show up in the morning. The Bishop missed supper and was observed still in front of the altar shortly before midnight. In the morning, he called the Diocesan attorney.

Father Jon went whistling up the stairs. He was met on the second floor by the gang, who indicated to him that he needed to be quiet. He laughed. It may have been the first time they ever saw him laugh. "It is my house, and I can make noise."

They nodded, still maintaining their silence. Scar saw a true brother in Jon for the first time. Patch posed the question, "What are we going to do?"

"Work!"

"Hey, come in here," called Mighty.

Obligingly, they moved to Mighty's room.

"Work," Jon said for the second time. He looked at the boys and saw what he hadn't seen before. They all needed clothing of some sort.

"Hmmm. Guess we will have to find you something to work in. A couple of you can wear my sweats, but I have only two pair. None of you are big enough to wear any of my pants." Jon laughed heartily then.

"Work?" Patch asked. "Where?"

"Ah, a good question. Glad you asked. Down in the cellar."

"Down in the cellar? Is that where you are going to hide us?" Don't Call Me Charlie asked.

"I am not hiding you. I am giving you sanctuary until it is time for you to safely talk with the police."

"It'll never be safe," retorted another.

"Maybe yes, maybe no. But first you must clean out the tunnel between the church and the rectory."

Patch moved in front of Jon. "Why the tunnel?"

"Well, if the Bishop is right, and Scar is right about sanctuary, the church and rectory are all one, and you can have sanctuary in all of the building, not just the church building. Right now I am housing fugitives up here, and that is wrong. To house all of you in the sanctuary/rectory all connected is an act of mercy. I like the sound of that better."

"Me too," several chorused.

Hilda had come up. "The Chancellor just called. You need to phone him back."

Jon nodded and excused himself after tossing two pairs of sweat pants and shirts to the boys. "Figure out how to divide these up and share the rest of your clothing. I'll find a couple more shirts after the phone call."

He listened to the answering machine before calling the Chancellor's Office. The urgent tone of the conversation impressed Jon with the seriousness of the situation at St. Ignatius. "Assure the Bishop I will not let *Restoration Now, Inc.* in. I do need to leave the house for a while this evening to go get groceries and some clothing. What? Do not leave? How? I will be expecting your delivery about 6 pm. Clothing sizes, boys, large and extra large, sweats, underwear, pjs, T-shirts, socks. Yes, that is right, probably half and half will do. Thank you very much." Jon hung up the phone, smiling for the first time that day. He wasn't in this alone. "Thank you, Lord!"

Upstairs, Hilda had taken charge, directing the boys to trade off and 'get decent'. They looked at each other and grinned. They had never taken orders from anyone, except Patch, and it sort of felt good being told to 'get decent'. Scar and Patch were the tallest, so they claimed the sweat pants. A few minutes later Jon tossed in several t-shirts. Soon they were all 'decent', having covered most of the dirt and holes in their clothing with the priest's.

Jon conferred with Hilda about the delivery arriving around 6 pm. They discussed how to handle it and decided that Jon needed to be the front person. She was still shaking her head at the miracles taking place when the doorbell rang. Suddenly fear invaded the house again. Silence reigned upstairs.

Jon looked out the parlor window. It was Agnes and Claire. "Hello, ladies."

They nodded. "You haven't been out all day. We were concerned you were sick. So here." They thrust two sacks of groceries at him.

Jon blessed them and took the offered sacks into the rectory.

"First-fruits from the ravens," he said to Hilda.

"Ravens?" she asked.

"An Old Testament prophet, Elijah, in First Kings. Read it sometime."

She nodded as she took the groceries to the kitchen. She scribbled the name of the prophet and First Kings on one of the bags. Hilda took stock of the contents of the sacks: eight cans of chicken noodle soup, two loaves of bread, a dusty box of crackers, and two jars of peanut butter, also dust covered. There was enough to give the boys upstairs a decent meal. She giggled at the word 'decent'. It certainly had its implications.

Jon came and looked over her shoulder at the provisions. "Definitely raven," he said, with a mysterious tone of voice. "Definitely raven. Praise

God for His goodness."

Scar had crept down the stairs. "Father, can we talk some more?"

They went into the office and closed the door. Hilda mixed half the cans of chicken noodle soup with a couple cans of mixed vegetables in a large pot. Soon the aroma made its way upstairs. Patch made a dash for the kitchen. Hilda looked up from her stack of peanut butter sandwiches. "Hungry?" Patch nodded.

"Get the others down here to the kitchen. I am not carrying hot soup upstairs to be spilled."

Patch took off in a flash. One by one, each boy appeared in the kitchen, followed lastly by Patch. "I told Mighty you would bring his up." He grinned at her. "He isn't decent, yet."

Enough bowls were found, and the boys set about eating the soup and slightly stale crackers. Hilda held back the sandwiches until they had finished all but one bowl of soup, saved for Mighty. "Oops, we forgot to save Scar any," Hilda laughed.

The boys quickly poured the remains of their soup into one bowl. They almost filled it. "Now we saved him some."

Hilda shook her head and laughed again. "You are something."

"We all stick together so we all have something. We took an oath," one of the quieter boys commented.

"What is your name," Hilda asked.

"Arabian."

"It really is Lawrence," another taunted. "Like Lawrence of Arabia."

"I like Lawrence for a name," said Hilda, "but if you want, I will call you 'Arabian'."

Arabian kicked at the floor for a moment and then looked up and smiled. "You can call me

Lawrence."

"Who's Lawrence?" Scar and Father Jon came in at the tail end of the conversation.

"Arabian," several chorused.

"I am," answered the boy. "You can call me Lawrence too," he said to Jon.

The others had shoved the bowl of soup and a spoon toward Scar. "She won't let you have the sandwich until you eat all of that."

After showing the boys the location of the tunnel in the cellar, Jon headed up the steps to the second floor. Voices could be heard wafting up the heating ducts from the furnace in the cellar. After a quick trip back down to warn the boys about noise, he resumed his upward climb. He wanted to shower before anything more happened. Hilda waylaid him to take a bowl of soup and a sandwich up to Mighty. The injured boy was pleased and ate the food eagerly. "I gotta get well so I can help them," Mighty said between spoonfuls.

Promptly at 6 pm a car pulled into the rectory drive. Father Damian, the Chancellor, was at the wheel. A Father Marvin, who had been recruited to help, was with him. After a quick conference at the front door, the Chancellor backed the car into the drive, all the way to where Jon's was parked. Hilda and Jon formed the inside conveyor line as Fathers Damian and Marvin pulled things out of the car. The clothing came in first, then bags and bags of groceries. Hilda kept expressing her joy at the abundance of food.

The three priests retired to Jon's office to talk. "How else can we help? The Bishop instructed us to get whatever was needed."

Jon was silent. He did not expect such

assistance. "Pray for me."

"Of course; anything else? Do you believe you are in danger?"

"The Bishop believes I am. Yes, there is a certain amount of concern on my part. I seem to have attracted someone's attention who isn't too keen on having an active priest at St. Ignatius. Is that why it has been so difficult to get anyone to stay here long?" Jon was looking at the Chancellor.

"I can't speak about that, but the threat on you is real. I saw the note."

Jon nodded. Angus, across the street! "There is something you can do. The custodian here at St. Ignatius lives across the street. He is not well, and of unknown age. The doctor escorted him home after I fed him in my kitchen this morning. The man often is demented. He has no family but lives alone in a rattrap apartment full of junk. I have tried to get the Social Services to come interview him, but they keep putting me off. Would you go across the street and check on him?"

Both Fathers agreed. "Of course, whatever we can do for him, we will. Social Services seem to put a lot of people off, often, I think, waiting for them to die without their intervention. Would you like for us to take him to St Elizabeth's Health Home?"

"I don't know that he will go. Everything seems to be a big issue, even going to the bathroom."

The priests laughed.

"He is in apartment 4D; it is the second door on your right after you get to the fourth floor."

Fathers Damian and Marvin moved toward the front door. Jon stopped them and told them to breathe well outside because the stench inside the building, and especially in Angus' apartment, was overwhelming. The two looked at each other.

"My first assignment was inner city. I think I

have smelled the smell," Father Marvin ventured.

"Probably not this one," Jon replied. "Here is a pack of gum. Split it between you. It will help cover up some of the odors." Jon tossed the package to the Chancellor. They shrugged their shoulders but opened the pack and started chewing anyway.

Moments later, on the way up the stairs, a ragged, longhaired youth passed them. "Are you looking for someone, Father?"

"Angus, fourth floor, 'D'."

"You'll find him up thar."

They continued their climb. Apartment D was clearly marked. There was no answer when they tapped on the door. Father Jon had said the door would be unlocked, so they turned the handle. Even with the preparation that Jon had given them, they were stunned at the inside of the apartment. Junk was piled in the corners. Angus sat on a dilapidated couch that he obviously used as his bed. The TV was on, but all that was on the screen was snow. And the stench was much worse than they had imagined.

Angus looked toward them. "Father Jon sent us to check on you." If the eyes blinked behind his glasses, they couldn't tell for the dirt and grime on the lenses. How are you feeling?" Still there was no movement of recognition that anyone was in the room. "Have you eaten anything lately?"

Suddenly Angus spoke, as he tried to get off the couch. "Bathroom!" The plea was urgent. Both priests moved quickly to him, helped him up, and headed him toward the only other door in the apartment. Angus was trying to take down his trousers as they steered him into the room and onto the toilet. In the bathroom was even a greater stench than in the apartment. Both men turned their heads aside to breathe. Father Marvin thought he was going to throw up. The Chancellor was wishing he could.

After the urgent task was taken care of, and Angus was cleaned and redressed, the priests gladly closed the bathroom door. Angus shuffled toward the couch. "Would you like to go visit with Father Jon?" Angus stared but changed his direction of travel from toward the couch to toward the door.

"What do you have in mind, Chancellor?" Father Marvin asked. "What can Jon do? He has his hands full already."

The Chancellor nodded as they helped Angus down the four flights of stairs. Once on the street they inhaled deeply, keeping their heads averted from Angus.

Jon saw them coming and opened the front door. Carefully he steered Angus to the one wooden chair in the parlor. Father Marvin and Chancellor Damian took seats on the opposite side of the room. "This man has no business living alone in all that filth!"

"I know that, but Social Services say they are backed up on new cases at least a month. I have checked, and there does not seem to be any family either. I started the process of being declared guardian for him so that something could be done. It is a long, drawn out affair."

"Would he go to St. Elizabeth's?" Marvin asked.

"I don't know, but then how are we to get him in there? They seem to have a waiting list also."

"May I use your phone in the office?" The Chancellor stood. "I am going to call there right now. Something has to be done for this poor man."

Angus sniffed and wiped his nose with his already dirty shirtsleeve.

"What will a phone call do?" asked Jon.

"When it is from the Bishop's Office, a lot."

140

The Chancellor left the room.

Jon moved closer to Angus, "Angus, would you like to go to live where you have a good bed to sleep in and good food every day and people who care for you?" Angus hung his head.

Father Marvin spoke. Jon looked up, startled at first, and then a big grin came to his face. He answered in the same manner he was spoken to, in Pig Latin. "I haven't talked this way since grade school."

Jon was almost sitting on the same chair with Angus, his arm extended around him. Angus stirred for a moment but then seemed to recognize who Jon was.

The Chancellor returned, smiling and with the news that a room would be ready in 30 minutes. Jon leaned in closer to Angus, "Would that be alright with you, a new clean room, people to talk to, good food, and a real bed?"

Angus nodded his head ever so slightly. "No riff rats?"

"No riff rats," Jon promised solemnly.

Father Marvin asked in Pig Latin how Father Jon could sit so close to Angus and not gag. "The chewing gum helps some, but mostly it must be God's grace. I don't know." Switching to Pig Latin, Jon explained that the first couple of times over at Angus' apartment, he could hardly wait to get back outside to the polluted air of the city.

"How are you going to get him to St. Elizabeth's?"

The Chancellor smiled wanly, "We will take him."

Father Marvin made a dash down the hall to the bathroom. Gagging could be heard.

"He worked inner city?" Jon asked.

"Never had this kind of exposure, I can

assure you, but neither had I. He was available and a little experienced, so I brought him along tonight. He'll be OK, I am sure." The Chancellor looked with compassionate eyes on Angus. "We should be doing more for men and women like him."

Jon nodded.

Angus was safely fastened into the back seat of the car. The Chancellor and Father Marvin, armed with more gum and a 'just in case' plastic bag, left for St. Elizabeth's.

Jon had the urge to throw open the doors and windows to air the front part of the rectory. Hilda said 'no' and came out of her quarters with a spray can of air deodorant. The perfumed spray barely covered the lingering odor.

Hilda pointed to the basement door. "The boys are through down there and are waiting on the steps."

Jon greeted them and gave each a pile of new clothing to carry upstairs. While he supervised the showers and changes of clothing, Hilda fixed supper. She then supervised the boys while Jon took a second shower for the day, hoping to remove some of Angus' odor. He made a mental note, when all he got was tepid-to-cold water, he would have to remember to shower before the gang.

Fed and tired from their work, the boys retired upstairs. Jon put two on pallets in Mighty's room and the other four in the other bedroom. Soon all that could be heard was a few whispers. Jon lay on his bed waiting to make sure all were asleep, when the phone rang at his elbow. "St. Ignatius, Father Jon," he answered. It was the Chancellor.

"All is well for Angus. He is settled and cleaned up. They fed him, and he devoured everything in front of him. Tell me, Father, do you know Angus' last name? I signed him in as Angus Ignatius, just so they had a first and last name." The Chancellor chuckled. "Hopefully he will not pass away tonight so that my doing that doesn't have to be on his death certificate."

Jon murmured, "Downstairs, on those papers I showed you, is his name. I can call it to you in the morning."

"All is well at St. Ignatius tonight?" asked the Chancellor.

"Yes, Father Damian, all are asleep, I hope."

"Good night, then, and God bless you."

Jon hung up the phone and turned out the small lamp beside his bed. He was asleep instantly.

A Season of Mystery

Jon woke Scar to serve Mass in the morning.
The gun still lay in the sacristy. Jon put it inside a
small drawer, along with the five bullets. Scar rang
the bell as they entered the Sanctuary. Seven were
present. Jon told those present that Angus was now
in a nursing home in order to explain the new person
who was assisting at the Mass. Several nodded.
One, a stranger, looked vaguely familiar. When Jon
served Communion and looked more closely at the
man, he saw it was the doctor, with a hat on.

The doctor lingered until the other six exited.
Jon told him briefly how the day before had ended.
Scar made a point of reminding Jon about the gun
before they left the church for the rectory. Jon took it
and the bullets with him.

After a quick check of Mighty, the doctor
and Jon talked for a while in the office. The boys
were having breakfast in the kitchen. "Mighty seems

to be healing as I might expect. Having his friends with him has definitely lifted his spirits."

"That, and the excellent care Hilda gives him, should get Mighty on his feet pretty quickly."

"Don't let him rush it. I do not want to stitch him up again," the doctor warned.

Jon agreed.

"What are you going to do about the gun?"

"I don't know. It is an old gun. Angus probably had it for twenty years or so. The mystery is why five bullets and no empty shell."

"I wonder if that is all he had, five." The doctor puzzled. "You remember, I've been in his apartment. There are all those boxes filled with what looks like trash in the corners. Wonder what else he has in there."

"Someone is going to have to clean out that trash, and there might be more guns and ammo," Jon mused.

"Yes, and that should be done immediately. As soon as the news circulates that Angus is gone to a nursing home, the pilferers will be at work."

"I guess I could go do it," Jon said, thinking of the stench. "I am not too eager, though."

"Does Hilda have extra plastic trash bags?" the doctor asked. "I will go and remove anything of value, and anything like that also." He pointed at the gun, "I'll leave the rest there. If anyone wants that stinking mess, they can have it."

"Do you suppose anyone will notice you are in there?"

"Probably, but I am known as 'the doctor' around these parts, and the local residents will not think too much of me being there. After all, I did take him home and put him to bed yesterday morning. They noticed. Nothing much goes unnoticed in this area, but mostly they don't care to say or doing anything about it."

Jon nodded. "I'll get the plastic bags. How many do you want?"

"Three or four, and I probably won't need that many. I'll leave by the front door like yesterday. That way I can go straight across the street. No one will think too much about that."

While the doctor was away, Jon called the Chancellor's office and left Angus' last name. "That is correct, Angus Cosstilla, spelled A-N-G-U-S Angus, C-O-S-S-T-I-L-L-A, Cosstilla." The secretary repeated the spelling back to Jon.

Before he could place the phone back on its hook, it rang. "St. Ignatius Rectory." The voice on the other end identified the caller as being with **Restoration Now, Inc.** and was inquiring whether he, the pastor, knew the reasons for the cancellation by the Bishop's office of the work that was to begin that day. Jon feigned ignorance and said that would have to be taken up with the Bishop, not a parish priest. The caller persisted, attempting to get Jon to let them come anyway. Jon said "no" for what was the third or fourth time. The caller then informed him that the church building was in immanent danger of falling in, and he would be responsible for any repercussions. Hilda must have heard his repeated 'no,' for she appeared at the office door, telling him that he was needed elsewhere. Jon bluntly excused himself from the increasingly abrasive caller and hung up.

Hilda just grinned at him and said, "Did I do alright?" Jon nodded. "Anytime, Father. That caller should have been hung up on at the beginning of that call."

"Probably," Jon acknowledged. "Is the doctor back, yet?"

"No, that was a big job he went to do."

"Only smelly, and most, if not all of that, will

remain over there."

"I hope so. I've run out of room deodorizers."

"Where are the boys?"

"Upstairs. Two helped with the dishes, and I found a Monopoly game in the closet. I told them how it is played, but I think they are making up their own rules. Scar is reading. Did you know he could read? He found a couple books that interested him. He is in one corner of the room reading, while the others are fighting over the railroads and avoiding jail!" Hilda laughed.

Jon grinned. "Is Patch playing also?"

"No, he is in talking with Mighty. They seem to have a lot in common, although I am not sure what it is."

"Could be the serious injuries each has had, you know, with Patch loosing his eye."

The doorbell rang loudly at the front door. Jon pointed to the upstairs. Hilda nodded and went up to ensure the boys remembered to not make a sound. The bell knob was twisted and rung again.

Jon took a quick look out the parlor window before opening the door with the security chain still on. A *Restoration Now, Inc.* truck was parked on the sidewalk in front of the church building.

A big, beefy man growled, "How do we get inside of that blame church, with that fence and all locked up?"

"I am sorry, but the Bishop cancelled the work for today. Did you not get the message?" Jon asked.

The man pushed against the door so as to open it wider.

Jon said, "The chain is on, and I have not invited you to come in."

"We were told to get in there and get the

work started, tearing out the old walls. We have a contract with a . . .", and the man fished into his jacket pocket for a piece of paper. "It says here that Father will cooperate by opening the church property to the workers from *Restoration Now, Inc.*, and it is guaranteed by someone by the name of Father John Mark."

"I am Father Jon Mark, and I have not guaranteed anything. This project is under the auspices of the Bishop's Office. Only he can give permission for you to be here, and I understand he has not given permission for the work to go ahead today."

The man stuck his foot into the opening between the door and the frame. "I am not leaving until you open up the church doors."

"I cannot do that. The Bishop has told me not to allow entrance to *Restoration Now, Inc.*"

Foul words came out of the mouth of the large man as he tried to shove the door open more.

Hilda appeared at the bottom of the stairs.

"Who's she?" the man growled.

"My housekeeper." Jon turned his head slightly toward her and said, "Bring me the telephone. I think I am going to have to call the police."

Seconds later, Hilda handed him the phone. "Are you going to leave peaceably, or do I call the police?"

More foul words issued forth from the man, and a threatening gesture. Jon pressed the 'nine' and then two quick strokes on the 'one' key. The man bolted away and got into his truck. "You haven't heard the last of this!" he hollered, as he rammed the side of the truck into the chain link fencing in front of the church before driving off.

Jon turned the phone back on. "Good move,

148

Hilda." His legs were shaking as he closed and bolted the door shut.

"I know that man," a voice from the top of the stairs announced.

Jon looked up at Patch. "Are you sure?"

Patch nodded. "He works for Buddy's Salvage."

"Oh great, and what does Buddy's Salvage have to do with *Restoration Now, Inc.*?"

"I don't know, Padre, but it ain't good."

Jon looked at the telephone in his hand and handed it back to Hilda. "Keep it handy. I am going to use the one up in my room to make a call."

A light tapping at the front door startled all of them. Patch bolted out of sight. Jon looked out the security hole and saw the doctor. Hilda had turned white as a sheet. "It's the doctor." Jon hastened to let the man in. "Only one bag?"

The doctor nodded and blew his nose. "I can't seem to get the smell out of my lungs and taste out of my mouth." He accepted the cup of coffee Hilda offered. In the kitchen he carefully laid out what of value he had found in Angus' apartment. Besides the lingering odor there was a bank savings book, birth certificate, a naturalization document, and a few trinkets of personal value to Angus. "And then there is this," he said with a smile. "The reason the gun did not go off when it was aimed at Patch." He laid one bullet, the missing one of six, on the table.

"Patch won at the game of Russian Roulette. What a miracle," Jon said.

"Russian Roulette?" the doctor asked.

"Yes, it is when you put one shell in the gun, spin the chamber, and pull the trigger, with the gun pointed at your head. There are five empty spots and one shell. You are betting on an empty one when you pull that trigger. Only this time it was five shells and one empty. What a wonderful God we have! Angus did not become a murderer, nor did Patch die!"

Hilda was now seated at the table with the two men. She was still very pale. The doctor asked, "Are you alright?" She nodded as she put her head down and cried. The men, only a little discomforted by her tears, sat alongside her, quietly talking with God. The doctor spoke in his native language for a long time.

"Padre." A soft-spoken Patch stood at the kitchen door. "I," the boy looked so young and vulnerable, "I think you ought to call the police about that man." And after a moment he said, "Is she alright?"

Jon nodded as he rose from the table. He placed his hand on Hilda's head and prayed a blessing. Then he placed his arm around Patch and guided him to his office.

Detective Janski had spent several hours in a debriefing at Central Headquarters. His Precinct Captain sent him as a representative from their area. Back in his small office, his mind awhirl, his habit of worrying a paperclip around his desktop went on, as he thought. His conversation with Sally last night was serious and frightening. After the visit with his Bishop, the detective was certain that he would not be in police work much longer. He was uncertain about the future, and, after this morning's meeting, he was even more concerned. The Police Commissioner spoke at great length about certain controlling elements in the city who were undesirable. It didn't take the Commissioner saying that for Larry to know the truth of the statement. Since he knew more than most in his Precinct, he understood why he was selected for the meeting.

150

The paperclip fell into the wastebasket. Normally he would take the time to dump the basket and retrieve the clip. But, as it fell, he thought about the acute dangers to the priest at St. Ignatius and wondered how much the Bishop had understood of his double talk at the Chancery. Oh, the Bishop had understood him, but did he realize that Vincent Sardoni had set his sights on destroying the historical church, if necessary, in order to drive out the priest?

Yes, Larry answered himself, *the Bishop did understand.* With the added knowledge from this morning's meeting, it was evident that Buddy's Salvage was the focal point of considerable criminal operations within the city, and possibly beyond.

It was then that Larry noticed a memo on his desk to call the Bishop's Office as soon as possible. A few curse words raced though his mind as he punched in the number. An efficient secretary answered the phone. "Detective Janski here, returning the Bishop's call."

"One moment." There was not even a 'please' before putting him on hold, and no soothing music in the background. Larry could hear his heart pounding.

"Bishop James Paul. Detective, thank you for returning my call. I received a report from the priest at St. Ignatius this morning that he was threatened by a man from **Restoration Now, Inc**, who tried to force entry into the rectory. I have been in contact with the Diocesan attorneys also, who will step in and legally represent all those staying at the rectory."

"All?" The detective was pulling a notepad toward him. "Do you mean to say there are more than the priest there and his housekeeper?"

"I have instructed Father Jon Mark to cooperate with you. It would be best to see him in person. I also have the documents before me that allow those fleeing from danger to have sanctuary in the church complex. I think you know of whom I am speaking."

"That gang of hoodlums."

"I don't think that would be the proper terminology to use for underage, frightened boys who fear for their lives."

"Bishop, you don't understand the gangs in that part of town."

"I will leave the legalities to the attorneys. They are on their way to St. Ignatius Rectory as I speak. I expect, if you want to protect the innocents and my priest, you will be there shortly. Is that clear enough, Detective Janski?"

"Yes." Larry hung up the phone. He was shaking from the encounter with the Bishop while at the same time wondering how all of this would work out. It had been apparent in the morning meeting that a concerted effort was going to be made to do something about the stranglehold being put on the city by the undesirables. And, in spite of having considered the gangs as undesirables, Larry was already beginning to see that they could be victims also.

"Where are you going?" another officer called, as Larry donned his jacket and gun holster.

"Down on the streets. There is business to take care of."

"You're going alone?"

"Might as well, I can call for backup if needed. Be ready!"

Picking a street-battered car from the pool of police autos, Larry took a deep breath and prayed. "Lord, help me. This could get out of hand." As he circumvented the streets so that he could park on the church side of the street, he realized that he was unusually calm, and, for a moment, it occurred to him that the Lord had heard his prayer.

Inside the rectory, life had been disrupted after Father Jon had called the Bishop and reported the attempt by the man from *Restoration Now, Inc* to enter the rectory. The Bishop said he was sending the Diocesan Attorneys and that they would deal with the issue of sanctuary in the church complex for the boys. Jon informed Hilda of the upcoming visitors before a quick chat with Patch. It stretched the friendship of the priest and gang leader momentarily before Patch agreed to talk first with his gang, and if need be, with the lawyers. Jon and Patch went upstairs and informed the others of what was about to happen.

"I knew it! The fuzz is comin'!"

"I don't think so," Jon offered cautiously. "The lawyers will know best how to handle this."

Amid other disgruntled comments came the call from Mighty's bed. "Hey, fill me in!"

Patch looked at each of his gang and said, "If any of you wants to split and run, think again. We are in this together, all of us, including the Padre."

All muttering ceased immediately when the front door bell rang. Jon looked out the window from Mighty's room. An expensive but not flashy car sat in the drive. "Excuse me. I think our visitors are here." He looked at Patch. "Are you?"

Patch nodded. "We are with you, Padre. You are our blood-brother." The others remained mute, but without any signs of hostility.

Downstairs, after they had shown her their identification with the Bishop's seal on it, Hilda invited the gentlemen into the parlor. Jon prayed with each step as he descended the stairs.

"I'm Father Jon."

After a short discussion behind the closed

parlor doors, Jon called for Patch to join them. Before their leader left them the boys joined hands in their secret pact. Mighty clung to Patch for an extra moment.

The attorneys were impressed with the clean, one-eyed young man in sweats who entered the parlor. Patch was attentive to what they were telling him, nodding his head as they explained about sanctuary at St. Ignatius, and what might happen if they were truly guilty of those rumors circulating about.

"I understand that a Detective Janski has been notified to meet us here." Patch's eyes grew narrow. "He cannot take you from here," assured the lawyer. "However, he has the right to know you are here and can talk with you here. Father, or one of us, must always be present during any conversations with the detective. These papers, which are recorded in the courts of this city, give you protection as long as you are in sanctuary here in St. Ignatius." The lawyer held a copy out to Patch.

"I can't read that much," muttered Patch.

"Scar can," Father Jon spoke up.

"Scar is here also?" the lawyer inquired.

"All of them are." Jon answered.

"Ask him to come down. If he can read, then he can assure Patch that what we say is in these papers is."

"I think we are about to get more company," volunteered the other lawyer, nodding toward the car being parked in front of the rectory.

Patch clinched his fists and then looked at Father. "Padre, can I take the papers up to Scar?"

With a quick nod by one of the lawyers, Patch scurried up the stairs before Detective Janski got to the door.

Jon opened the door, introduced the lawyers,

154

and invited the detective into the parlor. There was a moment of awkwardness and uneasy silence. For a few seconds Detective Janski wondered what he was doing there. It seemed like a setup. He had been in a couple of those in his career.

One of the lawyers cleared his throat. "We are here to represent the Diocese and St. Ignatius church complex. We are not here to interfere with law and justice but to state and prove the rightfulness of this church complex to be a haven of safety."

The detective raised his hand to silence the lawyer. "I have no quarrel with that. I have spoken with the Bishop and know that this is perfectly legal. What I am here for is to identify those who are using this place as sanctuary and to ensure that no criminal activity is being housed here. In other words, that this sanctuary is not being abused."

"What do you mean by 'criminal activity being housed here'?" asked Father testily.

Larry looked at the priest and shrugged his shoulders. "Are they continuing their gang activities from here, using this place as a base of operations?"

"Ask them," Father Jon said. On the stairs stood seven young men. Mighty clung to the rail and another boy. Jon marveled at the solidarity of the gang, then remembered he was their blood-brother. It was solidarity with him also. He was almost overwhelmed with emotion.

Detective Janski stared at the young men. "This is highly irregular."

"What, sanctuary, the gang, the lawyers, what?" Jon asked.

"Face-to-face with them."

"They are people, just like you and me. Does that surprise you?"

"Do you wish to interrogate them, detective?" one of the lawyers asked.

The detective nodded as he reached up and turned his lapel mic off. "One at a time, and one of you," looking at the lawyers, "will be present?"

"Yep."

"Use my office. If the phone rings, I will take it out here."

"Who do you want to talk to first?" Patch broke the silence.

"You."

Two hours later, a tired but still unconvinced Detective Janski took his leave. The lawyers had taken turns sitting in on the interviews. All of the boys told basically the same story, except for Mighty, who had been in bed at the rectory the night of the robbery at Buddy's. The story about giving the dogs knock-out potions with a dart gun was hard to believe, but they insisted on that truth and that they did not slit the dog's throats.

The lawyers waited until the police officer had left before also leaving. "I don't think you will have any trouble as long as the boys do not leave the complex. That detective is not convinced that they did not do the deed, but there is enough doubt for him not to press the kids as long as they are in your custody, Father. We will report back to the Bishop as soon as we get back to the office. We are also prepared to issue a protective document that will legally prevent intruders from attempting to enter the church or rectory. Parishioners and those who reside here," with a hand wave toward the stairs, "will be permitted."

"Thank you for your time. I know you are paid well by the Diocese, but that hardly expresses my deep thanks. God bless you." Jon blessed each man before he left.

Hilda appeared from the kitchen. "Coffee, Father?"

"How about a celebration cake for the guys upstairs." Jon grinned. "And a long rest for the resident priest."

Revelation

Vincent Sardoni twirled around in his thousand-dollar office chair. He looked at the phone and screamed into it, "What do you mean the priest would not let you in!" Whatever was being spoken on the other end did not satisfy him, and he slammed the phone down.

A hot-tempered man who had trained himself to appear calm, cool, and in control in public, Vincent had built a kingdom for himself. He owned half of the office buildings in town through various front organizations. With protection insurance and expendable muscle men, he managed to control his money, both inside and outside the law.

When the parishioners of St. Ignatius had prevailed upon a local politician some years back to have the building declared a historical site, he funded the politician's pet project under the table until the man retired from politics. The church had been a good investment for Sardoni until the Bishop actually decided to have it properly restored to historical standards. A string of priests came and went. None ever stayed long until Father Jon Mark came. This priest was different. He was making progress with the local residents, and with one young gang in particular.

The gangs had their territories. Vincent watched them for particular usefulness to his organization. They were the future bullies and toughs, the expendables, as they grew older and more skilled in street knowledge. Vincent was not particularly interested in anyone from the gang that the priest had taken an interest in. It did make him mad when they broke into his salvage yard at Buddy's and took the fuel tank back to the church. True, he had never paid them for it, but they had no right to take it back. Once it was at Buddy's, it was his. How dare they switch their allegiance from the street that he controlled to that man at St. Ignatius.

He hated all priests, nuns, religious 'do-gooders', anyone who tried to change the way the people lived in his territory. As a boy, he had quit school, and quit church, and quit being nice to everyone and anyone when he figured out he could make them pay him for protection, and pay him to do things they wanted done but were afraid of being caught doing.

His mother always said he was a smart boy. *Bless her,* he thought sarcastically. He remembered well the day he buried her after killing the man who had killed her. As they threw the dirt onto her coffin, he pledged to himself never to have a soft or kind person near him again. And he hadn't. Well, almost. There was his wife, a dainty, innocent morsel, that he had built a fine house for out in the suburbs. He had it fenced, he told Melinda, to protect her, but it served his purpose of keeping her there and not bothering him when he was not there. She believed he was a successful businessman, and he was, only not in the way she thought.

Now this abominable priest had entered the picture, and the property of St. Ignatius was rapidly slipping through Vincent's fingers. He knew that, if he waited long enough, the church would deteriorate to a state of no repair, and he could buy it from the Diocese for a song. He didn't want the church, but he did want the land it sat on and what had been hidden away for years in safekeeping on the property. It would give him great satisfaction to see the old monstrosity destroyed. He could almost see the day the bulldozers plowed down the walls and the cement trucks backed in to pour cement to seal away any evidence left there.

Sardoni drummed his fingers on his imported, massive mahogany desk. That priest had to go! He wasn't going to stop Vincent Sardoni's plans! "Little boy priest, your days are numbered, just like that stupid church building. And that gang that has taken refuge with you will wish they never heard of you when I get done with them." Sardoni frequently spoke aloud his plans of hatred, before putting them into action. It gave him a sense of purpose, knowing he spoke the words. He treated what he spoke like a sworn oath. To anyone hearing him, chills ran up their spines.

Chills did run down the spine of the man monitoring the sophisticated spy mic hidden within Sardoni's office. He had heard the priest's name mentioned before in phone conversations, and when someone had actually been in Sardoni's plush office, but never with the vehemence and hatred and threat that he had just heard. They had been collecting

160

information for some time and had heard Sardoni finger more than one of them, who later turned up dead. This time, maybe they would be ready, and just a little more prepared than Sardoni knew.

The noose to get Vincent on tax evasion was ready to be tightened at any moment. As the man monitoring the spy mic reported what he had heard, he resolved to be even more diligent at his listening post.

"You interviewed the boys and left them there?" the Captain of the Precinct hollered. The detective sighed and repositioned himself on his chair.

"I told you they have legal sanctuary there. It is all in those papers." He pointed at the pile in front of the Captain.

"What were the lawyers doing there anyway?"

"I think the Bishop sent them. You know that the law does allow for certain privileges for a recognized church and church leader. I think the Bishop . . ."

"Oh, hang the Bishop! These are the hoods that broke into Buddy's Salvage, stole money, and killed his dogs."

"Captain, what if the boys did not kill the dogs or steal the money? What if the boys took something else that they had tried to sell to Buddy and had never been paid for? They just took it back to its rightful owner."

"You aren't making any sense." The Captain was now more relaxed than a few minutes earlier. "Tell me about it."

Larry Janski knew his Captain well. He knew that, after the explosive start, the conversation would become rational, and all aspects would be considered. Like himself, the Captain walked cautiously around anything related to Buddy's Salvage.

After an hour or so of conversation, considering the problem from several points of view, the Captain agreed with his detective that there was much more to the situation than had been exposed up to now. Larry looked at his watch and commented that he could beat the evening rush if he left immediately. As he rose to leave, a call came in to the Captain's office. With raised eyebrows, the Captain said, "It's for you. I don't think you are going home very soon."

Larry shrugged his shoulders. "Detective Janski," he answered. He didn't say anything more. The conversation was one-sided. "I'll be there in about thirty minutes. Yes, sir, I do think that is true."

The Captain smiled at Larry. "The Commissioner?"

"Yes, more about the meeting this morning. It looks like things are changing rapidly. Maybe the mouse will go for the bait."

"Translation?"

"Later, Cap, see ya later."

Jon's nap was interrupted by a phone call from the Bishop. Since everyone was on the same ground, so to speak, at the rectory, he had told Hilda to monitor any in-coming calls and alert him if need be. Hilda had interrupted the Bishop recording a request for a call back and asked him to hold while she called Father Jon to the phone.

Somewhat groggy, Jon answered. He was instantly alert when he heard the Bishop's voice.

"I am sending you some Swiss cheese. It should arrive at your door within the next twenty minutes. My seal on the label will be evident. It is

162

Ramon cheese."

Jon thanked the Bishop and fell back on the bed, wondering why in the world the Bishop would send him some Swiss cheese, Ramon cheese. He didn't have to wonder long when the doorbell rang. Hilda waited for him to answer it. Using caution with the security chain on, he opened the door just a few inches. A stranger stood on the doorstep, grinning. He had on a bright yellow work uniform with the name 'Ramon' stitched on the pocket. He handed Father Jon an identification card upon which had the Bishop's imprint. In his left hand he had a stuffed gym bag. "You were expecting me?" he asked, with a slight accent.

"Just one minute." Jon closed the door. "The telephone, Hilda." He punched in the Bishop's phone number.

"Bishop's residence, James Paul here."

"Your Excellency, who is Ramon?"

"A multi-talented custodian, since you lost your obstinate one. Hand the phone to him."

Jon opened the door, with the chain still attached, and said, "Here, someone wants to talk to you."

Ramon nodded and took the phone. "Ramon, your Excellency. What do I need to do to convince the Father that I am who I am." Ramon eyes seemed to be laughing at Jon. "Sure," and he handed the phone back to Jon.

"Yes, your Excellency, I see. Thank you, and forgive me if I seem to be overly cautious." Jon punched the off button and closed the door long enough to release the chain. Ramon entered, still smiling but with an air of purpose. He watched as Jon refastened the chain. "It has been a rough day," Jon said by way of an apology.

"I know something about it. That is why I

am here. I will appear to be the new custodian, but I am more." He unzipped his jumpsuit to reveal a shoulder holster and a very modern revolver. He pulled out a sophisticated, high-powered radio from inside the jumpsuit. In his gym bag, under some personal clothing, he had more equipment.

"Take me to the church proper and I will find a place there to sleep. I understand you have all your beds already filled." Ramon's glance at the priest gave way to a big smile. "Relax, Father, the cavalry has arrived."

Jon shook his head as though he was trying to wake up from a bad dream. "What I am wondering," Jon said after a moment, "is why the Bishop thinks I am in danger?"

"I can't tell you that, but I do know that others besides the Bishop think so also. Trust me, Father, and tell those kids up there to trust me also." He turned toward the kitchen where Hilda was standing, "And you, too, Ma'm."

Jon was still in a daze as he led Ramon into the church. He pointed out where the floor was weak and showed him the two furnaces, the barred front doors, the padlocked side door, and the surrounding chain linked fencing. They climbed up into the choir loft, scaring a few pigeons on the way. "Rats in here?"

"Probably in the basement," answered Jon.

"OK, I can manage. Now I think I need to meet the kids so I know who is here, and they have seen me also.

"Ramon, tell me if you can. What is it that makes this place and my being here so important to everyone?"

Ramon only shook his head. "Trust me, Father, believe me it is important!"

Some of the boys were in the kitchen

164

helping Hilda bake a cake. They had never seen one made from scratch. Several of the others were arguing over who owed whom in the Monopoly game. Jon called them together in the parlor and introduced the new custodian for St. Ignatius. He then excused himself and went up to bed. The activities of the day had drained him.

Ramon quickly had the boys' attention and allegiance. He shared how he had grown up in another part of the city and had run with a gang until a local preacher asked him if he wanted to be buried or baptized. He told them he didn't even know what the man was talking about, but he quickly realized that what he was doing was going to get him killed. They all nodded. So he made friends with a Catholic priest and learned about Jesus Christ and the joy of being a part of the Catholic Church. Someone had befriended him and sent him out of the area to school. "The rest is history, as they say. I have a good job and hope to have a family someday." Ramon stopped talking. The gang held on to every word he had spoken.

"So why are you here?" Patch spoke up.

"To tend to the physical part of the church. I am another man living in this compound. Right now, that is important."

The boys nodded, each thinking his own thoughts and aware that the situation that they all were in, Hilda, Father Jon, themselves, was certainly not normal.

Mighty broke up the session when he asked Patch and Scar to help him back upstairs.

When the Police Commissioner studied the transcripts of the monitoring system used with Vincent Sardoni, he immediately called all who might be involved and asked if a change of action was warranted. This included Detective Janski, for it was in his Precinct the problem would arise. Normally, the Commissioner would have briefed the Captain, but, at this point, the fewer who knew the problem existed, the less likely there would be a leak.

Detective Janski made good time, arriving within twenty-seven minutes after being called. He left his cell phone at the security desk. No devices that could transmit or record were allowed in the 'safe room'. A couple more police officers entered after Larry came in.

"We have a major event about to take place, and it is our job to see that it is foiled without looking like we knew it was planned." Every eye in the room was riveted on the Commissioner's face. "Let me play this short excerpt that came in an hour or so ago. I think the time is about 11:38 this morning when this was recorded." He pushed the play button on a recorder, and a voice was heard to say:

> *"Little boy priest, your days are numbered,*
> *just like that stupid church building. And*
> *that gang that has taken refuge with you*
> *will wish they never heard of you when*
> *I get done with them."*

"You all know whose voice that is, and how we got that. The priest is Father Jon Mark at St. Ignatius, and we can assume that is who he was speaking about. You remember, I mentioned about a note threatening that priest received by the Bishop yesterday. We also know from past experience that, when the speaker has muttered about a termination of someone, it has happened, repeatedly."

"Detective Janski, that is in your Precinct isn't it?" The Commissioner was looking directly at Larry.

166

"Yes, sir, and I can confirm that there is a group of boys, gang – if you will, who have taken refuge at St. Ignatius. Also, the Bishop had the Diocesan attorneys making sure the refuge is legal and that the boys have legal representation."

"Oh great!" someone muttered.

"When did you get this information, Larry?"

"This morning and afternoon, sir."

"The report hasn't been filed yet?"

"No sir, the steno is working on it right now. It . . . I had a lengthy interview with all parties concerned, with the legal representatives listening on."

"What is going on in there?" asked another person.

Detective Janski shrugged his shoulders. "I can only guess, but what I said about refuge and the 'legal beagles' is true."

"Let's get back to the tape recording. We have a potential murder on our hands, correction, several murders – right Larry?" The Commissioner looked at the gathering. "I am open to suggestions. Anybody got any ideas?"

"Why doesn't the Bishop just pull the priest from the church?"

"Do we have any idea of a timetable on this thing?"

"How close are you guys to getting the noose tightened on the tax thing?"

"Should we put a police patrol in the immediate area?"

"No!" thundered the Commissioner. "We have to work at this in such a way that VS does not catch on that we have knowledge. Remember, we must protect that spy mic until he is behind bars."

"How come this man is so powerful?"

"Does the Bishop know of this additional

threat?"

The Commissioner's nod wasn't missed by those in the room.

"Does the Bishop have any ideas?"

"We didn't ask him," was the reply.

"How can we disable VS, or get him sidetracked?"

"Can we get a search warrant for that business, Buddy's Salvage, and put up a flack screen about the theft?"

"Weren't those boys accused of that theft?"

"Why didn't you bring them in?" This question was aimed at Larry.

"There isn't enough evidence," he replied lamely.

"Oh, come on now, we know you guys down there pick people up on weaker information than what was given about the break-in."

"Two reasons," Larry began, "one is that having them in our protective custody would not protect them from VS. You all know that. We have tried that in the past and lost. Secondly, and this information is in the report coming in, there probably is not enough evidence about that particular theft to hold them very long."

"You seem to be protective of that gang, Detective Janski."

"Probably so, I work that area all the time. Something does not ring true in the Buddy's Salvage complaint about the theft. And I did interview all of them, the boys, today. I probably heard the truth."

"When the report is in, we can talk about it. My concern is that there are seven boys, a priest . . ."

"and a housekeeper," interjected Larry.

". . . in that complex. Are they all in danger? It would seem so." The commissioner refocused the group.

168

"What about VS's wife. Could we do something that way to move the focus off St. Ignatius?"

"He has her under guard all the time. Her chauffer even goes into the beauty parlor with her. The excuse is that he is there to protect her."

Another said, "I figure he has a bullet in his gun with her name on it if she gets out of line."

"Do you think she is really all that dumb?"

"In the few encounters we have had with her, she firmly believes her husband is a successful businessman."

"Unfortunately, that is true; it is just the kind of businesses he is in."

"Yeah," several echoed.

"We need to have an action plan," the Commissioner pulled the group back to task. "I, we, can't just sit here and discuss without coming to a possible plan. It would be unconscionable."

The men nodded gloomily. "But what can we do without tipping our hand?"

"That is precisely why I called you all together!"

For several more hours, the group discussed and laid aside one idea after another. Finally they agreed on an action that would look like a general crime sweep of the area around St. Ignatius Church. It would keep a police presence on the street for a time, while the tax people made sure they had VS in their hands. One thing none of them wanted was VS to slither away. They all could remember things, people, places, and events that VS had destroyed. They wanted him, and they wanted him badly.

Larry went home late to his wife. Her face had worry lines on it, as he had not called. "I was in the 'safe room'," he explained.

"Could you not have called before you went in?"

"Yes, I suppose, but I was thinking of all the things that have gone on today, and our conversation last night. Then I was there, and I had to check my phone at the desk. No phones or recorders in the 'safe room', you know."

Sally nodded. "I was worried."

"I am sorry, baby; it looks like things are going to get rough before they get better." He gently kissed her. "How are your flowers doing?"

"Better. How rough?"

"You know I can't say anything."

"Does it have to do with that thing at that church?"

Larry looked down. "A lot."

"Dangerous?"

"Hmmm." Larry held his wife close to him. "Life seems to be mostly dangerous. That is why we have our faith. Would you like to spend some time at the Faith Renewal Center soon? I think we both could use a renewal of our faith."

"Are you still wanting to leave police work? Is that it?"

"Renewal, whatever happens. We have to know what we believe in, and believe in it fully. I have just begun to understand that. I know that what I am doing right now is very important, and I am supposed to being doing it. But after it is over, I don't know."

"Do you want to move away from the city?"

"I don't know yet. I don't want to take you away from your flowers and your friends."

"I can always grow flowers, and as long as you are my friend," Sally hesitated, "You are my friend, aren't you?"

Larry kissed her again. "Forever."

170

Janette looked at her husband. "I haven't seen you this deep in thought during our favorite dinner in years. What is bothering you?"

The Commissioner smiled. "Always direct! Is that how you settle so many legal cases so quickly?"

"Irish!" she baited him.

He grinned. "Touché!"

"Back to the question. What is bothering you?"

"A major case."

"Can't talk about it, huh?"

"No, attorney wife, I can't. Lips are sealed." He winked at her. "You can read about it in the paper, or better yet, we can watch the late newscast and see what they are making of our announcement."

"Oh, now I am intrigued. Are you sure you can't tell me?" she playfully probed.

'Operation Clean Sweep' was announced in the newspaper the next morning. It was explained that, because of considerable crime, drugs, and gang-related activities, the police were going to target certain sections of town for special patrols. These patrols would not be announced and could vary from place to place, as the Police Commissioner explained. The object was to make the presence of the police visible and curtail certain activities. 'Operation Clean Sweep' would go on for an undefined length of time, said the Commissioner.

The local television stations carried the same information. It was suggested by some news announcers that this was coming too late, or just on time, or not enough or not soon enough. A general vagueness in the announcement left the citizens of the city wondering who, what, when, where, and how? It was exactly as the Commissioner had

171

planned: general, specific, and vague.

Jon woke from a very restful sleep. He leisurely showered and got ready to go over to the church. Scar was waiting for him in the kitchen. He was keeping Hilda company as she washed up last night's cake utensils. "I guess it was a long day yesterday," she quipped. "I did not finish all my chores."

Jon just nodded as he left through the side door. Seven parishioners came to Mass, plus Ramon. Jon introduced him to the congregation, saying that he was the new custodian, since Angus was now in the health care center. The old people eyed Ramon in his bright yellow jump suit. At least they would know him by his outfit, Jon thought. That was good. He gave a short homily about the gifts of God and served each member in the pews as usual. Scar moved flawlessly along beside him.

After Mass, when all had left except for Scar, Ramon, and the priest, Jon gave Ramon the key to the outside padlock. "See that it is secure before you bar this side door."

Back in the rectory, Hilda had produced a large breakfast. All the others were waiting for Father and Scar to return before eating. Even Mighty was downstairs again. He walked with a gimp and screwed up his face in pain periodically. Otherwise he kept up with the others. Jon cautioned him about overdoing his activities. Mighty grinned but nodded. Ramon joined them a little later. Grateful for a break, Jon retired to his office to pray and consider all that had happened the day before.

About nine, the Chancellor phoned and asked for specific things they needed. He said he would come about noon with several days of food supplies. Jon asked Hilda what she needed. She had a

172

list of household supplies already prepared. "Do the boys need more clothing?" asked the Chancellor.

"Yes, several changes for each lad would be appreciated. Sizes? Let me ask Hilda and the boys."

Jon laid the phone down and found Ramon already making a list of clothing needs. He seemed to have a good idea about sizes. Jon sure didn't know how to guess what sizes. After Father Jon communicated a long list of clothing and sizes, along with Hilda's list of household supplies, the Chancellor stated again he could be there about noon.

Returning to his meditations, Jon became aware the house had grown very quiet. He stuck his head out into the hall. Hilda was cleaning the parlor. "Where are the boys?"

"Over in the church with Ramon. He said he needed help cleaning up one of the furnace rooms. They all seem eager to be with him. He really made a hit with them last night after you went upstairs."

"How is that?"

"I guess he grew up in an area like this and ran with a gang when he was younger. They held on to every word he said. I think he is more than a custodian."

"Could be," Jon answered, smiling to himself. "Could be." Jon thought of the shoulder holster and gun inside the yellow jumpsuit and let his mind wonder about why Ramon was there. Since the police knew the boys were at St. Ignatius, and the Bishop knew, why the protection?

"Did Mighty go with them?"

"No, Ramon insisted he go back up to bed, and I think he was glad to go. He was pushing himself again. We sure don't need a replay of the other night."

"That's for sure," Jon replied and went up to check on Mighty. He was sleeping soundly.

Through his many informers, Vincent Sardoni had known for a long time that the police had been at the rectory. He also knew that the Police Commissioner had held a late meeting downtown in the 'safe room'. The best he could find out, sometimes, was who attended those meetings. He was more concerned with the police being at St. Ignatius rectory and not removing the gang. That puzzled him. He did not like this kind of game. When he had called about the break-in at Buddy's Salvage, he had fully expected the gang to be picked up and held in Juvenile Detention unless they found guns on them, and then they would have been held in the adult jail. Either way, they would have been out of the way and at places where he had influence. Who would have expected those kids to hide so well, both from the police and from his informants, and then boldly go hide in St. Ignatius Catholic Church. And that priest had let them! The more he thought about that, the angrier he became. He did like a cat and mouse game when someone actually tried to outdo him. So while the gang and priest thought they were safe, he could devise ways to spring a trap. And after the trap was sprung, they would wish they had died sooner.

Just this morning Melinda had asked him about the old Catholic church near Buddy's Salvage. Vincent was abrupt with her, telling her that the old building was condemned. He did bother to ask her why she asked. She had just said 'oh' and then prattled on about her hair appointment later in the day. Her asking upset him more than he cared to admit to himself. He had been waiting and waiting on the day he could get into that property. How many years had it been, he wondered. Too many, knowing what was buried there. He would be the ruler of the city! Yes, that sounded good. Ruler, that was like a King or something. He thought about what kind of title would be most fitting for him.

The failure of **Restoration Now, Inc.** to start the so-called restoration of the old building yesterday annoyed him also. Why had the Bishop chickened out at the last moment? And that priest, Father John something or other, refusing to let his men into the building. It would have only taken a day or two, and he would have been assured that the old decrepit structure was a goner.

Looking out his Penthouse windows, he could see the salvage yard and railroad yards out one way. In the other direction stretched the major part of the city. He could see almost every building he owned. A map under glass on the coffee table was marked with bright red dots where he had property. Much of the downtown was marked in red. Like a spider web, red marks extended out every direction. He often laid his hands on the map and marveled that he could not cover even a tenth of the red dots with his hands. He was successful! Mom always said he was a bright boy. His lip curled in derision at the memory of her.

Then there was that news account of 'Operation Clean Sweep'. It seemed almost funny, because he knew his people would not be the ones picked up by the police. He was good at protecting them. And if they were picked up, they were expendable.

A dark blue van backed into the driveway at ten 'til twelve. The words on the side said, 'Martha and Mary's House', which was a ministry to the poor of the city. At the wheel was Father Marvin. When he rang the front doorbell, Father Jon answered.

"I've got quite a load in there for you, Father. And I think I can be better company than I was the other night." He grinned. "See, I brought my own chewing gum!"

"I'll get the back door open. Do we need any extra help? I can get some of the boys to assist."

"I think that would be a good idea."

Jon made a quick trip over to the church to find Ramon and the boys. They were sitting in the front pews, talking. Ramon lifted his head up and smiled. "We were just taking a break before lunch."

"Well, lunch will have to wait," Jon responded. "I need the guys to help unload a van from 'Martha and Mary's House'. The Chancellor has sent some more food and other things."

"Sure, Padre, lead on," Patch got up from the pew.

At the back door Father Marvin waited patiently. He was delighted to see several extra hands to help unload. Since he had filled the van full of food, household supplies, and clothing single-handedly, he really appreciated help at this end. They made a human chain and passed packages, bags, and boxes into the kitchen. Hilda directed, keeping the food in the kitchen. Household supplies were stacked on the washer and dryer, while the boxes and bags of clothing were taken upstairs and placed in a long line along the hall wall.

Hilda had set the dining room table for ten but quickly added an eleventh plate. She was wondering where to find another chair when Ramon pulled out a folding chair from behind the parlor door. Father Marvin was pleased to be asked to eat with them. Father Jon offered a blessing for the meal and for the new provisions. It was then he noticed Mighty was not present. Ramon volunteered to go up to get him with Father Jon.

Mighty whimpered when the two men came into the room. Jon knelt down beside him. Mighty

176

was feverish. "Oh oh."

Mighty hugged him and cried. "I did too much."

"Let's look at your wound," Father said as he pulled the covers back. Blood had soaked through the bandage. "Not good, Mighty."

Ramon held the covers clear as Father Jon placed a second bandage over the first. He was praying for Mighty and wondering where he would find the doctor today. There was almost as much blood as when they had repaired the wound a few days before, and the fever worried him. That indicated infection.

"What can I do, Father?" asked Ramon.

"Pray."

"Do you need to get medical attention for him?"

Jon nodded. "But not through the normal channels."

"Like?

"The doctor who saved his life and is caring for him is a doctor without a country, so to speak. He lives somewhere in this part of town. I do not know his name. He is competent, though, and would be here in a flash if we could get word to him. Go ask Hilda to come up."

Ramon nodded and left.

"I'm sorry," Mighty whispered.

Jon nodded and continued to pray. Hilda came. "It looks like you are going to have to nurse him while I try to figure out how to find the doctor."

Patch appeared at the door. "I know where to find him."

"But if you leave here, the police will pick you up. And then what good will you be to Mighty?"

"His sister."

"The girl who had me pick him up off the

street?

"Yeah, I could go there. That is just across the street, and she knows how to find the doctor."

"Can't take a chance with you going even that short distance. Once you leave this property, you have left the sanctuary."

"Do you know the girl, Father?" Hilda asked.

"Hmmm," was Jon's only reply. He left, two steps at a time down the stairs. In the dining room, all eyes turned to look at him when he came in. "Father Marvin," Jon beckoned to him. Together, they entered the priest's office and closed the door. A few minutes later the two went to the front door. Father Marvin locked it after Father Jon went out.

Back in the dining room, Ramon looked at Father Marvin and asked, "What should we do?"

"Pray." No one dared to ask what was happening. "Father Jon has gone to get the doctor for Mighty," he told the wondering boys.

The suspense that kept the boys quiet a few moments before now erupted with questions. Ramon held up his hand for silence and told them briefly what he had seen upstairs. Mighty was just having a setback, it appeared, and Father Jon was making sure that everything would be OK for Mighty.

Patch appeared suddenly back at the table and sat down. "Padre will take care of Mighty. They are blood-brothers, remember?" He pushed his fork around on the plate in the now cold spaghetti and then laid it down. "I'm not hungry now," he announced.

Ramon and Father Marvin nodded. "Warmed up spaghetti with cheese on top can be served later."

Father Marvin pushed his plate away too. "I guess this might be the best time to learn how to pray, if any of you guys don't know how." He first led them in the 'Our Father' before he pulled his Rosary from his pocket. "Some people misunderstand why we finger these beads, sort of thinking they are 'worry stones' or something. Really, they are a reminder of the mysteries of our Lord and Savior, Jesus, and help to keep us focused on the prayers when our minds might wander elsewhere. Right now, we want to remember God and his mysteries so that our prayers for Mighty are not in vain. Ramon went into the hall and picked up a Rosary he had seen hanging on a hook. Together the two men knelt, and the boys, one by one, knelt beside them as Father Marvin and Ramon quietly prayed.

Father Jon casually crossed the street and headed toward Claire and Agnes' store. The ladies greeted him and tried to get him to buy something. He picked up some fruit, some of it almost beyond use, and laid some money on the counter. Claire stared at him. "We don't need charity." She shoved the twenty-dollar bill back at him.

He looked at her and smiled. "It isn't charity; it is payment for some information."

"Oh, sort of like spy money?" Agnes asked.

"No, I need to find someone in a hurry."

"If we can help," Claire said, pushing the bill back toward him, all the while lovingly smoothing it out.

"We will help." Agnes finished the sentence.

"Where do I find the girl who helped the boy who was stabbed the first week I was at St. Ignatius?"

The two women looked at each other only for a moment. Claire left the store almost on a run and disappeared around the corner. For a moment Jon wondered if he had said something that offended her, or was she going to tell someone else what he had just asked.

Agnes pulled a stool around the counter and motioned for the priest to sit down. She went to the cooler and got out two 12-ounce bottles of juice. She carefully wiped the top of the bottle with her skirt before trying to open it. It resisted, and she handed it to Father to open. She wiped the other bottle and also handed it to him to open. She then sat on her stool behind the counter and smiled and smiled. She looked like a big Buddha, sitting there sipping her bottle of juice. Jon felt silly sipping his drink with her when he really wanted to find that girl or the doctor. No one had said anything since he mentioned the girl. Claire's behavior was out of the ordinary as much as Agnes'.

He heard running feet before the skinny girl, who had begged him to pick Mighty up off the street that day, burst into the basement store. Claire was close behind her.

"My brother? Where is he, is he alright?"

Jon nodded, "I need your help for him?"

"Has he been hurt again?"

"No, but he needs the doctor to come to see him."

"Where is he?"

"The doctor will know. Can you find the doctor without everybody else knowing you are looking for him for your brother?"

The girl had caught her breath now. "Uh huh. I know where he lives. Mighty, will he be alright?"

"I think so when the doctor gets to him."

Claire smiled, and Jon went back to the rectory.

The girl left and wandered up the street, like she did not have a care in the world. In the next block she stopped to tie her shoes before changing her direction and heading in the direction of an old

180

bakery.

Upstairs, a hushed group of boys sat in the room next to Mighty's. Ramon sat on the floor with them. Next door, Hilda kept cool cloths on Mighty's fevered brow. Patch worked beside her, dipping and wringing out the cloths. Father Marvin called the Chancellor and reported the turn of events before he knelt in prayer in the parlor, keeping watch at the front door.

Twenty minutes later, a tapping at the back door of the rectory revealed a beggar woman. Jon almost shut the door before he recognized the doctor. "You do like your disguises," he said with a chuckle.

"I thought I might need a few things with me, so my beggar's bag is useful," the doctor replied.

"Penicillin. What a wonderful drug when infection breaks out. It may take a more serious antibiotic, but we will start with this," he said as he gave Mighty an injection. He motioned to Hilda and Father Jon to step out into the hall with him. He saw the boys in the next room and stepped in to assure them that Mighty was still with them. Jon took the two into his personal room so they could speak without being overheard. "I am going to stay. That is another reason for the beggar's bag and disguise. It does not look good for me to come and go. The people are beginning to talk. So I stay."

"I can sleep in my office; you can have my room. That way, you will be close to the boy."

"No, make me a pallet, and I will sleep in there with him. It is better that I am there. She," he pointed to Hilda, "has much to do with all them." He pointed across the hall.

Jon nodded and thought, so do I.

Father Marvin left after learning that Mighty was showing some recovery. He promised to pray

181

for him and the others. Before leaving he offered his help to Father Jon in any way he could.

After getting the Chancellor's report following the delivery of items to St. Ignatius, and the accompanying receipts, the Bishop wondered briefly if he had heard what the Lord was telling him to do. Since the time two nights before, when he had spent most of the night before the Cathedral Altar, he sensed the urgency to put all available resources into the situation at St. Ignatius. He had no peace whenever he vacillated in his thinking away from this particular action. He decided to stay the course, no matter how it appeared. And then there was Father Jon Mark, a priest who so faithfully put his life in line with what Jesus would do. Occasionally Bishop James Paul wished he could just go and do as this unconventional priest was doing.

The conversations with the Police Commissioner and Detective Janski were uninformative on the surface. The Bishop had felt prompted to ask an old friend to go and stay at St. Ignatius under the guise of custodian, since the old one was out of the picture. The Bishop marveled at the timing that allowed him to send in protective help. He wondered what the Police Commissioner would think if he knew.

Melinda spent several hours at the hair designer's. She wanted a new look that wasn't drastic but complimented her face. She could see some aging lines on her face and neck. She knew Vincent would be distressed by them.

The chauffer checked on her constantly. He seemed more agitated than usual. Her hairdresser spoke close to Melinda's ear. "What's with him today?"

182

"I don't know. I think he had a fight with his girl friend."

"Over you?" the hairdresser asked.

"Don't be silly," Melinda smiled at the idea. "Vincent would kill him if he tried anything with me." She spoke these words innocently.

The chauffer noticed the conversation between the two women and wandered back one more time to see if the 'new look' was done. The hairdresser shooed him away, telling him it would be soon.

He continued his vigil in the waiting area at the front. He saw several police cars go by. He did not remember ever seeing any before while he waited on Melinda. It would be just his luck to be stopped today by a random police check. Sid looked in his wallet to confirm he had his gun permit right next to his driver's license. He knew they would notice his shoulder holster, and he sure didn't want any trouble.

"Voila! Done! What do you think of it?" The hairdresser gave Melinda a mirror and spun her around so she could see the back also.

"It's perfect!"

Her chauffer ambled back and gave his nodded of approval. "Ready?" he asked.

"One last light hair spray and you can take the princess." Flourishing a spray can, the hairdresser did a quick sweep all around Melinda's hair. The overspray caught the chauffer in the face. Sid turned away, coughing. "Sorry about that!" bubbled the hairdresser. "She is all yours now."

Melinda flashed her a big smile and handed her a sealed envelope. She always tipped the beautician well. Sid seemed in a hurry as he escorted Melinda to the car. "Can we stop at . . ." Before Melinda could finish her sentence, the car was in motion and headed back to the suburbs. She didn't bother to finish her question.

A car followed them. Unknown to either driver, a man in a third car relayed their movement ahead to a waiting police checkpoint. "There are two cars. One has the Mrs. in it, the other appears to be a tail."

"Roger."

Up the road five police cars sat, barricading the traffic. Efficient officers were checking licenses. Occasionally they had a car pull off, and they did a random check of all persons in the car and of the contents of the car. It was part of 'Operation Clean Sweep'. They allowed the cars in front of Sid to go on, with just a license check.

The first officer noted the gun permit and stood slightly behind where Sid sat. He politely asked Sid to step out of the car when another officer had joined him. On the other side of the car, a third officer opened the back door. "Ma'm, would you please step out. We need to search this car."

Melinda was bewildered. She had never been asked to get out of a car by a policeman. "I have a new hairdo. I need to put on my scarf."

"You can do that outside, Ma'm."

Melinda scooted across the seat toward the officer. He stepped back while she got out. She reached for her purse. He picked it up first, opened it, and glanced inside before handing it to her.

"I don't carry anything in there but personal stuff," she said sweetly.

He nodded and watched his partners on the other side extract a gun from a shoulder holster of the chauffer. It made him tense. Sid was arguing with the officers about taking his gun. They just continued and asked him to pop the trunk and hood. Grudgingly, he did. They kept him separated from Melinda. A female officer came up to her. What in blue blazes did they think they were doing? If

184

Vincent found out they harassed his wife, he would be livid, Sid worried to himself. In the next lane, the car that was tailing them passed through without a hitch.

The female officer explained that, out of a number of cars, they were doing a deep search of a few. She told Melinda that she need not worry, "It was just a routine check. I am sure you have nothing to hide. You would be surprised at how many people have things they don't want anyone to know about in their cars. Do you have any personal identification with you, like a license or photo ID?"

Melinda fished into her purse and pulled out her checkbook. Stuck inside was her driver's license. She used it only for ID when writing a check someplace where she was unknown.

The lady officer called in the numbers on her lapel mic. Shortly the OK came back that it was legitimate. "A surprising number of people either have an outdated license or one they have purchased under the counter. Yours is OK."

"I should hope so. I renewed it just this year."

"We are all through, Ma'm, sorry for the delay and inconvenience." The officer who had asked Melinda to get out of the car held the back door open while Melinda got back in.

Sid's white-knuckled fingers gripped the steering wheel. He said nothing as he drove straight home. He did not notice the car that followed him.

Vincent was angry. His wife and chauffer were ordered from the car by the police. It seemed to him that the police were overstepping themselves in this 'Operation Clean Sweep'. As Melinda told him about it, she could not imagine why it so upset her husband. "After all, they are running this campaign called 'Operation Clean Sweep' in the city right now," she said.

"That doesn't give them the right to pick on you," Vincent yelled. "It should have been obvious to them that you were not who they are looking for."

"Whom are they looking for?" Melinda regretted asking after the words were out of her mouth.

"Prostitutes, thieves, drug pushers, whatever fits their fancy. But not my wife!"

"Well, no harm was done. Do you like my hairdo? It took her over three hours to fix it."

"Three hours for that?" It wasn't hard for Melinda to figure out that, whatever she said, Vincent would scorn it, so she tried to cuddle up to him.

He shook his head, "Not tonight, babe, I got some things I have to do."

Hurt, but not showing it, Melinda picked up a book and went to another room. Vincent stewed a while before going out, presumably to his office downtown.

Later that evening, she watched the news reports on television. The police reported that they would be continuing 'Operation Clean Sweep' and gave the number of drug peddlers and prostitutes picked up so far. Melinda shook her head in wonder at the large numbers.

Life became almost routine at the rectory. Mighty was not allowed up by the doctor. Hilda had the other boys helping with the chores. Father Jon was able to get serious prayer and study time in. Ramon puttered around the church building, usually with two or three of the boys following him closely. The bird droppings in the choir loft had been cleaned up and the holes plugged where they had gotten in.

186

He had a scare when he found Scar and Patch up in the loft where he had hidden the radio and other things. They assured him they had not been into his stuff, and he believed them. He told Father Jon about it. Father suggested that he leave his things in the priest's office as that was 'off limits', even to Hilda. Ramon moved the sensitive objects, except for the holstered gun he always wore inside his yellow jumpsuit. Jon showed him the old revolver that Angus had, and the six shells. He told him the story. Ramon was amazed that Patch had not been shot.

After the noon meal, Jon began a Catechism class with the boys. Scar always had questions and sometimes answers for the questions the boys had. By now they all had normal names, except for Scar and Patch. There was Lawrence, formerly Arabian; Charles, formerly 'Don't Call Me Charlie'; William, the boy with the blonde hair that curled around his ears now that it was clean; Little Roy the smallest preferred Roy; and Mighty, whose name really was James.

"Father," Charles asked, "In that game we play, Monoplay, how come there is no church?"

"It's called Monopoly!" Scar interjected.

"That is a good question. How do you feel about each other when you are playing that game?" Jon asked.

"We hate the guy that owns the railroads and Boardwalk and Park Place."

"Why?"

"'Cause we are always having to pay rent!" blurted out another.

"Yeah, that guy always has all the money!" spoke up Roy.

"Then how do you feel?" probed Jon.

"We told you, mad!"

"What if there was a church? Who would

own it? Would you have to pay rent?"

They didn't know.

Jon gave them an assignment for the next day. "Consider what that game would be like if there was a church property." He dismissed them to help Hilda or Ramon as needed.

Mighty's sister, Irene, lived across the street, in one of the tenement buildings. She kept pestering Claire and Agnes to find out how he was. The old ladies pretended they were hard of hearing. They figured, if Father wanted them to know, he would come tell them. After Mass one morning, Agnes couldn't hold it in anymore. She went straight up to Father Jon and asked him about Mighty. Claire was shocked.

"Why do you want to know?" Father Jon asked.

"You came and asked us to get that girl, and she got the doctor, and we know the doctor is still there!" Claire had come up by her sister.

Father Jon smiled. "He is mending. The doctor is keeping him in bed. What is that girl's name? And is she his sister?"

The two old ladies nodded their heads vigorously. They turned to leave without saying anything.

"Whoa, wait a minute. I asked you a question, also? Does the girl have a name?"

"I ring," is what it sounded like.

"Irene?" asked Jon. "Is she his sister?"

"Maybe," Agnes was coy. "And maybe not."

"OK, OK, does she want to visit Mighty?"

Vigorously nodding, Claire ventured, "She asked us to find out."

"Tell her 'yes' he is getting better. And if she wants to see him, have her come to the front door

188

of the rectory." Father Jon watched the two old ladies scurry away. He was amazed to see Agnes actually almost keeping up with Claire and not clinging to her arm for balance. "Women on a mission," he said to himself and grinned.

"What was that all about?" Ramon arrived as Claire and Agnes rushed from the church.

"I think Mighty is going to get a welcome visitor. Where did the doctor go?"

"Back to the house. May I show you something?"

With a nod, Jon followed Ramon down the stairs. They stopped in the old furnace room where Ramon had opened the wall between the two furnaces. "Look at the difference here and there in the concrete."

"It looks like it wasn't poured at the same time." Jon observed.

"Right. Sort of odd, isn't it? The church history says the whole basement floor was dug when they put in the old furnace. And that they concreted the whole floor."

"Where did you find that out?"

"One of those books I borrowed from your library," answered Ramon.

"I wonder why the patch." Jon stated.

"There are more 'patches' like this over in the rectory basement also. They look like they were all done about the same time."

"A mystery to be solved?" Jon asked with a grin.

"Possibly," Ramon answered. "Patch and Scar are the ones who first noticed this one. Then Patch said there was one like it in the rectory basement. It turns out there are several over in the rectory basement."

Vincent stalked back and forth across his office. He looked out at his city, at his kingdom. Here and there he could see flashing blue lights, indicating the work of 'Operation Clean Sweep'. On his computer and coming in on the fax line were cryptic messages from his various enterprises. They were written so that the ordinary person would not know what they really meant, but he did. All over town, drug dealers were being locked up and prostitutes jailed. A few would not have concerned him, but some were in key positions in his vast organization. The police didn't know it, of course, but he had pinpointed some very good operatives, and they were the ones being picked up. It annoyed him that the nickel and dime drug peddlers and prostitutes were not. Anything that took money from his investments worried him. These investments were hidden in his multiple holdings, but they were living, breathing investments.

About two in the morning, Vincent took a walk over to the salvage yard and looked over the monstrosities that were sitting there, never used. Some were unpaid for, like that oil tank that gang had stolen right out from under the sleeping noses of his dogs. He could hear the dogs still breathing as they were when he found them that night. But with all the activity picking up his people, the police had not been able to catch a mere gang of teens. The rage that crept into him that night came back. Slowly, Vincent went into Buddy's Salvage office, opened the safe, and stuffed the records into a plastic bag.

Later, back in his penthouse office, he watched as police cars and fire trucks raced to the undesirable street location of Buddy's Salvage. It was burning nicely. Then he went out to the suburbs and crawled into bed beside a sleeping Melinda. He looked at her face and new hairdo briefly by

190

moonlight before turning on his side, away from her. In the morning, he would make love to her. He was too tired tonight.

The jarring ring of the telephone woke Vincent about seven. Melinda was not in bed with him. He swore as he knocked the phone on the floor in his first attempt to answer it. "Vincent!" a voice screamed in his ear.

"The Salvage yard is gone. It burned to the ground last night. The fire marshal is here now! They say it was arson. And the safe was standing open. I swear, I closed and locked it before I left. Vincent, say something!"

Vincent hung up the phone. He could hear water running in the shower. That must be Melinda. The phone rang again. He punched the answering machine to take the call.

The water was still running in the bathroom. Melinda was taking a long shower. He pounded on the door, but she did not answer. Twenty minutes later he tried the door, as the running water did not stop. It was locked. He pounded on it. No answer. Finally, he broke it open. The shower was still running, but there was no sign of Melinda.

With a roar, Vincent checked all the rooms in the house. Melinda was not there. He picked up his cell phone and called Sid, who lived in the apartment over the garage. No answer. He stood looking out the backside of the house. The dogs were in their kennel. He rushed to the garage. Both cars were there. Where was Melinda? He pounded on the door to Sid's apartment, and it came open. Searching the apartment, he found no one.

Back in the house, he showered with cold water and then dressed. He put on his best slacks, imported shoes, and a causal shirt that made him look ten years younger. He then called the police to report that his wife was missing.

During the night, as Buddy's Salvage burned, the constant sirens had awakened everyone in the house. The boys had seen the glow in the sky from the upstairs window. The doctor crept out into the wide-awake neighborhood. He slipped back inside just when Father Jon came downstairs, checking on the church.

"Something big is on fire."

The doctor replied, "They say it is Buddy's Salvage."

"They can't blame this on those guys upstairs. They are up there, aren't they?"

"They were, Father, when I went out to see what I could find out."

"Good, I hoped they wouldn't go out."

All the local television stations interrupted their morning programming to bring the story about the missing wife of the wealthiest man in town. The early news had reported the fire that totaled Buddy's Salvage. A reward was posted by some corporation for the arrest and conviction of the arsonist. And a grieving Vincent begged for his wife to come home. He indicated that a substantial reward would soon be offered for her safe return.

Father Jon heard the news from Hilda, who had watched the early morning broadcast. She had left the television on and caught the news about Melinda Sardoni. The picture of the missing woman showed her a few years younger than she was now.

Hilda muttered all morning about Vincent Sardoni. "They ought to check him out carefully," she kept repeating to herself.

Larry Janski had been called at 3:13 am about the fire at Buddy's Salvage. By nine that morning, he was weary of anything that had to do with Vincent Sardoni's holdings. When Sardoni's wife disappeared the same night that the Salvage yard was torched, Larry was betting on a corpse being found in the charred ruins. It was only later in the day that Vincent Sardoni had reported that his chauffer, Sid, was gone also.

The Police Commissioner called a meeting in the 'safe room' for noon. As the various police and federal investigators filed into the room, they noticed the Commissioner was in an upbeat mood. "Gentlemen and ladies, 'Operation Clean Sweep' has put a damper in the drug and prostitution traffic. This morning's court was full of those who were picked up in the past two days. Many who have slipped through our fingers in the past are included in those arrested. A few are willing to talk, but mostly they seem to be resigned to being abandoned by whoever normally would see they were bailed out. The judges, yes, it is taking several judges to set bond, are going for top dollar. The usual milling around of attorneys is not apparent. We have hit upon something! And you are to be congratulated for your hard work.

"However, we are not done. More time is needed by the federal tax investigators. Then there is this thing of the suspicious fire at Buddy's Salvage, and the disappearance of Mrs. Sardoni and the chauffer the same night. One might say we have just begun."

Larry Janski raised his hand like he was inschool. "Sir, the fire has been declared 'arson' by the state fire marshal. Also, I would think we would be wise to sift through what remains of the salvage yard, examining carefully for human remains."

193

"Are you suggesting that Mrs. Sardoni and the chauffer were murdered there?" asked someone on the far side of the room.

"I think we would be stupid to not look for human remains. The fire was set, and set in such a way as to destroy almost everything. But fires have a way of leaving behind evidence. Take the teeth of Mrs. Albertson, you remember. They didn't burn up in that fire, and the forensic lab was able to positively identify them as hers."

"I think Larry is right. We should concentrate on the fire site as a possible murder site."

"We don't know if we have a murder yet," another said.

"Yeah, but we have good reason to believe that, since the owner of the salvage yard has a track record of disappearing persons."

"Gentlemen, ladies, let's not argue over should we or should we not examine the fire site. It is a good place to start. You all have a copy before you about the missing person reported by Vincent Sardoni. He later noticed that the chauffer was missing also."

"Funny thing, he didn't notice that earlier," someone quipped.

"I assume most of you have already read the initial report. Any suggestions we have not tried yet?" The commissioner was fingering his copy.

"Yes, he said he and she went to bed about 11:30 pm, which would place it just after the Nightly News. What was reported on the news last night that they might have discussed?"

"'Operation Clean Sweep'."

"Do you know if his wife has any clue as to his involvement with . . .?"

"She'd have to be pretty dumb, or well trained, or something not to suspect something amiss

194

somewhere."

"She and the chauffer were stopped in one of our roadblocks. Their car was searched and their identities verified. The chauffer was carrying a handgun that he had the proper permit for. He was upset; she seemed to be very nescient of everything."

"OK, hot shot, what does that word mean, 'nescient'?"

"Ignorant," someone replied. "I had to look it up once."

"So she is a dumb blonde. I've seen her picture on the news."

"Not really, that was when she had highlighted her hair. It is more a honey brown now."

"So where do we start?"

"With a long nap, you guys. I've been on this since 3 am." Larry yawned.

"Get some rest, Larry. We can start sifting the salvage yard ruins without you. We'll call you if anything turns up." This was spoken by one of the forensic experts.

"Yeah, Larry, why does everything interesting happen down in your part of town."

"I'm lucky, I guess," Larry retorted.

"What about that gang of toughs. Could they have done it?"

"What, murder or the fire," asked someone.

"I checked on that. They were safely tucked away in their little beds at St. Ignatius. Father Jon called me before I could call him."

"Can you believe him?"

"Who, the priest? Sure." Larry yawned again.

The Commissioner who had also been up since the early morning hours called a halt to the discussion. "I think we have enough to go on and to keep us busy. We don't know if we have a murder or

195

two also. That remains to be discovered. Does everyone have a plan of action appropriate to your assignments?" Nodding heads answered the question. "Then you are dismissed until later. Larry, get some sleep."

"Sure."

All that the city and the neighborhood talked about was the fire that totally wiped out Buddy's Salvage, and the coincidental disappearance of Vincent Sardoni's wife the same night. The presence of yellow-vested police sifting through the ruins fueled the gossip that Sardoni's wife was murdered and disposed of at the salvage yard. Her chauffer was missing, also, which kept everyone guessing, from the police investigators down to the local clientele in the bars.

Inferno

At St. Ignatius, life had a regular pattern. Scar was teaching Patch to read, Hilda had kitchen help, while Ramon mostly stayed in the belly of the church. He was discretely digging up one of the patched areas. Sometimes, a chill ran down his spine when he hit odd items buried under the floor. By careful digging, he had dislodged one patch whole so he could replace it after sifting through various items he discovered there. He talked frequently with Father Jon about his findings. They decided that by mid-week they would have to inform the Bishop that there was a problem in the basement of St. Ignatius.

After lunch, Catechism classes continued. The boys were interested in everything about the Church. As often happens, they had learned many misconceptions about the Catholic Church in their short lifetimes. Jon pointed out that, since they were being given sanctuary by the Church, it was prudent that they learned about why this Church could do this, its history, traditions, and dogma. The word 'dogma' upset them at first until Father explained what the word meant. This opened a whole new area of thinking for the boys as they began to question other words that were new to them or that they had used all their lives without really understanding them. Father Jon found their eagerness to learn exciting. He guessed that all the boys had better than average intelligence.

The Bishop called before Ramon and Father Jon were ready to talk about the findings in the basements of the church and rectory. Jon hesitated only a few seconds before filling in the Bishop. "Does this cause a problem here?" Father Jon asked.

"I am not sure. It is evidence that the police will want to investigate at sometime. The findings are not involved in the current picture. Given all the other conditions there, tell Ramon to stop digging. We will tackle that later. Detective Janski phoned today to urge us to keep our vigil up there at the church. I am not sure what he is learning in the investigations of the fire and the missing persons. However, he stressed strongly that we continue to consider the church, you and all there, to still be in grave danger."

Jon thought a moment. "Could what happened at the salvage yard be done here?"

"The fire?"

"Yes."

"It would be difficult with the stone structure of the church and no access for outsiders. However, it is a thought to pray about. The rectory is more at risk than the church building. I'll order additional chain link fencing so the backside of the church and the rectory can be more secure. Tell Ramon to measure and phone the Chancellor the measurements."

After a short prayer of blessing by the Bishop, Jon cradled the telephone. His expression must have been somber as he passed through the kitchen, headed for the church building. Hilda asked, "Problems?"

Jon stopped a moment to snatch some raw cookie dough that William and Roy were working on. "Now you stop that, you are setting a bad example for these boys."

"Yes, Ma'm," Jon said. The boys grinned at him as he left hurriedly out the side door to the church.

"Don't you guys get any ideas," Hilda admonished. "Otherwise, there won't be enough dough left to make cookies." They each grinned and popped a cookie shaped dough piece into their mouths.

"What cookies?" came the call from the dining room. Lawrence and Charles were locked into a cutthroat game of Monopoly.

"Later," Hilda hollered back.

Lawrence and Charles took the break in the game to continue their discussion of where a church would have been if part of the Monopoly game. Ever since Jon had given them the assignment, they had been in discussion about the possible street location on the Monopoly board.

Over in the church proper, Ramon and Father Jon talked about the instructions from the Bishop. "He really does believe we are in danger, doesn't he?" Ramon ventured. "I don't have any problem waiting with what we are finding downstairs. He is right; it isn't of current police action, although it might solve something back in history. How soon does he want the measurement?"

"From his tone, immediately."

"OK, one of the guys would be helpful."

"They all seem to be busy. I'll help. All you need is someone to hold one end of the measuring tape while you read the other end, right?"

Ramon nodded. "I'll get the tape and meet you out behind the rectory in about five minutes."

Across the street, a man loitering near the corner observed the priest and a man in a yellow jump suit measuring behind the church and rectory. He wandered down the side street, trying to get a better view of what the two men were doing. Ten minutes later, the information came in on the fax machine in Sardoni's office. And an anonymous call was received at the police Precinct about suspicious activity at St. Ignatius.

Larry looked at a telephone memos stacked on his desk. They were the usual, people who thought they had seen something the night of the fire, someone who heard a woman scream. The bottom one he almost tossed aside before he read it the second time. Someone had called anonymously to report suspicious activity behind St. Ignatius. There was nothing behind St. Ignatius, except the recently returned oil tank, and besides, who would be in the position to notice anything other than the priest. Thinking a little more, Larry realized that, to see behind the church and the rectory, one had to be on the side street that dead-ended halfway past the back of the rectory, where the city had built the foundation for a freeway project and then abandoned it. Who in the world would be back there and interested in the backside of the church. He placed that memo on top, sensing that it was the most important one.

He had hoped to get away early because it was their wedding anniversary, and he wanted to take his wife out to eat at a nice restaurant. Ever since the 3 am call announcing the fire at the salvage yard the week before, he had hardly been home to even sleep. Catnaps on a cot in the backroom had carried him for a couple of days. Last night, he got home at midnight and was back at the Precinct by 9 am. It certainly did not give him much time to talk with Sally, but he did promise her they would celebrate this evening.

Now he wondered. That phone memo could be a forerunner of a lot of activity around St. Ignatius. He hoped not. It worried him that the Bishop chose to leave the priest, housekeeper, and that gang there. To his practiced and experienced eye, it was like baiting the situation. Soon something had to give somewhere.

If they could get a lead on Sardoni's missing wife and/or chauffer or find something that was concrete at the burnt out salvage yard, he would feel like some progress was being made. The Commissioner had Vincent Sardoni interviewed, but only as it pertained to the disappearance of his wife and chauffer. The manager of the salvage yard was unhelpful about the open safe. He swore he had left it closed and locked. When questioned about what had been in the safe, he stuck to his story that the day's receipts and a few miscellaneous papers was all. The cash for the day was confirmed to have been deposited at 7 pm in a night deposit at one of the banks. The rest of the record books were kept in a locked, fireproof file cabinet that did survive the intense fire.

When the expected phone call came from the Police Commissioner's office about a meeting in the 'safe room', Larry sighed before calling Sally. "Sorry, sweetheart, the Commissioner called a meeting. I don't know when I'll get away."

Sally was not surprised but, of course,

disappointed. She assured Larry he was doing what he was supposed to do and promised him that she would be waiting for him when he got home. "I'm going to order in a pizza and indulge in the whole thing."

Her remark reminded him of pizza anniversaries when they were newlyweds. He smiled. "Keep your chin up, I love you."

As Larry sat down in his place in the 'safe room', the Commissioner looked at him. "It is your wedding anniversary, isn't it?" Larry nodded.

"How did you know?"

"Your wife called," the Commissioner smiled, "and she asked that I deliver this to you. It is highly irregular, you know." At that point he pulled a large pizza box from under his desk. "She said you would understand. Oh yes, there is enough here for everyone." Pointing to a side table, Larry was just then aware that a hand printed sign hung on the wall, declaring his wedding anniversary. On the table were several more boxes of pizza. As the others arrived, they all joined in the pizza feast.

The next hour or so was spent getting everybody informed about what the investigation of the fire and disappearances had uncovered to date. Larry introduced the idea that they were probably at the brink of another event. All eyes turned to him.

"How's that, Larry?"

"You sure it isn't just too much pizza?" someone else kidded.

"No, I've worked that area for the last fourteen years. I have seen some serious things, and I have watched patterns develop. I think I am seeing one such pattern now. We received an anonymous tip at the Precinct today. It didn't seem like much until I considered how someone could have seen the area spoken of. The area is blocked by the freeway

202

construction that went bottom up a few years ago. And yet, someone told us about something going on in that area that was suspicious."

"So what are you driving at?"

"That area is clearly visible from the penthouse office of Vincent Sardoni."

The restlessness in the room ceased. Larry had everyone's attention.

"What do you think will happen, Larry?" asked the Commissioner.

"That's just it, I don't know. The events that occur are so unpredictable. Like, who would ever think that Buddy's Salvage would have been torched with such professionalism?"

"First time I ever heard an arsonist called a professional." That comment came from across the room.

"Yeah, I know. What have your guys found from all their sifting of the wreckage?" Larry asked.

"Well, we haven't found any body remains, if that is what you mean."

"What made it such a hot fire that there is little left? Do you know that yet?"

"Sort of. The fire burned internally for some time, producing a very hot core, so when it got to the acetylene tanks, it just melted their values and voila, the explosion that consumed the rest of the yard."

"What was in the core to burn that hot?" Larry asked.

"Classified information," was the less than helpful reply. "Sorry, we can't tell that yet."

"Classified by whom?" someone else challenged.

"The buck stops here," the Commissioner responded. "Although, in this case, I don't even know."

"Oh, now you really have us wondering."

The Commissioner shrugged his shoulders. "Let's get back to Larry's point. You really feel strongly about this?"

"Yes, sir. Experience should teach us something, and I have experience down in that area. Remember when that street preacher disappeared about three years ago? At the same time several of the apartments and business that had supported him were destroyed within a few days of his disappearance. That kind of language the people of that area understand. So no one made a big fuss about the man's disappearance or even filed a statement about him. I had to go out and pry what information I could from a few who have trusted me in the past. It is still an open case."

"Yeah, but Larry, didn't we pull a man's body from the river about a year ago that everyone said must have been the preacher's?"

"That's just it. It could have been any of a number of missing persons we have had listed in the last several years. And decomposition left us no way of knowing how he died."

"So what are you driving at?" asked a thin forensic officer.

"Just a hunch, just a hunch."

"We could beef up the 'Operation Clean Sweep' closer into the area where St. Ignatius sits," someone said.

"How soon are you guys going to have that tax loophole case ready to go?"

The federal tax sleuths shrugged their shoulders.

"Well, until we find a body or bodies at the salvage yard, or something else to snag VS with, we are just spinning our wheels, watching and wondering each day what will happen next, Gentlemen."

204

"Commissioner, if I may, I would like to go home and see my wife."

"Go ahead, Larry," the Commissioner said. "We will continue the discussion, and I'll brief you tomorrow."

"Thank you. That is assuming tomorrow does not have a whole new set of events and problems, I suppose." Larry closed his papers before him and left the room.

"What's with him?" someone asked. Within the hour the others also left. The Police Commissioner wished he didn't have such a foreboding about the next few days. He respected Larry's hunches. He had seen them played out in the past. Larry was a good man and knew his area.

The chain link fencing arrived within an hour after Ramon had telephoned in the measurements. He had wondered if it would come with tools for him to install it. He was happily amazed when a truck of men also arrived with the fencing and prepared to have the area enclosed by dusk. He had always known the Church could get anything done it wanted. He almost felt useless as the crew expertly fenced in the area around the rectory and the back of St. Ignatius. His only task was to show them where the property lines probably were. Included in the load of fencing were several gates, with sturdy padlocks. The driveway was even protected. They handed Father Jon the keys, saying, "Here, Father, you might want to get you car out sometime."

Inside the house, the boys were upset at the outside activities. They wanted to help, but Father had said 'no'. Then one of them noticed that St. Ignatius Church and rectory now were inside the fencing, with the exception of the front door. "Looks like a prison," William said.

Scar snapped, "Shut up." There was a brief scuffle before Patch intervened. Jon had heard the remarks and was starting to join them when the scuffle broke out. He watched Patch. The boy was a good leader. He knew when and how to respond. Scar backed off, while William sat down nearby with a sullen look on his face.

Good time for the cookies, Jon thought and hurried to find Hilda. "They'll spoil their supper, eating cookies at this time," she said.

"Spoil it," Jon ordered.

"Yes, Father," she said as she piled a plate full of cookies and headed to where the guys were watching the construction from the second floor. She paused at Mighty's room and left him a couple. The doctor looked up from the book he was reading. Hilda handed him two and went on to the others.

Another message came in on the fax in Vincent's office. He turned and looked out his windows toward the church and swore. He could see the shiny new fencing gleaming in the late afternoon sun. Vincent sent his secretary home early and spent the next hour or so ranting as he paced back and forth in his office. The man on the other end of the spy mic listened in astonishment and telephoned his contact at police headquarters. The Police Commissioner had left for the day, he was told. He left a cryptic message. "Something is up." He then dialed another number.

The Commissioner was just pulling into his drive when his cell phone rang. He thought of Larry's hunch as he answered it. "Something is about to happen." The voice was the man on duty on the spy mic. The Commissioner continued on into the house. Janette had dinner ready. He was glad. As he sat down to eat, he looked fondly at his wife.

"You know, for an attorney, you are a good wife."

"'Operation Clean Sweep'?" Janette asked, gently probing.

"No, counselor, that won't work." He grinned at her.

"Thought I might drum up some business with the new clientele who are residing in the city jail now."

"Don't. It is bad enough that I am in the middle of all of this. Can you imagine what the news people would do with Police Commissioners wife defending persons picked up in 'Operation Clean Sweep'?"

Janette laughed. "It certainly would give the talk shows around here something to talk about. On the serious side" she continued, "our firm has been approached by one or two of those clients. I told my partners that I would take a leave of absence if they took any of those cases. I think they got the message."

"I hope so, since you are one of the senior partners."

"Don't worry, I do have veto power when it comes to taking criminal cases. I will exercise it if need be."

"Good, and this was a good supper. You do wonders with food. I'm going to rest in the den for a while, hopefully for a long while. I'll catch the phone in there if it rings." He kissed his wife on the cheek. "And no cases involving 'Operation Clean Sweep'."

"Gotcha, Commissioner. No soiling of the Police Commissioner's wife."

At supper the boys wolfed down their food, in spite of the late cookie treat. Father Jon asked them all into the parlor after supper. Ramon lounged at the door, while Hilda fussed about needing to clean the dining room. Jon waited until everyone was settled. "This is our first official house meeting. Everyone who is living here in the St. Ignatius complex needs to be present at each meeting." He looked meaningfully at Hilda.

"We have never set any ground rules around here but have figured out what was acceptable as the need arose. Being kind and polite to one another is essential for this many people living together."

"Padre?" Patch interrupted. "What about Mighty and the doctor?"

"When Mighty gets better, he will be actively involved in the house meeting. And the doctor will leave."

Patch nodded.

"A fence was put up around the rest of St. Ignatius and the rectory this afternoon."

"We know that," Charlie said.

"But you don't know the purpose of the fence."

"It looks like the juvenile detention center," William blurted out.

Father Jon looked at the boy. It was obvious that William was angry about the fence. "The Bishop had the fence put up to protect you, us. You know that the fencing out front of St Ignatius and the single side gate has kept the church from being destroyed by some members of the community."

"Like us!" Charlie said.

"Only now you are inside, and the Bishop does not want this place to be a battle ground or any of us injured, including you," Jon looked at William.

William looked down at the floor. His shoulders still were tight with pent up anger, but he was listening.

"You all have clean clothing, a place to

safely sleep, and more than enough food to eat. You are intelligent guys. And most of the time you are peaceful. You are learning things about yourselves, and about life, and about God. The authority here, although it may seem to be me, or Ramon at times, or even Hilda, rests in God. The Bishop is concerned about our welfare so he made it a little less easy to have anyone bother us."

"I still don't like the fence," retorted William. "It still looks like a prison."

"Is the Bishop, God?" Roy asked.

"No, he is a representative, and it is in that role that he decided on the fence. Like it or not, we will have to live with it until the danger is past."

"What danger? I don't see any danger!" William was still in a defiant mood.

"Who were you hiding from when you came here for sanctuary?"

The limp 'oh' told Father that William was coming to an understanding of the need for the fence.

Jon continued talking with the group. He complimented them, kidded them, and encouraged them. When the meeting broke up, Hilda commandeered the boys to clean the dining room and to wash and dry the dishes. She had asked for extra help from the boys, and possibly a day off, during the meeting. Father Jon promised her that she could have all of the next day off if she wanted. Ramon told her he would cook sometimes. Hilda was happy.

Sometime after they were all asleep, screams were heard outside. Jon sat up in bed and was aware of more light out on the street than usual. There was considerable commotion somewhere out there. He pulled on his pants and shirt. He heard running on the stairs. As he came out his door, he saw Patch and Scar at the open front door. There was more noise on the street, breaking of glass, and screams, and he caught a whiff of smoke. The boys turned and said, "Don't stop us" as they ran out the front door. Jon wasn't far behind them when he realized that the whole block across from the church was on fire. Patch ran toward the burning buildings and straight into the one where Jon had carried Mighty weeks before.

Jon turned toward the basement store of Claire and Agnes. He could hear cries for help. Scar was right beside him. For a moment or two they tried unsuccessfully to yank the barred door from its rotting frame. Jon heard Claire cry, "Try the coal chute."

Scar was halfway around the burning building before Jon caught up. Embedded in the foundation was an iron door covering the old coal chute. They pried it open, and smoke billowed out. Coughing but alive, Agnes was being pushed upward by her petite sister. Jon and Scar reached down and pulled her up. Agnes coughed and vomited as she sat down hard on the ground. The two reached for Claire. She wasn't there anymore. Jon started to climb into the chute when he was stopped by "I'll go, Padre." It was Scar, not Patch, who pushed past him and slid down the chute. A fireman appeared at Jon's elbow.

"Who's down there?"

"Her sister and a boy named Scar who went to get her sister."

Another person moved Agnes out of the alley. The fireman called for an assist on his walkie-talkie. With gas masks on, they were ready to descend down the chute when coughing was heard below. Scar appeared, carrying a limp Claire. The firemen pulled her up and placed an oxygen mask on her face. They reached for Scar. He handed them a leather satchel. "Here, Padre, this is what she went for." Then he accepted their lift up to the alley.

The two firemen moved them out and away from the building just before parts of it began to fall. Patch appeared with a scantily dressed girl. "Mighty's sister," he said.

"Take her to the rectory and up to Mighty's room."

Scar was out in the street helping someone. Jon spotted a fireman with a lock cutter trying to open the front of Claire and Agnes store. He told him they were rescued. At that moment the fireman was called to help another. He left the lock cutter beside the fire hydrant. Jon walked with purpose to the cutter, picked it up, and started back toward the church. "Hey you, where are you going with that?"

Father Jon did not answer as a large section of one of the middle buildings fell in and out. During the commotion, Jon walked up to the chain link fence barring the front door of St. Ignatius and snipped it open. Ramon appeared. "Go in and open the doors," Jon ordered. He cut a big opening so that people and equipment could enter the building. Moments later Ramon threw the doors wide open. Jon walked back to one of the fire trucks and set the lock cutter down before going into St. Ignatius.

Already some had turned to the open doors and entered. Scar brought Agnes in. "Where is Claire?"

"I think she is in one of the ambulances," Scar replied. "I'll go see if I can find her. You still have that satchel, don't you?"

Jon nodded. He had placed it inside as soon as the doors were opened.

"I think it has all their money," Scar commented as he left to find Claire. Jon moved the satchel to the sacristy for safekeeping.

When the call came in to the Commissioner, he was dozing in his favorite chair. Janette went to the door with him and wished him safety and success in whatever was going on. He could see the fire from the interstate that cut through the city. It wasn't hard to tell that it was close to where the other one had been. He wondered how soon Detective Janski would be there.

The Fire Marshal was already calling the blaze 'arson'. The news media were there with their cameras and video equipment. Someone tried to get the Commissioner's attention to talk on camera. He walked the other way. The smell of the old buildings as they burned was nauseating. As he heard the numbers rescued, versus the numbers who were believed to have occupied the buildings, he got sick. Some of the stench had to be flesh burning. He would cry later, but at that moment he intensely hated whoever it was that had torched the whole block. He snarled at anyone who tried to talk to him. 'Operation Clean Sweep' seemed to mock him in the fire.

Larry and Sally were getting ready for bed when the call came in. He hurried into his clothing, unaware that his wife was also dressing. "What are you doing?" he asked.

"An anniversary gift. I want to go too."

"Are you crazy?"

"No, I just want to be a part of you tonight in whatever happens." She had pulled on blue jeans, a dark t-shirt, and her hiking boots.

"OK." Larry tossed her a yellow t-shirt marked 'P-O-L-I-C-E'. "Wear that under your jacket. Only show it if you need to. Let's go."

As they sped toward the city, they could see the glow from the fire. Larry turned on his scanner and listened to the reports. Two blocks away from the fire area, Larry parked his car and locked it. He took his wife's hand, and they ran to the fire site.

"You can't go there," a policeman stopped them.

Larry identified himself. "Oh, sorry Detective Janski, I did not recognize you in the dark and with this smoke." Larry nodded and moved ahead with Sally. "Excuse me, who is she?"

Larry turned, "My assistant." The two moved on toward the fire. He noticed lights on in St Ignatius and the front door open. He was relieved to see that the wind had blown the fire away from the church. He found the Fire Marshal. "Arson?"

"Your professional," replied the Marshal.

"How many hurt?"

"Better question, how many got out alive."

Larry's stomach churned. "Oh God."

"Speaking of God, the priest over there has opened the church to those we were able to get out on this side, who were not injured." The Fire Marshal hooked his thumb toward the church.

Sally's lips were set tightly together. Death was not a stranger to this part of town, but collective death, and by fire, was horrific to even think about. Larry guided her to the front of St. Ignatius. He thought he recognized the young man who helped them climb through the cut in the fence. Inside the building, scattered about on the pews, were men, women, and children who had escaped the fire. Most were now wearing sheets or blankets or assorted clothing that seemed to be coming from the rectory.

Hilda appeared, bringing more blankets, sheets, and extra clothing into the church. Larry recognized her from the meeting in the rectory.

Two of the boys he had interviewed stood near the front of the sanctuary, off to one side. Jon came up to Larry and noticed that he was looking at Roy and William. "There is a weakened part of the floor behind them. You saw Charlie out front."

"Amazing. And they were all inside and in bed when the fire started?"

"Always the policeman," the priest replied. "Yes, we all were asleep."

Larry turned to introduce his wife to Father Jon, but she was no longer beside him. He looked around and saw her over to one side, comforting a distraught woman. He pointed her out to Jon. "My wife. She wanted to see for herself what I deal with. I was afraid it would be too much."

"Looks like she has found something to do."

"Yeah," Larry smiled. "Today is our wedding anniversary. We will always remember it."

Jon touched Larry on the shoulder. "It has been hard for you to work this area."

"Fourteen years. Some job."

"Detective Janski, the Police Commissioner would like to see you."

The interruption seemed to change Larry before Jon's eyes. He turned to hurry off and then pointed at his wife, "Tell her I'll be back for her later." Jon nodded.

A second interruption occurred as Hilda came toward him carrying the phone. "The Bishop!" She thrust the instrument into his hand.

"Father Jon, St Ignatius."

The reception was poor, so Father Jon retreated back to the rectory. The Bishop waited until they could talk clearly. "What is going on there?" By way of apology, the Bishop explained, "I couldn't sleep tonight, so rather than pray, which I usually do, I decided to watch some television. What is going on there?"

Jon briefed him on the fire, but the Bishop

214

kept interrupting, saying he knew about that. "It is all that is on the television right now." Jon mentioned he had opened the church so that the barely dressed victims could have shelter from prying eyes. "Are there many of them?"

"Fewer than I would have expected."

"The news reporters are saying that many perished," reported the Bishop.

"I pray that that is a false report, but I do not see enough people to account for all those apartments. We got out the two parishioners who lived in that little basement grocery. And the sister to one of the boys."

"That Detective Janski was afraid something big was about to happen." The Bishop paused. "Have you seen him yet?

"Yes, he was here a short while ago. He is really grieving."

"So am I," responded the Bishop. "We all should feel deep sorrow for this disaster. They are saying on television that it was arson. The Detective was so much concerned that it would happen to St. Ignatius."

"Well, in a way it did. You see, I have seven young men, a housekeeper, a foreign doctor, and Ramon living in this complex. And I can look around and see all of them, except the injured boy, doing what God would want us to do."

Jon was interrupted by the Bishop's "Praise the Lord! I am lifted up by that testimony. My heart can sing praises now." The Bishop went on to give Jon some instructions and cautions before blessing him. Jon returned to the church building with a lighter spirit.

Upstairs in Mighty's room, a tearful reunion had taken place. Mighty urged his sister to put on the sweats he had never worn yet. Patch left to see what else he could do down on the street. Crying, Irene and Mighty held onto each other as they watched the fire burn across the street.

About an hour later, after Scar located Claire being treated for smoke-inhalation, he convinced a Red Cross worker to let him take her back to St. Ignatius. "Her sister needs her," he said. The worker did not want to let a teen take her. That made him mad. "Look," he said, "I am the one who went in and got her out!" Finally two workers, basically carrying Claire, accompanied him to St. Ignatius. They were amazed at the number of people in the church and the care they were being given.

A short time later an official from the Red Cross arrived. Her job was to get the displaced persons to a safe shelter. Several motels had offered free rooms. The people in St. Ignatius did not want to leave the church building. It was a safe place, a sanctuary, they felt, and since it had always been there, they wanted to stay in the neighborhood. No amount of persuasion could budge them. Finally she spied the priest and asked him if the Red Cross could operate a shelter in the church. She was starting to give all the reasons when Father Jon stopped her. Pointing to those sitting and laying on the pews, he said, "They have made the choice. Yes, the Red Cross is welcome."

Hilda went back to the rectory and to bed about four in the morning, taking several of the boys with her. Jon stayed until five when Ramon pushed him toward the side door. "I'll be here, go to bed Father." Jon had been on the streets, anointing bodies and some of the injured. He was almost a walking zombie. So were many of the fire, police, and civil defense workers. The intensity of the fire, the large number of fatalities, and small number of living victims stunned even the toughest civil servant.

216

Detective Janski found his wife still caring for the stunned and disoriented women in the church about six. He took her home. She didn't say much until they got home. He took her in his arms in the privacy of their home, and she cried. She smelled like the poverty of those she had comforted, and he smelled like the putrid stench of the smoldering fire. For an hour, they both cried. "Now I know," she said.

"Know what?"

"What has kept you working in that Precinct for so many years."

"Umm," he replied as he kissed her tenderly. They fell asleep in each other's arms, too exhausted to notice that the sun was coming up.

The shock in the city that morning was nothing they had ever experienced before. The newspapers ran black banners on top of the front page, like they did when a president or other high political figure died. Pictures of the fire had been shown on the television stations all night. The Fire Marshal and Police Commissioner were quoted as saying that the fire was arson. The editorial page was full of criticism of the city officials for not preventing the fire.

When the Police Commissioner arrived home to change clothing, Janette looked at him. She had never seen her husband so tired, both physically and emotionally. "What can I do to help you?" He just stared at her.

"Tell me it didn't happen," he said.

"I don't think that will work."

"Tell me why it happened."

"Only God knows," she answered.

He pulled his smoke-polluted clothing off. "I am not sure he even knows." He went in to shower.

Janette sat on the foot of the bed until he finished. "Here, let me give you a backrub."

"If I lay down now, I probably won't get up."

"Just sit on the edge of the bed." She began kneading the tight muscles of his shoulders. He leaned into her as she worked.

After a few minutes, he stood up. "I've got to get downtown."

"I know. I will be available anytime today if you need me. I didn't have any cases pressing. Besides, I don't think too many people are going to be thinking of anything else. Oh, yes, I shall direct the firm to refuse any cases involving 'Operation Clean Sweep' clientele."

"Good," he grunted as he buttoned his shirt. He tucked a necktie in his jacket pocket. "Just in case I need to look proper."

"Take my car," Janette offered, pulling her keys out. "The press and others probably won't know it is you for a while anyway. I can pick it up later in the day if I really need it."

Pulling his portable radio and cell phone from his car, the Commissioner settled into Janette's car. She was correct. They won't expect him in it. The press would be vultures today, so arriving without them knowing would be best. Her car had darkly tinted windows. He smiled at himself as he neared the downtown. It would be hard for anyone to see him in his wife's car with its dark tinted windows. Pulling into the police garage, the watchman yelled at him as he pulled into his usual spot. "Oh, it's you," the watchman said as he came up to the car to confront the person daring to park in the Police Commissioner's spot.

"Thought I would be less visible coming in, and I guess it was a pretty good disguise."

"Sure was, I was ready to raise an alarm."

"My wife will pick the car up later today if she needs it."

"Sure, do I have to check her ID?"

"You'd better if you want to keep you job."

"Yes sir."

It was around noon when Jon got up. He wasn't rested, but he felt he should be available. When he got to the kitchen, he found Hilda setting out boxes of dry cereal, bread, peanut butter, and jelly. She had a hand-written sign taped to the table. It said, 'Serve yourself, and wash the dishes you use.'

"Morning," she said.

"I thought you were going to take today off."

"Fat chance!" she retorted. She scribbled another sign and taped it to the outside of the refrigerator. It was a rough drawing of a bottle of milk. Another she taped to the outside of her door. "Knock, if you REALLY need me!"

"Feeling rough?" Jon commented.

Hilda nodded. "Just look out front!" She went into her private area and closed the door.

Jon wandered to the parlor area and looked out. What a shock to see across to the next block. The rubble was still smoldering, and firemen were standing around just watching it. Yellow tape had been strung, closing the street. He could see policemen standing at the perimeter of the tape just down from the church and rectory. There was so much junk on the street from the fire that he knew he wouldn't be taking his car out soon.

He crossed over to the church by the side door. Scar was asleep on one of the pews. Ramon, in his soiled yellow jump suit, was talking to someone with a Red Cross armband. He saw Jon and waved him over. "There is food available." He pointed to near the open front door. "I wouldn't let them set it up inside the main part of the church. Those rest rooms that were added off the vestibule some years ago aren't very good, but the toilets work, and the water runs. They must not have been used for years. I did some emergency plumbing down under that part during the night. We'll have to do a cleanup job later."

"Have you slept any?" Jon asked. Ramon shook his head 'no'. "Go up and use my room in the rectory. I'll be up for awhile."

Ramon did not have to be told twice. He nodded and started toward the side door but turned and came back. "All the kids are in and, I suppose, asleep over there. Patch is back there asleep." He pointed to the sacristy.

"Yeah, and I saw Scar."

This time Ramon left the building. Jon was relieved that all the boys were accounted for. The Red Cross worker assured him that all was well, and everyone was being cared for, and he could go back to the rectory if he wished. Jon nodded. He wanted to see those who were his parishioners before he went back. He found Claire curled up asleep on a pew and her sister sleeping in the aisle on a cot. He saw another of his sometime regulars, an old man, eating something. There seemed to be plenty of workers to care for everyone. He prayed at the altar before leaving. He wanted to lie on the floor, prostrated before the altar, but didn't. He was certain it would cause some distress and confusion.

In his office, he thought about what had happened. He wondered who had started such a fierce fire. True, the buildings were old, and firetraps, but the thought of an arsonist sent waves of anger through Jon. It was not an emotion he entertained very often. He lay on the floor of the office, beseeching God to do something about the madness of the deliberate inferno of the night before. When the phone rang, he was reluctant to get up to answer it but knew it would wake Ramon if he let it ring. "St. Ignatius Church."

"You're next," a voice said, and Jon heard the phone click. For a moment he didn't move. Then it sunk in. He dialed the Chancery Office. As soon as he identified himself, he was transferred directly to the Bishop.

"Father Jon, are you all right?"

"For the moment. I just got a phone call. The person said, 'you are next', and hung up."

"Do you have the direct phone number for Detective Janski?"

"No."

"Let me see here, oh, here it is. Call him immediately." The Bishop read off the numbers and had Jon repeat them. "Call me back after you report the call to him. This has got to stop, in the name of Jesus. What kind of person or persons are we dealing with? Make that phone call and then call me again."

Jon only pushed the disconnect button on the phone before calling the Detective.

Larry Janski wasn't in. However, when Jon reported who was calling, his call was transferred to someone else. He told them about the phone call. They said they would be at the rectory very shortly to take all the information and asked if Jon felt threatened.

Jon could hardly think of a civil answer to the question. "Yes, you would, too, after last night," he shouted into the phone.

A tap of the office door nearly unnerved him. Jon paused and reminded himself that this was not his normal behavior. "Yes?" he responded. Ramon opened the door and came in. "I heard the call. Habit or something. I had picked up the phone when you answered. Did you recognize the voice?"

Jon shook his head. "The police will be here to interview me, like I am a celebrity or something?" Jon was angry again.

"I heard the caller," Ramon said again.

It slowly sunk into Jon's mind. "You heard the threat?"

"Yes, I did. Like I said, habit or something. I picked up the phone after it rang, and then you answered it."

Jon relaxed a little. "Then I really did hear it. For a moment or two something in me wanted to say that it was just my tired mind after last night."

Ramon nodded. "I know. I could hardly make myself lay down I am so keyed up. But when I did, I went to sleep until the phone rang."

The phone rang again. Both men jumped. Ramon stepped forward beside Jon as he answered it. The Bishop's voice was a welcome sound. "Father Marvin is coming to be with you. Did you get a hold of Detective Janski?"

"No, your Excellency, he was not in. The call was transferred twice, and the police are on their way to 'interview' me. That was their word: 'interview'. However, the good news is that Ramon picked up the phone upstairs when I answered and heard the threat."

"Father Jon Mark, I don't doubt you were called and threatened." The Bishop's voice was fatherly and soothing. "Remember, I got the first threat against you by courier. Everyone is jumpy and touchy right now. They may not say what they really are feeling, or they may spew out stupid things." The Bishop prayed for Jon and gave him his blessing. "Father Marvin is on his way," he repeated. "I thought it would be good to have two of you there praying. And Ramon isn't such a bad prayer person,

222

either. Call me after the 'interview'."

As Jon hung up the phone, Ramon came back from the kitchen with instant coffee. "Did Hilda take the day off?" he asked.

"No, you read the signs. She is pretty upset by all this." Jon waved his hand toward the front. "She was barely civil when I saw her."

"Sugar?" Ramon pulled the paper sugar packages from his pocket. "Forgot the spoon!" He picked up a letter opener and stirred his coffee.

Jon was beginning to relax when the front doorbell rang. "I'll answer it," Ramon quickly said, "You stay here."

Jon could hear voices at the door and then the door shut. Ramon came back, smiling. "Just the Red Cross, telling us that they had gotten all of the persons sheltered here to agree to move to the other shelter."

"Claire and Agnes?"

"Guess so, they are better set up over there for a long term shelter. They understood why these folks did not want to leave their block. Most haven't been more than a block or two away in their lives."

Jon nodded. "I know the boundaries of this area seem to have invisible wires on them, as if they were fenced in. Even the boys upstairs had difficulties the few times they were picked up by the police and taken someplace else. Interesting, isn't it?" The doorbell rang again. "That should be the police."

"Stay put, I'll get it," Ramon was out the door. A few minutes later two detectives entered Jon's office.

"Detective Janski is on his way. He just wanted us to take a statement from you."

"The statement is that the phone rang, and when I answered it, a voice said: 'You're next.'

Then, I heard the person hang up." Jon looked at Ramon, who was standing in the hallway. "And he heard the same thing."

"I was barely asleep up on Father's bed when the phone rang. Habit or something, I picked up the receiver and heard a voice say what Father has told you."

The two men were taking notes and nodding their heads. "That is all?"

"That is all." Father Jon echoed.

Ramon exploded. "WHAT MORE DO YOU WANT!" Jon thought of the Bishop's comments about how, due to the current distress, people would say things they might not say normally.

"We believe you, we believe you," the older detective said. "I guess that was a dumb question on my part. This whole thing has us all jumpy. I am sure Detective Janski will be talking with you. Thank you for your time." Almost apologetic, the two men left the rectory.

After locking the door behind them, Ramon went back upstairs to try to sleep.

Jon phoned the Bishop and reported the 'interview' to him. The Bishop chuckled. "We all are edgy."

Too tired to stay awake but knowing someone needed to be up in the rectory, Jon laid his head on his desk and slept. Sometime later, the doorbell rang many times before the doctor came down the stairs and let Father Marvin in. "I had to park eight blocks away and go through a security check point to get into this area. I am glad I had worn my collar and not a sport shirt. I think they did call the Bishop's office to see if I was supposed to be down here. That," pointing to the smoldering rubble, "is unbelievable." The doctor nodded.

"In this country, the land of freedom and

224

security, it is. In my homeland, I see it often, only we knew who burned the people out there. Here, in America," the doctor shook his head in dismay. "I find hard to understand."

"We all do," Father Marvin answered.

Jon sat on the front steps looking at the destruction across the street. The firemen and others were still probing through the ruins of a two square block area. Every so often, they would call for a black body bag and remove still another victim of the holocaust. Jon would walk over to the black bag, anoint it with oil, and pray, as solemn men removed it to a waiting morgue ambulance. Father Jon was beyond tears and nearly spent of emotional resources, but he stayed available hour after hour. Patch and Scar often sat near their friend, watching him grieve and wondering what kind of man this was that had so much compassion for them and all the people of the area. Father Marvin kept an eye on his fellow priest also. So far all but three of St. Ignatius' parishioners had been found alive. Jon kept his vigil on into the next night, when Father Marvin and Ramon finally coaxed him to try to sleep.

Sleep seemed to escape Jon, even when he went to bed after two days. He knelt in prayer in his room, his heart broken by what had happened. He wondered if his coming to the parish had been the cause. He hoped not. But, then, when the boys had recovered the oil tank, they had been accused and persecuted. If he had not asked them to get it back, would the buildings across the street and the lives lost not have happened? The doctor heard his sobbing and quietly entered the priest's room.

"Father, you must rest."

Jon nodded but remained kneeling, tears running down his face.

"Take this," the doctor handed the priest a glass of liquid. "Then, in a little while, you will be sleepy."

Jon looked at the glass. "What is in it?"

"A mild sedative. It will allow you to sleep for a while. Then you can go back to assisting across the street. Father Marvin is sitting out there, watching. Ramon is with him. I sent Scar and Patch to bed. They have been out there beside you most of the time."

"I need to talk with the Bishop," Jon said.

"After you rest. It is the middle of the night again. Drink the liquid."

Jon drank the contents and handed the glass back to the doctor. "How soon will I go to sleep?"

"Twenty minutes or so. You have time for a warm shower. I'll check on you again in a little while."

Jon nodded and headed into his bathroom. When the doctor looked in thirty minutes later, Jon was sleeping. "God, you are so good. Give him a refreshing sleep and let nothing happen to awaken him until you are ready for him to get up." The doctor quietly closed the door and tiptoed downstairs to let Father Marvin and Ramon know that Father Jon was finally sleeping.

The early morning sirens did not awaken Jon but disturbed the doctor. He ran toward the flaming buildings where he and his wife lived. The police and firemen were angry with everyone, victims and perpetrator. The doctor sought information about his wife and found her in a temporary Red Cross shelter. Everyone was in shock and disbelief that another two blocks had been torched. The news media were excited. This fire had been detected almost at the onset. The baker had just arrived in his shop when he heard something and looked out. The flames were

226

just starting. His quick action spared those who were asleep in the buildings. The television cameras were showing the rescued people, with flashbacks to the fire scene and to the baker who was a hero.

Larry Janski and the Police Commissioner stood shoulder to shoulder. Neither had had much rest since the fire across from St. Ignatius. A grim Fire Marshall was telling them that this fire was started just like the other one. Very hot incendiaries were set in strategic places which, barring the good fortune this time of the early morning baker, would have caused as much damage and loss of lives as the one earlier. The Police Commissioner looked into a waiting television camera. "There is no doubt these fires, probably all three, including the salvage yard, are the work of the same demented arsonist. We will find you." The Commissioner then took Larry Janski aside and said, "Go get some rest. We will meet this afternoon at three. I want you refreshed. We are going to get this arsonist."

Larry did not have to be told twice to go get rest. His body ached from the lack of sleep. He tapped a fellow officer on the shoulder. "Drive me home. I'd be a danger on the road." Permission was quickly granted.

Father Marvin, Ramon, and the doctor were sitting at the dining table when Father Jon came down the next day. Jon was sniffing the air. "The fire across the street is still smoldering?" From Hilda's room, a strange woman emerged. The doctor stood up and introduced his wife to Father Jon.

A look of amazement crossed Jon's face as the doctor's wife and the doctor told of the fire a few blocks away. Father Marvin nodded as Ramon told of what he had observed and what the television stations were reporting. Jon slumped in his chair. The doctor immediately sprang to his side to check his pulse. Jon waved him away.

"I'm OK, just still very tired. I find it hard to imagine."

Father Marvin pushed the morning edition of one of the papers in front of Father Jon. It showed the flames and destruction from the night. The center article was about the baker who had discovered the fire and had gotten all the people out safely.

"It did happen," Father said quietly. "I wonder how likely it is that the threat on me will happen also."

"The Police Commissioner called at daybreak to alert us," Ramon answered. "The Bishop also called."

"And you did not wake me?" Jon asked.

"We would have had to get past the doctor here first." Ramon grinned. "He slipped you a good 'Mickey' last night. You were in a deep sleep."

Jon looked at the doctor, who nodded. "Oh. Where are the boys?"

Ramon pointed to the cellar stairs. "They are down there, clearing out the junk from the basement room. It is dry down there, so as soon as supplies arrive from the Bishop we are putting up partitions and cots for four of the boys to sleep on. The doctor and his wife will be going to a shelter, since Mighty is doing fairly well. Father Marvin will take the other room upstairs. One of the boys, probably Patch, will sleep in Mighty's room."

"And I have Irene in with me," Hilda added.

"I'll stay over in the church, probably taking Scar over there," Ramon added.

"You seemed to have things all planned out." Jon responded. "How long did I sleep?"

"About twelve hours."

"It is afternoon?" Jon shook his head in disbelief. "I suppose I had better phone the Bishop."

"He said he would take your call whenever you were awake and rested."

"Well, I am awake."

"And rested?"

"I doubt I'll be that for some time," Jon answered. The doctor nodded.

"How many days have passed since that across the street?"

"It happened three nights ago." Father Marvin stood up and stretched. "I have said Mass the past two mornings for thirty or forty people. Tomorrow they need to see the resident priest back at the altar. Will you concelebrate with me?"

Jon nodded. "Thirty or forty? There were only a dozen or so when I came here."

"The fire," Father Marvin commented.

Shared Hearts

Jon retired to his office, currently Father Marvin's temporary bedroom. Only the folded bedding and a large suitcase in the corner indicated that it was being used this way. The telephone rang. "St. Ignatius Church," he answered.

A stranger's voice greeted him. "Praise the Lord! Is this the pastor, Father Jon?"

"Yes, what can I do for you?"

The voice continued. "I am another pastor of the same area as St. Ignatius." Expressing concern and sorrow over the intense disasters, the pastor offered his church facilities, which included a small dorm, classrooms, and a kitchen, for the use of any displaced persons in the area surrounding St. Ignatius. His congregation, one of color, was grieved over the terrible events. His people were ready to assist any that Father Jon would recommend.

Then he asked Jon, "May I come over and meet with you and pray with you? It is a shame I waited until all this happened before reaching out. I have grieved the Lord greatly by my lack of action."

At first Jon thought he would say 'no', but he felt the nudge of the Lord. "I, too, have failed to reach out to my fellow Christian brothers. Yes, please come. There is another priest staying here also. We all need to pray together."

An appointment was made for later that afternoon. Before the pastor hung up, he prayed on the phone with Father Jon. "I will be there at 5 pm," he promised.

Noise in the hallway indicated that materials were being moved toward the basement. Jon stuck his head out the door. "Watch your head!" a voice sang out. He ducked back in as a sheet of paneling passed by. He phoned the Bishop. The call was satisfying and reassured him of continued help from the Chancery. The Bishop's concern for the welfare of all now residing at St. Ignatius was apparent.

"When will all of this end?" asked Jon. It was just a rhetorical question.

"When God has His way," answered the Bishop.

"I have a lot I would like to talk about, but I know there is not time to talk. It seems like I have been propelled toward this since the first moment I stepped out of my car in the driveway."

The Bishop agreed and reminded him that he, Jon, did not choose this plan of action. The Bishop blessed him before hanging up. It was then that Jon remembered the black pastor who was coming by to visit. He had forgotten to tell the Bishop. He considered calling back to the Bishop but didn't.

A tap at the office door before it opened revealed Father Marvin. "They just uncovered another body across the street. Do you want to go anoint the bag and pray?" He was holding the bottle of oil in his hand.

Jon nodded, "Yes, I will go. How many did they find while I was asleep?"

Marvin held up his hand, his thumb touching his forefinger making a circle. "I guess they were waiting for you to get up again."

Jon took the bottle and went out onto the street.

The boys were carrying cartons of food and clothing into the house from a large white delivery van parked in front of the rectory. Jon had noticed a collection of boxes in the parlor as he went out. "Hey Padre!" Patch was carrying several boxes at one time.

The mood was as somber as usual as the body bag was lifted from the basement area of one of the charred buildings. The men paused. Father Jon came, anointed the bag, and prayed over it. They nodded a greeting and continued on to the morgue ambulance. "Are you expecting to find many more?" Jon asked the worker who climbed out of the hole that once was a basement.

"I don't think so. The dogs have stopped showing much interest in the ruins. This one was well buried under the debris. He wasn't burned, only crushed."

"Have any idea who he was?"

"Yeah, the owner of S & S. His wallet was on him."

Jon remembered Bill and the last time he was in S & S restaurant with Angus. "I knew him. He was not a very happy man."

Jon returned through the church. Ramon had trimmed away the sharp edges of the chain link fence that Jon had cut through that first night. The front doors were open. Inside he found some workers praying. Several of them acknowledged him as he went up to the altar and genuflected before it. He looked in the sacristy before going back to the rectory.

It was a sober group that gathered in the 'safe room' that afternoon. Larry, refreshed but still very tired, arrived, carrying his suitcase. "I am staying in town for several days. My wife encouraged me to save my energies for here and not travel back and forth."

The top two lab techs for the Fire Marshall arrived with a stack of papers, reports on the analysis of the incendiary used to start the fires. Basically, the incendiary was high school chemistry, they said. The arsonist was starting multiple fires with a hot fuel, which heated the rest of the fuel so that, when the fire department arrived with their water hoses, the fuel burned even hotter, thus consuming the buildings, which were constructed with interior wood beams and air ducts of the type that sucked the fire up as it heated up.

"OK, guys, what is that fuel that burns hotter when doused with water?"

Silence was in the room, as they all racked their brains to remember when water was not advisable to put out a fire. "Car engines a few years ago, when they tried to make a lighter engine. If the engine caught fire, the car was a goner."

"Right. Our arsonist is using that as a source of intense heat, letting us contribute to the fire."

"Boy, that points to the fire at Buddy's Salvage."

Larry Janski, still groggy when he came in, was now alert. "Are we looking at VS?"

"Could be," retorted one of the fire techs.

"It could be anyone with access to a salvage yard and old cars."

The Police Commissioner was rubbing his forehead. He had rested but, like Larry, was still exhausted.

"So why don't we pick him up?"

"'Cause we have no evidence that he is the perpetrator," answered the Commissioner.

"What about the threats to the priest at St. Ignatius?"

"Yeah, what about them? Are they a diversion or are they real."

"They are real." Larry interjected. "Not because they are in my Precinct but because that priest is the target. Too much else has happened to indicate this. I think he and that church building/rectory are targets. The mystery is why."

"Why doesn't the Bishop pull the man out and close the doors there? It would be simpler."

"Not really. And the Catholic Church doesn't run from potential trouble, or at least this Bishop doesn't." Larry prayed to himself, hoping he was saying the right thing. "Besides, there are more people involved besides that priest."

"So move them!"

The Commissioner interrupted, "I think we are missing the point, ladies and gentlemen! If the priest is a target, he will be a target wherever he is. We know that he is. You heard the tape just last week." The Commissioner paused to gather his thoughts. "Our job seems to be to stop any more events like those of last night, or last week, and at the same time try to tip the arsonist's hand."

"Or VS'," someone added.

The Fire Marshall had entered the room while the discussion was going on. "I have instructed the individual stations in that area to treat any new fire with foam first. We may be able to stop the destruction and loss of life if we do not add to the intensity of the fire initially. These fires seem to have a psychological element in that the arsonist is using what would be the positive role of the fire department as part of the perpetration. Frankly, I am mad."

"Does the media know what you have discovered about the fires?"

"Not from us it doesn't, but it won't take long before some bright thinker will figure it out. Each of the fires got worse when we arrived. What does that tell you?"

"What are you going to tell them?"

"Nothing."

"Even if they figure it out?"

"Even if they figure it out. Our job is to stop our participation in these holocausts." The Fire Marshall was emphatic.

"I have asked the mayor to request National Guard help in the affected area. My men are tired and spread rather thin. We have all but stopped 'Clean Sweep' because of the fires. There are just not enough officers to do the job." The Commissioner looked around the room. "Security in that area must be maintained for the benefit of those living in the area and for the overall welfare of the city."

"Do you suppose the fires were set to tie up the ability of the police to continue with 'Clean Sweep'?"

"Possibly, that is why we need additional help policing that area so we can go back to what was being effective. After all, the courts are helping by setting high bonds, and no one has been bailed out. We are squeezing something."

"Or someone," Larry interjected.

"Yeah," multiple voices spoke up.

Rudy White arrived promptly at five. He had barely twisted the old doorbell when the door was flung open. Standing before him, Father Jon just said, "Welcome, brother. It has been a long road."

Rudy grasped his brother in an embrace. Turning to look across the two blocks now leveled by the fire, he said, "What a price to pay."

Jon ushered him into the parlor. Father Marvin came in and was introduced. Rudy clasped Father Marvin's hand. He was not as open to other denominational clerics as Father Jon and stiffened. He quickly relaxed as he felt genuine love flow from the black man.

Ramon was standing in the doorway. He just grinned. He knew Rudy from years ago. Rudy was the young Evangelist who had asked him if he was going to be baptized or buried, the pivotal event in his young life. When the two men saw each other eye to eye, Pastor Rudy White began to cry. The two men held each other for a long time. "It is well with you, my boy?"

Ramon laughed a light airy laugh, "It is very well with me, Evangelist!"

"Forgive me." Rudy pulled out a white handkerchief from his pocket and wiped his eyes. "I wondered if you were still alive. I see that you are. Praise the Lord!" Looking at the priests, he started to explain.

Father Jon raised his hand and shook his head. "I know the story."

"So do I," Father Marvin chimed in.

For a while, the conversation stayed on things of the past. Pastor White was eager to find out how Ramon found his faith and made the change

236

from a ghetto gang member to a respected adult. When Hilda announced supper, Father Marvin and Ramon excused themselves to supervise in the dining room. Father Jon and Pastor White continued talking in the parlor. Neither one was interested in food, as there was so much for them to share with each other about the fires in the St. Ignatius area.

Finally, after a time of prolonged prayer for each other, Pastor White left. He reminded Father Jon of the availability at his church for helping some of those displaced by the fire. Jon had told him a little about the doctor and his wife. Rudy extended an immediate welcome to the couple to use the dorm rooms and kitchen at his church. Father promised to tell them when they returned to the rectory. Pastor White knew of the doctor by the good works he had performed for various persons of the area. He expressed his anticipation of meeting him.

The National Guard moved in during the night. Father Jon awoke to the drone of heavy trucks out front. As soon as it was daylight, he went out to introduce himself. The commander was a medium-built man who had the respect of his men. He acknowledged Father Jon and told him he had been briefed about the possible danger to the priest.

Soon the National Guardsmen fanned out over the whole area, canvassing the neighborhood to see who was still there. They took names and photos and issued photo IDs. The boys were impressed with the very first photo IDs they had ever had. They found that IDs gave them a sense of status.

The Police Commissioner and Mayor had drawn up the boundaries for the area that included where Pastor White had his church. It appeared the police and Mayor were not taking any chances. Only those people who lived in the area were allowed in after dark. All visitors, delivery trucks, and

237

unofficial persons were to be out of the area between 6 pm and 6 am. A few people grumbled, but most were relieved the area was being made secure.

One thing about this disaster, there was no looting. The destruction had been so complete. This made the job of the Guardsmen easier.

In the meantime, activity in the 'safe room' went on nearly round the clock. Part of the briefings dealt with the resumption of 'Operation Clean Sweep', while the fire techs and other investigators pushed for the identity of the arsonist. The tax investigators looking in to VS's financial activities were relegated to the back corner. They believed they were nearing the time when they could go to a grand jury with enough evidence to get an indictment. Neither Larry Janski nor the Police Commissioner felt that this action would solve the more blatant problem of the fires.

Father Marvin took up the task of Catechism classes with the boys in the afternoons. Fathers Jon and Marvin concelebrated Mass every morning. Scar still served as altar boy. The discussion, brought on by the Monopoly Game, and what if there was a church on one of the game streets, was still bantered around by the boys. A sleeping room for four of the boys was created in the basement. Hilda took two days off. Her cousin's gaudy taxi came and picked her up. Ramon cooked and taught Scar how to make meatloaf and crustless apple pie. Irene learned to run the washer and drier. The Bishop or Chancellor phoned daily. Detective Janski visited the rectory whenever he was in the area, and that was often. The boys began to talk with him. And there were no more fires for over two weeks.

The doctor and his wife were living at Pastor

White's church complex and were welcomed by the congregation there. Jon and Rudy talked daily and prayed often together. Jon was grateful for a praying confidant who understood the area and its problems.

The media thought having the National Guard in the area was restricting the people and began a campaign to have them pulled out. This made both Jon and Rudy angry because they saw many of the local people more relaxed and secure than they had ever been. The city authorities did not seem very open to removing the Guardsmen.

They certainly have short memories!" snapped Jon as he read an article criticizing the National Guard's presence. "I guess we aren't creating enough news for them down here."

"Don't let it bother you, Padre." Patch was sitting at the dining table with the priest. He was looking at the ads for cars. "Do you think I will ever be able to read these?" He pointed to the words spread across the full-page auto ad.

"You want to learn to read, don't you?"

Patch fixed his single eye on the priest, "Of course. Scar taught me some things, but I can't read the paper, so what good is that?"

"I wonder if I can find a volunteer teacher for you guys. Do any of the others want to learn to read?"

Patch nodded. "Father Marvin reminds us everyday that we need to use our minds. Then he has to read out of that book what he wants us to learn. I want to read out of that book for myself."

"The book, which book?"

"The one that has the questions and answers about the Church."

Father Jon sat looking across the table at a crack in the wall. He wondered how long it had been there and if it was getting wider. He thought of how the crack in the boys was opening up. They wanted to learn. It was time to get them some schooling. They no longer were in hiding from the police, but they were living in the rectory. They were very useful during the days immediately following the fires. Now things were settling down.

"I think I'll walk over to Pastor White's church. Do you want to go with me?"

"That's Street Rats' territory!"

"So."

Silence.

"Do you think they will attack you when you are with me?"

Patch still said nothing.

"Are you coming?" Jon stood up.

At the front door he looked back. Patch was staring down at his feet. Jon shrugged his shoulders and went out.

He was at the corner when he heard Patch call out, "Wait for me, Padre." Jon felt a charge of pride because of the decision that Patch had made. Together they walked the nine blocks to Rudy's church. No one bothered them.

"Sure, you can use the classrooms for schooling. I even have a teacher or two in the congregation who could teach them. I will call them right away. When do you want to start?" Rudy's enthusiasm was contagious.

"Tomorrow!" Jon answered.

"Tomorrow?" Patch echoed.

"Sure, strike while the iron is hot," Pastor White laughed. "Let's go over and pick out a room or two to use. I have a few people around here who also could benefit from an alternative type school. And I have someone in the church who knows how to make one work. He ran one for a couple of years a few years back."

240

Rudy was up and out the door before Patch could ask about 'strike while the iron is hot'. It was a peculiar expression. He thought it probably referred to him, and he wanted to know what it meant.

Over in the classrooms, Father Jon and Pastor Rudy explored which ones would be best. They finally chose two that were halfway between the exit and the rest rooms. The two rooms were connected and outfitted with larger tables and chairs; a plus, the two men decided. One room down the hall had a sink in it and could be used for arts and crafts if they ever got so interested.

"Arts and crafts?" Patch echoed. "I thought that was kindergarten stuff."

The two men chuckled. "You'd be amazed at what happens when you are allowed to be creative." Pastor White said. "Take, for instance, the graffiti on the underpasses. Some of it is quite good."

"Art-wise, there is talent out there waiting to be discovered." Jon added.

Patch kicked at a dirty spot on the floor, thinking about some of the graffiti he had put up. "Talent?"

"Yeah, special abilities to do something." Jon answered. "Like, you have a talent for organizing and keeping control over the other six boys. That takes a special talent."

"Have you ever read the story in the Bible about the 'talents'?" asked Pastor Rudy.

"I can't read." Patch answered honestly. Jon was proud that Patch was able to state his inability to read. That should be the beginning of his learning to read.

"Well, we will just have to change that, won't we?" Pastor Rudy was looking straight at Patch.

"Yeah," Patch answered.

"I'll contact my people and see if they can be here tomorrow, let's say about 10 am, OK, Father Jon?"

"We will be here. Thank you for your willingness to have us."

As they walked back to St. Ignatius, a thousand questions were whirling in Patch's mind. They stopped to survey the second burned-out set of buildings. Jon seemed to be preoccupied, so Patch kept his thoughts to himself. As they approached the rectory, Scar came to meet them. Seeing the sober look on Patch's face, he fell in step with them. "What's up, bro?"

"Ask Padre."

Scar glanced at their friend and shook his head. "He is hurting too much to ask. You tell me."

"Later."

Jon sat on a pew in the front of the church. He had not realized how much just looking at the second set of burned out buildings would disturb him. His mind cried out for an answer to the senseless destruction. He thought he had come to an understanding, but something inside of him still churned and wrenched. He had to find an answer, a peace. He knew it could only come supernaturally, as the Lord healed. Some of the people seemed to be healing, but he wasn't. This was disturbing for Jon. After all, he should be leading them, not trailing behind them. At least that was the way he saw it.

Inside the rectory, Patch informed the others that in the morning they were going to go to Pastor White's church and meet a teacher or two who would help them learn. Scar stood behind the others, grinning at his leader. This was quite a step for them.

"I ain't going!" declared Charles.

Patch shrugged his shoulders, "You can say

242

that, but you will go with all the rest of us."

Charles turned to leave the group and found Scar blocking his way. "We are all together in this thing from the beginning, remember? Besides, why shouldn't you go?"

"Street Rats."

"I was over there today. They did not bother me."

"Yeah, Patch, and you had Padre with you." Charles retorted.

"And we will have Padre with us tomorrow, so get over it. We are going. Padre made the appointment, and we will be there, including you."

Charles, still looking defiant, nodded.

Father Jon missed supper and evening devotions. Ramon found him in prayer before the altar and advised Father Marvin to keep the boys at the rectory. They had lots of questions about going over into the Street Rats' territory and about learning. Father Marvin did not have any answers as he had not talked with Father Jon. Patch filled them in on the visit at Pastor White's church and the classrooms. He failed to mention about 'arts and crafts', figuring most of his gang wouldn't understand. He barely did. Father Marvin assured the boys that, if Father Jon did not walk over with them, he or Ramon would. This seemed to calm some of their fears.

"Where is Father Jon?" Mighty asked.

"Praying over in the church," Ramon answered.

"About what?"

"You should have seen his face when we went by the other burned out buildings over where the bakery was," Patch answered.

"What can we do to help Padre?" Scar asked Father Marvin.

"Pray for him."

243

"But how?"

"Remember the day we all prayed for Mighty?"

Heads nodded.

"Let's start there and see what else God would have us do." Father Marvin knelt on the floor. The boys followed. "Ramon, why don't you lead tonight?

The prayers of the nine rose to heaven in unison as they sought God's grace for their friend, Father Jon.

It was late when Jon crossed over to the rectory. He was feeling a little more at peace with the destruction of the neighborhood around St. Ignatius. Hilda looked up from where she was reading at the kitchen table. "I have your dinner in the refrigerator. It will only take a minute to heat up."

Jon pulled out a chair and sat down. A microwave was on the cabinet. "When did we get that?'

Hilda punched some buttons on the microwave. "It is mine. I brought it back when I took the days off. Thought it might come in handy, with all the food I prepare and reheat."

"I wondered if the Bishop had sent it." Jon blew on the heated food placed before him before he tried to take a bite.

"Well, we might ask him for one if this one proves to be very useful. I would like mine back eventually."

"Are you feeling better since your days off?"

Hilda grinned. "Yep! I can keep these guys all fed and behaving themselves now. Of course, Irene is a big help."

Irene had entered the kitchen from Hilda's rooms. She was carrying a pile of cleaned dishtowels. She had a shy smile.

"It is good to have you here with us now," Jon spoke. The girl ducked her head but nodded.

"It was an adjustment at first," Hilda spoke up. "She wanted so badly to stay with Mighty. Father Marvin insisted she sleep down here, so we put a cot for her in my room. It works out well. She hasn't had much loving care or teaching, but she is a quick learner." Irene was standing awkwardly by the kitchen sink.

"Sit down with us." Jon pushed another chair out. Irene looked to Hilda and her nod before sitting down. From where she sat, Hilda reached into the refrigerator and pulled out a bottle of soda. Irene hesitated before she accepted it. Jon passed the plate of cookies Hilda had placed on the table for him over to Irene. "I don't bite, but you can bite into these."

"Thank you." Irene's voice was almost a whisper.

Jon considered the thin slip of a girl sitting across from him. She had been determined and aggressive when Mighty was hurt. She had changed, or was she frightened of him now that Mighty was mending and she was being cared for in the rectory also. His mind was still too tired from all of the events to try to figure it out. He looked at Hilda to see if she would say anything more than she already had, but she had reverted back to the book she was reading when he came in.

Silently, Irene ate her cookie. Jon pushed the plate toward her again. She took one more. Jon finished off his coffee and the last two cookies.

"Where are the boys?" asked Jon

Hilda looked up. "In the parlor, I think, praying. At least they haven't come by here to go down to the room downstairs yet."

"Praying?"

"Father Marvin and Ramon were leading them. There was quite a discussion at supper about going into the Street Rats' territory tomorrow. Father Marvin and Ramon took them into the parlor to talk it out."

"I guess I dropped a bombshell on them, the guys and Father Marvin. Do you think I am needed to explain anything?"

"No, Patch did a good job, from what I could tell. Charles contested the idea, but Patch and Scar reminded him that they were all in this together. That is quite a bunch when they get all upset." Irene was nodding her head as Hilda spoke.

"Did you finish school?" Jon asked Irene.

"Do I look like someone who finished school?" Irene responded in her more normal voice.

Jon chuckled. "I can't tell."

"None of us went very far in school. Momma was sick all the time, and someone had to stay home. I was it. You don't think Mighty did, do you?"

"Were there just the two of you?"

Irene nodded. "Momma died last year. She made the manager of the apartments promise we could keep our apartment for another year. She had it paid for out of the disability money she got."

"Disability?"

"She got burned in a grease fire at S & S. She never got over it."

"S & S, that was across the street?"

"Bill said it was her own fault, but at the hospital someone said he was responsible for keeping the grease cleaned out of the exhaust fan. I don't know where the money came from, but she got a monthly check."

"Bill was the owner?"

"Yeah."

246

Jon found his thoughts going back to the last time he had seen Bill alive. It was that day with Angus. Bill seemed to be so unhappy. No wonder, Jon thought. If there was an accident in his place of business, he had to pay out a monthly stipend for it unless he had had insurance. No, probably not.

"So you and Mighty are alone and on your own?"

Irene nodded. "He's all I got."

The serious discussion was interrupted by a whoop and cheer as the guys came out of the parlor and spotted Father Jon in the kitchen. They descended upon him, all talking at once.

"Hold it, hold it!" Ramon yelled as he came up and started to herd the four that slept downstairs toward the basement door.

Father Marvin and Scar were in deep discussion in the hall. Patch just grinned at Jon. "Prayer works, Padre."

"Meaning?"

"We were praying for you to get better. And you are!"

Jon started to say that he didn't know that he was not well but considered it best not to as he remembered the hours he spent crying before the altar in the church. Instead he said, "Thanks, I needed that!"

Departure

Vincent Sardoni was in a near rage. The accountants had just faxed him a full report about the effect 'Operation Clean Sweep' had on his empire. The high-rise buildings were all rented to 85% capacity. That was nearly perfect. The operations at the nightclubs, bistros, and gambling houses showed a distinct lost. After a string of curse words, Vincent settled down to see how things could be changed. The record of deposits in national banks and international banks was satisfying. It was then that he noticed that one of the elegant pictures on his wall was crooked. This set off more rage before he finally got up from his chair to fix it. His finger caught a loose piece in the elaborate gold frame. At first he thought it was just a loose piece of gilt until he picked it with his thumb. He pried it loose and saw that it was hard and compact. As he turned it over and over in his hand, he saw the glint of sophisticated electronics under the gilt surface. It was a radio implant.

Lilly had gotten those pictures for him and put them up. He pounded on the intercom, paging her. In his right hand desk drawer he pulled his terminator with silencer forward. There was only one answer for what he had found. He wondered if he should have her questioned before killing her, or just kill her. She did not respond to his page.

In the outer office that was outside the sound proofed inner office, Lilly reached for the intercom button. The phone rang at the same time, so she picked it up first. A voice said, "Gold, get out!" and the line went dead. Lilly did not hesitate. She moved swiftly to the outer door and ran down the hall. She took the stairs two steps at a time, kicking off her heels at the first landing. She ran to another stairwell on the next floor before continuing her race away from Sardoni's office. She didn't stop until she was in the basement. She turned and headed down another flight to the boiler area. A man was waiting. A portion of the wall was pushed in. They both entered.

After closing the wall, he placed a steel beam across. Taking her hand, they ran down dark tunnels, with only a small flashlight showing them the way. Twice they ran head-on into a wall before they could stop their running and make a turn left or right. At last they went down into one of the storm sewer passages. They ran on until they reached a sealed grating between them and the river.

Breathless, they waited in silence to see if they could hear any footsteps following them. Dripping water in the storm sewer and river sounds were all they could hear. The man pressed a number into his radiophone. The luminous screen of the phone showed the call answered. "Now we just wait."

Lilly nodded. She had been prepared for this dash since she took the job with Sardoni. Her breathing eased while they waited inside the sewer. "At least it isn't raining."

The man grunted. A short time later, a dilapidated river tug pulled up to the grating. A package was passed through with a change of clothing. A welder, hidden under bulky canvases, cut two bars of the grate. The man and Lilly, now clothed in jumpsuits, climbed through. Twenty minutes later, the hole was welded shut and the tug moseyed down the river, seemingly with no specific purpose.

In the listening room, where all that took place in Vincent Sardoni's office was recorded, the two men on duty heard the oaths of rage, the finding of that particular listening device, the crushing of the device as Vincent pounded it into pieces on his desk, and then the rage when Lilly disappeared. They smiled. There were several devices in Sardoni's office. The one Vincent found and destroyed had been inactive for some time.

The 'safe room' was all abuzz as news came in that Sardoni had found one of the listening devices. The recording of events just before, during, and after his find was played for the gathered officers. Larry Janski arrived late. They were getting ready to play the recording again when two people wearing jumpsuits were ushered in. Everyone stood and applauded. Lilly smiled and turned to the Police Commissioner. "Have you a job back in the records department, where I can work without having to run for my life?" Several laughed, for Lilly had worked for Sardoni for over a year. The custodian had been there for a little longer than she, minding his business and doing police reconnaissance.

"Well, this should stir things up," someone quipped.

"I was just getting used to more normal activities."

"Yeah, me too."

"I might as well forget about a vacation this next week," Larry said.

"Where were you going, Larry?"

"You got that right. I won't be going now."

The Police Commissioner quieted the room. "Here is the tape of the last moments of finding that listening device."

The room was quiet as the men and women listened to Vincent's ranting and his subsequent find and discovery of Lilly's quick exit.

"What was that sound about the time he buzzed her office?"

"Sounded like the opening and closing of a desk drawer."

"Yeah, but there was a scraping sound too."

"Don't know," answered the Commissioner.

"I know," Lilly offered. "It could have been the drawer he keeps his gun in."

The group all stared at her. She paled and then said, "Be glad you didn't have to listen to him kill me, 'cause he would have. That rage always means bad things. And no one outside of that room would have heard it, 'cause he has that room double sound-proofed."

Larry clenched his fists and flexed them open again. He wondered when they would quit playing cat and mouse with VS and put him in jail for good. It was his territory, and he hated what that man had done to the people of the area.

"We are on a time-bomb again." The Commissioner looked around. "Got any ideas?"

"What about that priest?"

"There is a whole bunch of people living at St. Ignatius now, isn't there?"

"Shouldn't we warn them?"

"I will," Larry answered, "and alert the Bishop, also."

"I will be discussing the situation with the National Guard. They are pretty relaxed, and the people are content to have them there."

"The newspapers and media all seem to think it is time to lift the restrictions down there."

"To hang with the papers and media. They don't have to dig out people from underneath burned buildings or identify people in body bags!" The Commissioner was angry. "How many of them actually saw what we saw or the fire department had to contend with. They are even suggesting that all danger is over now!"

"They don't have the privilege of sitting in this room. That's part of their complaint. Of course, if they did, they would print everything and have a roving reporter reporting on the nightly news all the inroads we have made. And you know who would know it all." Larry took up the anger.

"Yeah, VS." several choroused.

"Right!" Larry answered.

For another hour or so, the officers and others hashed and rehashed what was the best next move. Larry excused himself to set up the alert system for St. Ignatius and the Bishop.

The Bishop took the new news in stride. He alerted the attorneys, the Chancellor, and St. Ignatius.

Larry arrived at the door later that night while Jon was hanging up the phone from the Bishop's call. "You know?" he asked.

Jon nodded. Father Marvin and Ramon came

to the office, where they sat and talked.

"What about your housekeeper?"

Ramon went to get her.

"Do you want to leave," Father Jon asked Hilda.

She shook her head 'no'.

"What about the boys?" Larry asked.

"Where would they go? Beside, they have been here all this time with this kind of danger, even before it started to be specifically aimed at me and St. Ignatius." Jon sighed. "I think they would be insulted to be moved now." Ramon agreed.

"They are to start schooling tomorrow over at Pastor White's church. How will this affect that?"

Detective Janski sat back a moment. "In the daytime?"

"Yes."

"Probably won't be a reason for alarm. These attacks seem to be done at night. How are these guys going to fare in the Street Rats' territory?"

"Patch and I were there today. We had no trouble." Jon replied.

"One of us will be walking over and back with them, or two of us. Do you think that will be enough?"

"With the National Guard around, yes," Larry answered.

"Just a point of interest, the boys prayed for their enemies tonight while in prayer for you, Jon," Father Marvin spoke up. "Ramon suggested it, with their fear of the Street Rats, and then they all seemed to come to a comfortable place with that prayer."

"That's a miracle, having them do that. Good job." Jon looked to Ramon and smiled.

"Maybe that is what we all should be doing about the arsonist and Vincent Sardoni."

The men looked at Larry. "Where have we

been?" Father Marvin asked.

"Let's pray now." Jon knelt, and so did the others. Within moments their prayers united in a heart cry to the Lord for protection for the innocent and conviction of the guilty.

The next day was sunny but cool. Fall had arrived. Father Jon and Ramon walked with the guys to Pastor White's church. True to his word, Pastor White had two retired teachers available and another man who had run an alternative school earlier in life. The three greeted the boys. Each boy signed a paper agreeing to abide by the simple rules of conduct as Pastor White explained to them. William balked, but only for a moment. The process of accessing their learning needs was begun. Since most could not read, everything was done orally. Time passed quickly, and soon it was noon. Each carried back to St. Ignatius a reading lesson to practice before the next day.

Father Jon and Ramon briefed Father Marvin after lunch. It was agreed that Ramon would accompany whichever priest was available daily. After lunch and Catechism class, Father Marvin would help them with their assignments in reading. After supper, Ramon would be available for any additional help. The three men considered the time left in the day's schedule to be free for the boys, other than the normal housework jobs that Hilda had trained them to do. The Fathers and Ramon prayed for protection and success for each boy before Father Marvin called them together for the daily afternoon instruction in the history of the Church and faith.

Hilda and Irene had used the time the boys were away to bake and clean the house. Both were happy with the results. Father Jon asked Irene if she would like to go to class over at Pastor White's. She shook her head 'no'. "Well, if you change you mind, let me know," he told her. She nodded.

Detective Janski listened carefully to the phone call. The Police Commissioner was elated that the night had passed quietly. Even more so was his elation that two bodies found in the river were checking out positive as being those of Melinda Sardoni and the chauffer. They were discovered several days earlier when a dredge, cleaning out the river channel, found their car. The information and find had been kept secret, even from the snooping press. This suited the Commissioner well.

"So we have murder charges pending?" asked Larry.

"No, apparently they skidded off the road in the car."

"Oh, oh," Larry responded. "Dead or alive?"

"Coroner says they had river water in their lungs, alive."

"Drugs?"

"Alcohol only, from what the 'corn' says. Deterioration was pretty bad. We'll see what the state and federal labs say."

"I thought there was no car missing at VS's."

"Yeah, that is one interesting thing. This car was registered to Mrs. Sardoni but not kept at VS's house. He may not have known about it. Makes for some interesting speculation, doesn't it?"

Larry laughed. "Sure does, boss. When is this going public?"

"Finding their bodies will be on the noon news. The rest is confidential at present. I imagine we will have a real drama on our hands as VS shows his remorse at his wife's demise." The Commissioner chuckled. "And then rage? Or what, when it sinks in that she was in the car with the chauffer."

"Don't count on the rage. We have never seen it in public. Has your office contacted him about the find?"

"That is going on right now." Wonder what the listening post is hearing. Should be a revealing tape, I would think. Keep alert. The usual meeting at five this afternoon will be hopping with information. See you there."

Larry hung up the phone. He wanted to shout and holler. At last something was happening with VS outside of his Precinct. He knew he shouldn't be so joyful, but it was about time. Calming his emotions, he leisurely strolled out past all the usual commotion in the common room and tapped on his Captain's door.

"Come in if your nose is clean!"

Larry walked in and straddled a straight chair. He just grinned.

The Captain looked up after a moment or two from the folder he was studying. "What brings you here? We had a quiet night, didn't we?" Larry nodded. "You look like the cat that ate the canary with that grin on your face. VS confess to all his doings?"

"No," Larry still grinned.

"Your wife is going to have a baby?"

Larry nearly rocked off the chair laughing. "They found them!"

For a moment the Precinct Captain looked puzzled. He started to say 'found who' when it dawned on him. "Alive?"

"No, very dead, and have been for awhile."

"Can you share the details, or does the Commissioner have a lock on that info?"

"Locked, but maybe not murder."

"When does all this hit the street?"

256

"It's on the news right now," Larry pointed to the clock. "Noontime edition."

"What do we need to do? Here I am, the Captain asking you."

Larry nodded. "Cancel any leaves. Double check our security ring. Wait. I don't know." Larry flung his arms up into the air. "The bodies were found outside this Precinct! Wonderful! Now some of the others will learn how hard it is to control anything VS does. Seriously, boss, I don't know what will happen. I just have that tingling in my bones that we are about to find out though."

The Captain nodded. "I guess I'd better start rounding up the troops.

"Do you have your usual meeting at five?"

"Yep."

"Keep us informed."

Larry nodded. "Here's hoping that this breaks open into something we can nail VS on."

Hilda informed the Fathers and Ramon about the breaking news at noon. She just shook her head. The reporters were careful not say to that this was considered a murder case. A clip showing Sardoni immediately after his wife's disappearance aired. "He done it. Why do they try to make it out that he was victimized by someone else?" she asked the men.

"He certainly is a slippery one," Father Marvin noted. "Never any blood on his hands."

Ramon snorted. "Excuse me," he said with an embarrassed grin. "Stories like that," he pointed to the television news, "always bring out the animal in me." Father Jon just turned away from the blaring TV.

Soon the guys were settled into a routine of classes over at Pastor White's church in the morning. During the afternoons, they studied. Father Marvin and Ramon tutored. The two Priests concelebrated daily Mass. Attendance was around thirty. On Sundays close to one hundred people attended St. Ignatius.

A call from St. Elizabeth's Nursing Home where Angus now resided informed Father that Angus seemed to be doing a lot of thinking and desired a visit from the priest and the "riff rats". "That is what he said, Father. Do you know what he means?"

"Yes," Jon answered. "I think we can arrange that. Could we visit about seven this evening?"

"Certainly Father. Shall I tell Angus you are coming?"

"Of course, and the riff rats too."

Jon requested a vehicle large enough to haul eight people. The Chancellor offered the station wagon that belonged to the nuns at the Cathedral School.

The boys all showered and put on clean clothing for the trip to the nursing home. They were excited about riding in a big car and going some place other than to the juvenile detention center. Hilda stood with her hands on her hips, proudly watching the boys as they left. It was quite a different group than the one she first met. Ramon volunteered to drive. This crowded the seating a little, but no one really complained.

At St. Elizabeth's, the group was escorted to a small parlor, as the aides got Angus ready for a visit. Father went down to his room first. Angus was anxious to see the boys also. After Father Jon heard Angus' confession and prayed with him, Jon sent for the boys. Shyly, they crept into the old man's room. They had never seen, heard, or experienced such

258

stimuli as they did now. Seeing a clean Angus propped up in a hospital bed, pale, thin, and shaking, caused some of them to want to leave. Ramon shook his head when William tried to leave.

"Who did I shoot dead?" Angus asked. A stifled giggle ran through the room.

"Me." Patch stepped forward.

"You're a nice looking boy, sonny. How'd you get that patch?"

Patch dug a toe into the floor and hesitated. "Tell him something, Patch." Jon encouraged.

"In a street fight."

"That's a dang shame," Angus retorted.

Nothing was said for a minute or so. Then Angus pointed at them and spat out the words, "Riff rats! You stole the oil tank."

More silence followed before Scar stepped forward. "Yes, old man, we did, and we returned it too."

"You're proud of that too!" Angus replied with almost a vehement sound in his voice.

"Stealing the tank, no. Returning it, yes." Scar was stand right beside Angus, looking him straight in the eyes.

"Weren't no good ever going to come of you."

Jon stepped forward. "They are going to school now, and some are getting ready to be baptized into the Church."

Angus blinked. It was then that Jon realized that Angus was wearing clean glasses. His eyes were visible.

"You don't say."

Patch stepped forward again. "I . . . I am sorry for all the trouble I caused you at the church."

Jon felt a shock of excitement course down his back. One by one, each boy stepped forward and said he was sorry for the trouble caused at the church. Jon looked over at Ramon, who was grinning like the Chestershire Cat.

Angus said nothing for a long time after the last one had spoken. He seemed to be in deep distress. Jon wondered if they needed to call the nursing attendant. When Angus finally spoke, his voice was broken by emotion, "God bless you." Big tears ran down the old man's face as he groped for the tissue box. Patch handed him one and helped Angus mop his face. "Thank you, boy," he rasped.

"We had better go," Ramon looked at Father Jon for confirmation. A quick nod, and the boys all left, calling 'goodbye Angus' as they went.

Jon, overcome with emotion, wiped his own tears. Angus reached out to him. "You will bury me from St. Ignatius?"

"Yes, Angus, you have my promise."

"And in the Little Flower Cemetery?"

"Yes, I will arrange it."

"God sent a good priest to St. Ignatius." Angus was staring at Jon as though he had never really seen him before. "Thank you."

Angus died in his sleep that night. Not a dry eye could be found at St. Ignatius when the news came. Jon announced to the morning congregants that the funeral Mass for Angus would be held the next day at eleven in the morning. In his homily that morning Jon spoke about confession and forgiveness, a healing balm.

Little Flower Cemetery was located at the edge of the big city. A section had been reserved for the indigent population of the city. Angus Costilla was buried there on a warm autumn day. Seven young men carried his coffin.

260

One More Time

Sitting in his office late one night rereading his notes for Sunday morning's Mass, Jon heard an explosion, and the rectory shook. Before he could get to the door, several more explosions shook the ground. Father Marvin stumbled down the stairs, pulling a sweatshirt over his head. Ramon burst through the side door into the kitchen. All three stood out on the porch as they heard sirens all around. Looking toward the river area, they could see a glow of light filling the sky. Then Ramon pointed to another glow near the middle of the city. They searched the sky and identified three more glows. Jon fell to his knees in agonized prayer. Ramon set off to circle the perimeter of the church complex. Hilda stood in the doorway wringing her hands. Irene clung to Hilda, as memories of the fire across the street raced like hot irons through her mind.

"What has happened, Padre?" Patch was on his knees by his best friend. Jon was weeping now. Scar joined Patch beside 'their' priest.

Mighty went with Ramon as he circled the church buildings. Father Marvin turned on the television in the kitchen. Shocked reporters were reporting that in a five minute period five separate explosions had hit within the city. As the details came in, the sense of panic increased. A normally unexcitable senior newscaster seemed to have lost all control as he screamed into his microphone about the multiple explosions. The network quickly moved to a calmer person who reported that the pleasure ferry on the river had exploded and was on fire. The side of the Cathedral was blown away, but there was not much fire, as the building was built of stone. One of the telephone substations was in total ruins and burning. The bridge over the river that carried the newly opened interstate was now twenty feet under water, as well as a number of vehicles and their occupants who were on the bridge at the time of the explosion. And the new high rise Mall near the center of town that was having its opening ceremonies was ablaze, with numerous fires on different floors.

"This is the work of a madman," someone exclaimed.

The confrontation between the Mayor and the Police Commissioner was loud. "Why could you not prevent this?" hollered the Mayor. "You are supposed to keep the city under surveillance, and you failed. Where were your men? What were they doing, sitting on their duffs? I thought after those disastrous fires down in the ghetto and having the National Guard in here for a while you could have gotten your officers in line. There is no excuse for

262

what happened last night!" The Mayor was still shouting.

The Police Commissioner agreed that what had happened in the last twenty-four hours was without excuse. However, his men had been vigilant, and whoever planned the explosions was very, very professional.

"It is unthinkable that this should happen in our great city in this great free country. It is almost like an act of 'terrorism'!" The Mayor's face was as scarlet as the red ink in the pen the Police Commissioner was using to mark the attacked spots on his map. If the man kept up his tirade much longer, he would have a stroke or heart attack.

The Mayor screamed, "Why don't you say something?"

"I will, when you quit screaming. Please sit down, Mr. Mayor, and calm yourself." The Commissioner watched as the Mayor sat, still fuming. "Here are the targets of this attack." He point to the red circles on the map. "Do you see any connection among these circles?" The Commissioner didn't wait for a response before continuing. "No, you won't. Each target was different from the next. The only target that seems to point to a common thread of the fires and the death threats on the priest at St. Ignatius is the one at the Cathedral."

"So why haven't you solved the fire crimes? And why is this priest so &^$%#* important? Who is he anyway, God?"

"I'll ignore that last comment," replied the Commissioner. "Rather, let's look at the profile of the man who has held much of this city in a vice grip for over twenty years. You know of whom I speak."

The mayor nodded and wiped his face with his handkerchief. "That, that . . ."

Interrupting the Mayor, the Commissioner

continued. "We had no more fires after the National Guard came in at our request to help us in the ghetto. During that time the police force was busy with the normal duties of the city. Note, we have been without the Guard just one week. Doesn't that say something?"

"Well, I don't see how that fits."

"Well, suppose we were living in a police state all the time. That is what those in the ghetto have been doing. Crime went down, and the people were feeling secure. Now the insecurity has been spread all over the city. Do you want to call the National Guard back?"

"No, of course not, that ruined our budget for several years to come. I really thought it was so unnecessary . . ."

Again, the Police Commissioner interrupted the Mayor. "George, you said right on television, in an interview, that you thought having the Guard in would help the people."

The Mayor did not say anything.

Continuing, the Commissioner said, "The whole city is afraid now. I am not suggesting any recall of the guard, but I am suggesting we get more aggressive toward our number one suspect. He has avoided jail, fines, and even court appearances over the years. He thinks he is invincible. Well, he isn't!"

The Mayor slid out of his chair onto the floor.

The Commissioner sprinted to his side. The Mayor was dead. He yanked the door open and yelled, "Call 911," but he knew it was too late.

The Police Commissioner opened the file that the Mayor had handed to him during their conversation. On top was a crude message: "You're next!" For a brief moment he wondered if the message was for him or had been for the Mayor. The

264

envelope under other papers answered that question. It had been sent to the Mayor. He retrieved the envelope and letter and placed it in his desk. There was no need for the information to be public yet.

After the Mayor's body was removed from his office, the Police Commissioner decided to pull out all stops to trip up VS, who he was certain was behind the explosions.

The Mayor was dead, and the city was in an uproar from the explosions, fires, and multiple deaths of the night before. The Deputy Mayor was sworn in as the new mayor. Reporters from all over the world were descending upon the besieged city. The Police Commissioner made a scathing statement to the media and said everything but Vincent Sardoni's name. There was no doubt in the minds of the public that this Commissioner was going to get his man, or the man would get the Commissioner.

Janette called him immediately after his interview was aired. "I'm scared," she said.

"For yourself or for me?"

"Both," she replied. "You know that you will be a target for any hoodlum who wants to get in good with VS, the poor souls."

"Well, that may be true, but it is time the people of this city quit having to live with so much insecurity."

"Do you have to set yourself up as an obvious target? I love you. I don't want to be a widow."

"Neither did the Mayor's wife. He was talking scared when he came to see me. That was not like George. He had been such a strong supporter of the efforts to curtail VS's activities."

"What made him scared?" Janette asked.

"I have a hunch, that is all. Maybe the same

thing that is making you scared, and most of the city. Keep me in your prayers, hon, and I'll see you soon."

Larry Janski had slipped into the Commissioner's office during the conversation with Janette. "Your wife too?"

"Yes. Let's get this madman!"

Larry looked at him sadly. "How?"

The two men stared at each other. The Commissioner pulled open his desk drawer. "Let's start with this." He handed the threat note to Larry. "Get fingerprints, etc."

"Probably nothing on it but the Mayor's and yours."

"Maybe we will get lucky." A slight smile played on the Commissioner's lips. "Maybe we will get lucky."

"I heard your statement to the media."

"Hope VS did also!"

"Would a reward help, do you think?"

"It would have to be large."

"How about $500,000?"

The Commissioner's head jerked up. "Where would we get that kind of money?"

"It is already donated."

"By whom?"

"The Diocese."

"They have that kind of money?"

Larry nodded. "I got a phone call from the Bishop after the explosion at the Cathedral. Only thing is, the donor must remain anonymous."

"Who will be holding the money from this 'anonymous' donor?

"The largest bank in town, in conjunction with a set of attorneys picked by the Diocese, although not their normal ones."

"How soon will it be available?"

"I understand by this evening."

266

"We've got work to do! Let's figure out how we can get VS to fall for the bait. That kind of money might just open a squeaky door for us."

Vincent Sardoni enjoyed the instability he had created in his town. The announcement of the Mayor's sudden death made him laugh and clap his hands together like a little child getting a bright new toy. The Police Commissioner's straightforward interview only served to stimulate him to think of greater and bigger ways to control his city. When the announcement was made on the late night news about the $500,000 reward, Vincent had already put his next plan into action.

For days the telephone lines set up to receive phone calls regarding the perpetrators of the explosions and fires were constantly ringing. All leaves, vacations, and any other time off were cancelled. The Commissioner had every possible lead investigated. The new Mayor lived at the Central Police Station when he was not out in the neighborhoods encouraging the people to believe that the terrible things in the city were about to come to an end.

This had gone on for over two weeks. A series of murders of lesser-known hoodlums were reported, which kept the coroner busy overtime. Auxiliary police were on duty in the Malls and on the downtown streets. Their presence helped calm some of the fears of the public.

The guys from St. Ignatius were rubbing shoulders with the Street Rats of Pastor White's area. Ramon and the pastor visited the classroom often and found that the teachers were having no trouble with the mix. The first few days were tense, but then they all were so busy trying to make up for the lack of previous learning that they hardly noticed the others' gang 'colors'. Those from St. Ignatius no longer had 'colors', thanks to the clothing donated by the Bishop's office. Soon the Street Rats seemed to be leaving off their 'colors' also. The many hours of prayer spent by Pastor White and Ramon for each boy may have helped make the transition easier.

The young former gang members were challenged to make a positive stand in the ghetto area. Jon thought it was probably something that Ramon had urged, remembering Ramon's testimony. As a group, they decided to patrol the area in the evenings up until 10 pm, which was the curfew set at St. Ignatius. Two young men, one from each gang, would team together and walk the streets from dusk until ten. As it was late fall, dusk came earlier, so the 'patrols' were on duty for four to five hours per day. They were required to keep their schoolwork at an acceptable level in order to be allowed to participate. A few starts and stops occurred.

It worried Hilda at first that the boys would get into trouble. Ramon and the two Fathers assured her that, if they did, they, Ramon, and Pastor White would know and would take the necessary action. Within a week Patch's leadership, supported by Scar and a boy named Tiger, had the patrol working well.

Father Marvin took over the daily administration of St. Ignatius. He had a knack for working with numbers and seeing to the overall needs of the parish.

This left Father Jon answering the phone and calling on new or returning Catholics to the Church. It was the phone calls that were troubling Father Jon. He did not tell the others about the persistent man who called, sometimes speaking rudely, sometimes challenging, sometimes threatening, sometimes laughing at the foolishness of the Church, and sometimes asking serious questions. It was always the same voice. At first Jon had been uncertain that the calls were from the same person. Day after day the calls came until he was certain it was the same person. One day, after an exceptionally threatening call, he remembered the voice that had called him months before. This was the same caller. Jon knew that Detective Larry thought that call had come from Vincent Sardoni. This caller was intelligent, shrewd, clever, and demonic. That fit the description of Sardoni.

Father Jon formulated a plan and waited for the time when the caller was somewhat friendly. Then he simply addressed the anonymous caller by the name of Vincent. The caller promptly hung up. "Bingo!" Jon chirped.

"What are you so happy about?" Hilda inquired when Jon came out to the kitchen to raid the cookie jar.

With a mouthful of cookies, Jon mumbled something before retreating back to his office. He called Larry Janski and told him of his suspicions.

"You have been talking to him how long?" Larry's voice sounded pinched.

"A couple of weeks. I just took his mask off today."

"I'm going to have your phone bugged," declared Larry.

"No you won't. Callers here need to know that what they say on the phone is in confidence."

"This is a police matter."

"No it isn't. Well, maybe yes it is. Ask the Bishop before you put a bug on this line."

Larry muttered something and hung up. The Bishop said 'no', and it was very apparent that he expected his response to be obeyed. Larry prayed and decided that he would not mention the caller that Jon was getting to the Police Commissioner until it was absolutely necessary.

The Encounter

Why he was going to the Chills and Frills Amusement Park in November was a mystery, even to Father Jon. When Vincent called the rectory and asked if he would make a pastoral call, Jon had felt a chill run up and down his back. This was the first time Sardoni openly identified himself since the anonymous threats, the two fires, and bombings. The place of meeting caused even more doubts and concerns when Sardoni suggested the amusement park, which was closed for the season. Vincent explained that he owned it, so it was suitable to meet there. It was not located anywhere near St. Ignatius, but Sardoni reminded him that, since his wife had disappeared, he had his residence in the tall, penthouse office building that overlooked St. Ignatius, and thus he was a parishioner of Father Jon. He said he wanted to talk and get some things off his chest. It would be like 'going to confession'.

271

"Oh, really," was the immediate response from Father Marvin. The Bishop inhaled deeply before blessing Father Jon. Detective Larry Janski said he was crazy to meet up face-to-face with the man.

Father Jon listened to all those concerned, including the guys living in the rectory. They were all maturing, but the idea of Padre meeting Sardoni face-to-face scared them. They had too many memories of his influence in their ghetto.

Larry set in motion one of the many contingency plans hashed and rehashed in the 'safe room'. The Police Commissioner asked, "Is he really going to go there to meet with him?"

Larry shrugged his shoulders. "Father Jon said there was a verse in the Bible, in Exodus, he thought, that spoke about the people standing a way off from where God was. As a result, they missed an encounter with God."

"Oh great, he is getting religious on us!"

"He is religious!" Larry retorted. "He lives his convictions! And, in this case, we have to do everything we can to see that he does live!"

"Don't remind me. Where in Frills and Chills is he supposed to meet up with VS?"

"At the pavilion, across from Spook Mountain."

"Right! Right in the center."

"Yep. Sardoni is keeping himself protected."

"Which makes it so much harder for us to protect the priest. Will he wear a mic?"

"He has turned me down on that. I have gotten him to agree to wear a 'man down' sensor. At least with it we can keep track of him."

"What you really are putting on him is the movement/tracking sensor, right?"

"I took the liberty to pick it up in the

storeroom on my way in to see you." Larry's grin was only slight. The stress of the moment was eating away at him. "I noticed that we only have one in there? I thought we bought several."

"They are in use," the Commissioner replied. "One is all you need, right?"

Larry nodded. "Can we get the snipers into the area without setting off the alarms in the park?"

"A power outage will give us enough time before the emergency power kicks in. Who knows, VS may have the power off there anyway to save money."

"I don't think so. Someone reported that the roller coaster was running last night." Larry replied.

"After dark?"

"Yeah. Weird. But no alarms went off, so it was not a bunch of kids breaking in and enjoying the thrill."

"Chris over in logistics has an 'accident' planned for there at the boulevard and the gateway to the amusement park. The media will be lending us their news trucks and helicopters, so we should be able to get in close. Only thing is, they are going to be mad if we have their equipment and this encounter becomes fast breaking news." The Commissioner was almost smiling.

Larry laughed. "They haven't been too overly friendly lately anyway. How did you get their cooperation and silence?"

"They don't know about it yet!" The commissioner laughed. "About twenty minutes before the 'accident' and the priest walking in there, we will declare an emergency."

"That should work. Anything more that I should tell Father Jon before he walks into the lion's den?" Larry asked.

"The less he knows, the better. I sense he

trusts that we will do whatever is necessary if need be. Just in case Sardoni tries to get something out of him, he is better off not knowing anything, except that he is carrying the sensor."

"I'm still going to call it the 'man down' sensor. That way he may not realize how accurately we can pinpoint his location at all times." Larry face reflected the seriousness of the proposed action.

"Let's hope and pray it doesn't become a 'man down' in reality." The Police Commissioner shook hands with his detective. "You are doing a great job, Larry. Hopefully, this whole thing will come to an end soon."

Father Jon approached the amusement park shortly before two. One of the pedestrian gates was slightly ajar. Jon went through, paused to tie his shoe, and left a small rock holding the gate open. He figured he might need to get out later. The place was impressive. He had never visited this park. Boarded up concession stands and closed small gift shops lined the main walkway. He proceeded toward the very center of the park. At the end of this avenue of enticements he found a great pavilion and a landscaped park area. Slightly to his left was Spook Mountain, a fun house full of terror, so he had heard. He sat down on one of the pavilion benches.

"Come on over here." A voice spoke through the public address system.

Jon looked around and finally saw Vincent Sardoni standing at a courtesy booth almost directly in front of Spook Mountain. Carefully, Jon made his way through the stacked picnic tables and benches. He kept in mind just where he had entered the pavilion in case he had to make a hasty retreat.

"You act like you are afraid of me." Sardoni spoke without the public address system.

274

Jon stared at a well-dressed man standing about thirty feet from him. "You have a bad reputation," Jon commented.

"Yeah, well the press hasn't been too nice lately. Somehow they think that everything bad that happens in the town is all my fault."

Closing the distance to about fifteen feet, Jon stopped.

"You said you wanted to talk." Jon pulled his stole from his pocket and draped it around his neck.

Vincent Sardoni laughed. "Look at you, prepared and all!" His sharp cackle reverberated off the empty buildings.

"You did say you wanted to go to confession." Jon felt a chill, as a sharp wind blew some leftover trash about the front of Spook Mountain.

"Yeah, I said that. I knew that would get you to come. What do you want me to confess to? The murder of my wife and her chauffer? Or how about the fire at Buddy's Salvage? I think they both occurred the same night. Then there was the fire in the buildings across from St. Ignatius, and the other one several blocks away. And the bombing of the chapel at the Catherdral. Is that enough?"

"Are these things that you are confessing?" Jon asked with a steady voice.

"Oh, yeah, and the fiery explosion at the ferry, and the one at the Mall dedication. And others." Sardoni cursed, "No! I am not confessing them! How do I know you aren't wired with a radio?"

"Because, I am a priest, and confession is a Sacrament, and I am bound not to repeat what has been confessed to me."

"Yeah, that is why I asked you to come to

275

talk to me. You know, I knew you would come alone and without a radio. You don't know how long I have waited for this moment." Vincent had moved forward about five feet. He looked up as he heard a siren off in the distance. "They'll not find you for a while inside there." He pointed toward Spook Mountain. "And that is just where we are going now."

A revolver in Sardoni's hand pointed at Father Jon.

"You are going to have a little accident and fall out of one of the cars."

Jon reminded God that he was ready to go home if this was God's plan. "Tell me, how did you get so good at arson and bomb building."

Sardoni laughed. "I didn't, but they did. He waved his free hand up toward the roller coaster stopped high in one of the loops. What appeared to be two bodies hung upside down. "They are tied in. It was a slow death. Now move it!" He swung his gun menacingly at Jon. "Inside the mountain. There is a special ride waiting for you!"

Father Jon Mark made a decision. "So you are the killer everyone thinks you are. If you are going to kill me, as I presume you are planning to do, I would rather die out here in the daylight!"

Sardoni swore again. "You are a fool. Inside, you will be in the dark and not know when it is that you die. Out here, you can see me taking aim at you." Slowing Vincent Sardoni raised this gun. "Are you really that brave? Or do you think you will become a saint when I pull this trigger?"

Jon stood very still and said, "Lord, forgive him, for he knows not what he is . . ."

A shot rang out, and Jon fell.

Voices called to each other, as several policemen ran to the spot where Sardoni lay dead. Someone knelt by the priest. "He's alive. What hit him? Did Sardoni's gun go off?"

"No!" An officer picked up Sardoni's gun. "It hasn't been fired."

Jon moaned. "It's OK, Father, an ambulance is on its way."

Detective Larry Janski and the Police Commissioner bent over the inert body of Vincent Sardoni. "The bullet went clean through him!"

"Look, here is where it ricocheted off the pavement."

It didn't take very long to see that the bullet had hit Father Jon in the thigh.

"Bishop!" exclaimed Larry, as a man in priestly garb rushed up to Father Jon.

Vaguely, through the pain and haze, Jon felt someone anoint him with oil and pray over him. Try as he might, Jon could not distinguish exactly who the priest was. He remembered hearing someone say something about a shattered bone as he was lifted on to a stretcher and place in an ambulance. Then everything went dark.

Back on the street, tears ran down the Bishop's face as he entered his car. Ramon clutched the steering wheel and asked, "Is he alive?"

"Yes! St. Margaret's Hospital, quickly!" Then the Bishop cried out. "Oh, God, thank you for preserving Father Jon Mark's life. Now give him the healing graces that he needs to be whole again."

Ramon felt heartbroken listening to the Bishop's deep cries for mercy for Father Jon.

At the hospital, two surgeons were called in to operate on Father's leg. His left thighbone, splintered by the ricocheting bullet, presented a critical problem. They discussed if it would be best to just amputate the leg above the wound. Jon drifted in and out. He thought he heard birds chirping above him, and then two larger birds were arguing. He thought it was interesting and wished he could understand their language.

When he awoke several hours later, his left leg was in an air cast and held securely in place, leaving him immobile. A nurse noticed that he had awakened and called the doctor.

"Hi, Father, I am Dr. Forbes, your surgeon. Your left leg was splintered. After a little persuasion, the other surgeon agreed to let me use a very new technique to try to save the leg bone. It may or may not work, but I think it will. There were an awful lot of tiny pieces of bone embedded in your thigh muscles. We did what a 'china' repair person does, who puts a broken plate or cup back together, piece by piece. It is a tedious job, but the results are always splendid when a person gets back the heirloom object looking brand new. That is what I, we, the surgery team, tried to do for you."

"I am an heirloom?" Jon mumbled.

"No, you are a very fortunate man, whose leg pieces have been 'glued' back together." The doctor chuckled. "It is a technique sometimes being done on wounded soldiers. So far the success rate, although not high, has been encouraging, considering the alternative of amputation."

"Then I still have my leg?"

The doctor patted him on the shoulder. "You bet, and you have several rather important visitors waiting to see you, now that you are awake. Nurse, get him moved to his room."

Bishop James Paul paced the floor in the

278

room where Father Jon would soon be coming. He was anxious to talk with the priest. A nurse asked the Bishop to go down to the waiting room at the end of the hall while they brought Father Jon in. That room was full, with single chairs all lined around the wall. Ramon sat praying for his friends, Bishop James Paul and Father Jon. The television newscast had described the death of Vincent Sardoni as quick but not without cost to the brave priest who had gone to confront him at the Chills and Frills Amusement Park. People all over the city were praying for the brave priest. Ramon felt deeply saddened that Father Jon had been hurt so grievously.

"I can't sit. All I want to do is pace the floor." The Bishop interrupted Ramon's thoughts.

"Is he awake?" Ramon asked.

"I guess so. They are moving him to his room right now." The Bishop pause his pacing to look down the hallway. "I think that is him now." He pointed at a bed being moved into a room.

Minutes later, a nurse stopped in. "He is asking for you, your Excellency."

"May I come too?" Ramon asked. The Bishop nodded as he followed the nurse to Father Jon's room.

Jon eyes brimmed with tears when the two men entered. "It's over now," he whispered to them. The Bishop and Ramon bowed their heads and wept with their friend.

The End

St. Margaret's

"A Chaplain?" Jon looked at the bearer of the news.

"Yes, the Bishop has decided to have Father Marvin stay at St. Ignatius, and, while you are in therapy here in St. Margaret's Hospital, you will be one of the Chaplains."

"Will I be going back to St. Ignatius later?"

The Chancellor shrugged his shoulders. "I don't know where the Bishop will assign you after you are well."

Jon nodded.

"There is a nice two-room apartment in the east wing for a resident Chaplain. You will have privacy and yet be available as needed. And, of course, you will have your daily therapy." The Chancellor stood to leave. He reached out and shook Jon's hand. "This would be a 'soft' assignment if you were able-bodied, which you aren't yet. Enjoy." Smiling, the Chancellor left.

280

For a full minute, Jon was dumb-founded. The Chancellor reappeared. "I almost forgot, here is the key to the apartment. The hospital staff will help you get settled. You are still a patient, just a working one."

Within the hour, he moved to the apartment. The sparsely furnished rooms contained a bed, a desk and a recliner.

This was to be his home for a while. Jon laid his cane down before he sat in the chair and prayed. He wanted to be prepared for whatever the Lord had in store for him at St. Margaret's.

From "Not My Legs", the next in the
Adventures of Father Jon Mark

www.ingramcontent.com/pod-product-compliance
Lightning Source LLC
Chambersburg PA
CBHW031103260626
47172CB00001B/194